Praise for the Deadly Series

Kate Parker (
a wonderfully str(
Escape with Don.,

DEADLY FASHION *is an impeccably plotted mystery*
filled with not only historical details but the atmosphere
and attitude of the people on the precipice of World War
II.
Cozy Up with Kathy

Books by Kate Parker

The Victorian Bookshop Mysteries

The Vanishing Thief
The Counterfeit Lady
The Royal Assassin
The Conspiring Woman
The Detecting Duchess

The Deadly Series

Deadly Scandal
Deadly Wedding
Deadly Fashion
Deadly Deception
Deadly Travel

The Milliner Mysteries

The Killing at Kaldaire House
Murder at the Marlowe Club

The Mystery at Chadwick House

Deadly Travel

Kate Parker

JDP PRESS

Deadly Travel copyright © 2020 by Kate Parker

ISBN: 978-1-7332294-2-5 {ebook}

ISBN: 978-1-7332294-3-2 {print}

Published by JDP Press

Cover design by Lyndsey Lewellen of Lewellen Designs, Inc.

Dedication

To my family and friends in the midst of a pandemic, may this book find you healthy and enjoying a little historical mayhem.

To John, forever.

Late March, 1939

Chapter One

A summons to Sir Henry Benton's office was one thing; a command on behalf of Sir Malcolm Freemantle was quite another. This was decidedly not the way I wanted to start a Monday morning. I was shown in by Sir Henry's secretary, who left me to stand on the thick carpet in front of the huge desk, the smooth, polished wood gleaming, while Sir Henry finished typing on low-grade yellow-beige paper with his beat-up Underwood.

Satisfied with what he'd written, despite the rows of Xs I could see from where I stood, Sir Henry pulled the paper from the typewriter and acknowledged me for the first time. "Olivia, sit down. As I said on the phone, Sir Malcolm Freemantle wants to use your talents on a Kindertransport from Berlin. I've decided to tell him yes. We can use your observations of Berlin, the trains, and the Kindertransport for a series of articles in the paper."

I did not like people making my decisions for me. It had been a bone of contention with my father, a stuffy Foreign Office diplomat, since I'd been old enough to talk. "What if I don't, or can't, go?"

Sir Henry held my gaze. "Of course you can. Think of this as another one of those special assignments you do for me. Besides," he gave me a sympathetic look, "I doubt either of us can afford to tell Sir Malcolm 'No.'"

The father of my best friend from school, Sir Henry had hired me at a far greater than adequate salary. It had taken me a while to learn how to write copy for the women's and society pages in the *Daily Premier*. But I'd proved my worth when he had me travel to Germany and Austria to help rescue his late wife's family, and part of their wealth, from the Nazis.

As owner and publisher of a powerful London newspaper, Sir Henry could hire whomever he wanted and pay them whatever he wanted. And give them whatever assignments he wanted.

In this case, he appeared to be lending me out to the head of Britain's counterintelligence service.

"Who's paying my salary?" I'd become accustomed to my wages from the newspaper. I didn't imagine Sir Malcolm would be as generous.

"I am, in exchange for our use of your notes and reminiscences."

"If Sir Malcolm will let you publish them."

Sir Henry raised his brows. "You don't sound like you trust Sir Malcolm."

"I don't." Sir Malcolm Freemantle was a clever, devious, brilliant spy, three steps ahead of everyone else, and not a man to be trusted with a ha'penny, much less my life.

"Wise girl. Neither do I. I've received some assurances from him, but who knows what they'll be worth if we go to war. In the meantime, you're to go to his office. You know where that is?"

I nodded.

Sir Henry rose and reached across the vast expanse of desk to shake my hand. Only when we both stood was our height difference obvious. He was several inches shorter than me.

"Good luck," he said as he released my hand. "Let me know what the old, er, ah, spymaster wants and when you leave."

* * *

Sir Malcolm's office was in what was originally an Edwardian residential block of red brick that had been turned first into a hotel and now an office building.

An army officer in uniform escorted me upstairs from the entrance directly to Sir Malcolm's private suite. When we approached his battered desk, the officer saluted. Sir Malcolm rose, towering over me, and told me to sit. The officer left, pulling the door shut behind him.

I sat in an uncomfortably hard wooden chair. The view out his window was lovely, with the tops of bare tree branches and the roofs of nearby buildings shining in the dappled sunlight. Perhaps Sir Malcolm hoped his visitors would be distracted by the view. I was not so foolish and watched him as I would a snake.

"Come, come, Mrs. Denis, I'm not that bad a person."

"I'm wondering why you chose me to do whatever it is you want instead of any one of a million other young women."

"Because you have the attributes needed to

convince the Refugee Children's Movement and the Watersons to let you go in Alice Waterson's place on the next Kindertransport."

"And those attributes are?"

"Fishing for compliments, Mrs. Denis?"

I shook my head. "I want to know what's expected of me. By you, by the Quakers, by the Watersons. Didn't I read that Alice Waterson was killed recently in a nighttime attack on an East End street?"

"Yes. Did you know her?"

"I met her at some parties before I was married. She didn't make much of an impression on me at the time." She had been quiet, with mousy brown hair and an unfortunate habit of dressing in dreary colors. Brown tweed with a beige blouse, sensible brown shoes, and a brown hat. She even had a brown ballgown.

But I remembered she could draw men to her with a forthright laugh and a cynical way of looking at them.

"She was engaged to be married. To a German."

My eyes widened. That was interesting, especially in light of Hitler's current behavior. "Is he also a Quaker?"

"Yes. And likely to gain British citizenship, or was, at least as long as Alice was alive."

I thought I saw where this was heading. "Her family doesn't approve of him?"

"Her father is a peer of the realm. The whole family is quite patriotic despite their refusal to fight. Lord Waterson served as a medical corpsman on the Western Front. Noncombatant, but brave nonetheless."

I guessed her father was about the age of mine, who

had also served in the Great War. "You want me to go on a Kindertransport, but why would the Watersons care who went in their daughter's place?"

Sir Malcolm's lips slanted upward, proving that snakes could smile. "You speak German. You've traveled to Germany before. You have a plausible reason to be there as a reporter covering the work of the Kindertransports for Sir Henry."

The Kindertransports were organized by Jewish leaders in Britain and Nazi-held territories to remove unaccompanied Jewish children under the age of eighteen to the safety of Britain, the only country that would take them. The Quakers were active in helping organize and chaperone the children on the trips as well as finding them places to stay once they arrived.

The first Kindertransport had arrived by ferry the preceding December. Not much had appeared in the newspapers since then, but with the Germans now occupying all of Czechoslovakia, there would be more demand from parents to rescue their children from the hell they found themselves in.

"And," Sir Malcolm added with a nod of his graying head, "you find killers."

"Do the Watersons think her fiancé killed her?" What had happened during their courtship?

"They suspect him."

"And Scotland Yard?"

"Can find nothing that points to anything but a random street robbery gone bad. She had her neck snapped on a dark street not far from the docks."

What was a peer's daughter doing in that neighborhood at night? "So I'm supposed to go on this Kindertransport and watch him to see if he's a Nazi agent. But even if he is, I doubt he would be stupid enough to kill his ticket to stay in England with a war coming."

Sir Malcolm watched me closely. "Her fiancé doesn't go on the Kindertransports. And I want you to keep an eye on everyone associated with this trip."

"Why?"

"The people on this transport knew Alice well and were in the area on the evening she was murdered." He steepled his fingers. "Every time this particular group has traveled together, British secrets end up in Nazi hands. I want to know if the Refugee Children's Movement is harboring a traitor, as well as a murderer."

"And I'm expected to figure out which one of them, if any of them, is the killer." I pressed my lips together in distaste. "What if I fail?"

"Then it probably means Scotland Yard was right, and this was a random attack on a dark street. Unusual, though, in that she was killed by having her neck snapped."

"Someone choked her?" That was unusual for a mugging. Normally, victims of robbery with violence were stabbed.

"No, she had her skull snapped off her spine in a very businesslike way. The way sentries are taught in the military."

"A strange skill for a group of pacifists." I would

consider that proof that this was a random killing.

"Yes. If they are." He slid a piece of paper to me. "Memorize this name. He's your contact in our embassy in Berlin. He'll give you your secondary assignment from me once you arrive."

I glanced at the name. *Douglas MacFerron.*

"You mean finding the traitor giving secrets to the Nazis in Berlin isn't my secondary assignment?" How many different directions did he want me to go in at one time?

He watched me. "I think if you find the killer, you'll find the traitor. I just wanted you to be aware of what you'll be facing."

"I might have guessed there would be more to this than just spying on some Quakers trying to rescue children from the Nazis." Sir Malcolm wasn't the sort to do things for only one reason when he could turn an investigation in multiple directions. Probably why he was in charge, I thought grimly. "What is this secondary task I'm doing for you?"

"You'll find out when you get there. I'm not sure at this point if it's even possible."

My heart sank to my heels. Sir Malcolm had something dangerous that needed doing in Berlin, and I was expendable.

No. My stubborn streak reasserted itself. He thought I was expendable. I'd look after myself, and if things got too treacherous, I would walk away. That choice was mine to make. Even if walking away from my assignment while in Berlin was hazardous on its own.

"I'm not going to throw you to the wolves," he added. "Don't worry. This won't be any more difficult than helping Sir Henry's mother-in-law leave Berlin."

Why didn't I believe him? I summoned up my courage. "When do I leave?"

"The whole group leaves for the Netherlands the day after tomorrow on the seven o'clock ferry train. Now, you'd better make yourself known to the Watersons as the investigator they requested and the Refugee Children's Movement as the reporter writing the story to help them gain more funding."

* * *

The Watersons lived in a wealthy area near Holland Park. I escaped the wind and the rain as a maid let me in, and I handed her my card. She took my coat and umbrella and led me to a drawing room done in art deco furnishings and paintings.

A thin, gray-haired woman in a plain rust-colored dress with a wide collar and cuffs in the same material came in a minute later. "This was Alice's favorite room," she said, looking around. "It seems strange not seeing her here."

Grief was etched on her face. I was sure sorrow would rest on her shoulders for the remainder of her life. "I'm sorry for your loss."

"Oh, please, don't be sorry," she said, sitting down as she gestured me to a seat. "You are here to investigate whether our suspicions are correct?"

Not exactly, but I needed to be diplomatic. "I've been directed to go on the Kindertransport in Alice's place, to keep my eyes open, and to talk to her friends and find out if any of them have any information about Alice's death."

Lady Waterson's eyes and lips narrowed. "They were all there that night. I just want you to find the man who killed my daughter."

She carried not only grief, but a deep burning anger.

"You're sure it's a man." I raised my eyebrows, having not heard anything that would make me certain of the killer's gender.

"Alice was a strong woman with a forceful personality. I don't believe another woman could have gained the upper hand and killed her."

"Even by surprise?" Alice had her neck broken on a dark, empty street in the East End. She had been alone. She was at a disadvantage that a determined killer could put to good use.

Lady Waterson sat forward, her legs primly pressed together to one side from the knees to the ankles. "Since she was attacked from the front, I doubt it was by surprise. I believe it was someone she knew."

"Do you have someone in mind?"

"Her fiancé. Johann Klingler. I've never trusted that man." She paused and stared at me for several moments. "It's not fair of me, telling you I believe Johann killed Alice and trying to turn you against him, when I don't have anything to back up my instincts. But the fact remains that Lord Waterson and I were against him from the start."

"Did Johann do anything that you can point to that

made you question his loyalty or his love for your daughter?" I'd be more successful if I had something concrete to consider.

"He always looked around here as if he were appraising the furniture." She shook her head. "He seemed to know the price of everything."

"What sort of work did he do in Germany?"

"He was a solicitor. That's why he had to get out of Germany. He tried to defend people the Nazis were throwing in prison."

This was getting me nowhere. I decided to try a different approach. "Can you tell me about Alice's close friends?"

Lady Waterson leaned back in the overstuffed chair covered in a tapestry print. "Her close friends were children she grew up with in our faith. Several of them will be on the Kindertransport with you. Shall I write down their names and addresses?"

"Please."

While she wrote at a small desk, I asked, "What about the staff at the Kindertransport office? What can you tell me about them?"

"Mr. Thomas Canterbury, the head organizer of the different transports, attended university with Alice."

When she didn't continue, I said, "Surely, that created some sort of a bond. Especially since they worked on the rescue together."

"Yes. Apparently, they worked well together," she said grudgingly. "But despite his college degree, he was only a research assistant when he left his position to manage the Kindertransport office. At the time I met him, he was living with his mother and younger sisters in what Alice called threadbare elegance. She said he didn't have the drive to get ahead in any field."

Without looking up, she added, "He wasn't Alice's type."

"What was Alice's type?" Was the key to her murder the way she saw people? Did her killer get to her because she saw him as beneath notice?

Chapter Two

"Someone from our class. Alice wasn't a delicate debutante. She could never have done the work needed on the Kindertransport if she was afraid to get her hands dirty. But the children on the Kindertransport weren't likely to become her friends." Lady Waterson gave me a smile. "Her friends not only had to be of our class, they had to have drive."

"Alice liked people with the drive to get ahead?"

"Only people with drive could keep up with Alice." She sounded proud of her daughter. She walked back to where I sat and handed me a paper with a dozen names on it. "I've put a check by the names of those who will be traveling on the Kindertransport with you."

I glanced down the list. Johann Klingler made the list, but without a checkmark. Thomas Canterbury didn't make Lady Waterson's list.

"How did Alice spend her time when she wasn't working on the Kindertransport?"

"She read, she went to parties with her friends, she played the piano, she played tennis, she helped with projects led by our Meeting. She led a very normal life." She scowled at me then. "She wasn't wild. She didn't have scandalous friends. This shouldn't have happened to her. She should have had a long, happy life."

I put a self-deprecating smile on my face, hoping to disarm her. "If I'm going to have any chance of helping to find out who killed your daughter, I have to ask a lot of frustrating, needless questions. I never know where the information may come from that will lead me to the murderer."

She took a deep breath, trying to regain control of her emotions. After letting out a deep sigh, she said, "Look at Johann. I think he killed her. I have no evidence. Just a feeling deep inside that he didn't love Alice. That he didn't want to be around any of us. But I want you to go on the Kindertransport and learn what you can."

* * *

The Refugee Children's Movement had an office in Bloomsbury for the Kindertransport. When I left the Watersons' house, the weather was still nasty. A half hour later, I had to fight a strong wind and a wintry mist catching at my umbrella to reach the outside door of their building.

Once I made it inside and repaired the wind damage to my hair and hat, I began a search for the office. It was on the ground floor in the back. I tapped on the door and walked in.

A young woman sat stuffing envelopes at a desk near the door. She looked up with a smile and said, "May I help you?"

"Yes. I'm Olivia Denis and I was told to see the person in charge."

She looked me up and down. "We were expecting the newspaper to send someone a little older. Oh, well, I'm sure you'll do fine." Her expression said she didn't believe it. "Hang your coat there. Tom!"

A man in his mid-thirties, his pale hair already

thinning, straightened from a search in the lowest drawer of a file cabinet across the room. "Yes?"

"Olivia Denis," the woman at the desk said. "The woman we were told would write the newspaper articles on the Kindertransports that would bring us funding."

Tom strode forward, his thin frame already beginning to display stooped shoulders. He stuck out one hand as he reached me. "Mrs. Denis? I'm Thomas Canterbury. We've been expecting you. Come into my office."

I followed him through a doorway into a small office crowded with a large desk, a few wooden chairs, and several file cabinets with two drawers half open and crammed with forms. Canterbury shut the door behind us before lifting a stack of papers off one of the chairs and motioning me to sit.

He squeezed around the end of his desk and sat. "Now, Mrs. Denis. Olivia, if I may?"

This appeared to be an informal organization. "Livvy, please."

"I'm Tom. Oh, I guess you knew that. I suppose you've been told what is expected?" He shifted a stack of papers, shifted it back, and then knocked the top sheets off.

As he grabbed for them, obviously nervous, I said, "To write a terrific article for the newspaper gaining you support for the Kindertransports. I'll be replacing Alice Waterson."

"A terrible tragedy. Alice will be sorely missed." He

took off his glasses and polished them on his tie.

I decided to copy some of Sir Henry's news reporters. "Who do you think killed her?"

Tom jumped and nearly toppled over in his swivel chair. He put his glasses back on before he said, "I—I don't know. Some thief."

"You know that I'm a reporter. And the Kindertransport isn't the only story here."

He shook his head with a shudder. "No one here would have hurt her. It had to be a robbery gone wrong."

I needed to put him at his ease, or we'd never get anywhere. "Tell me about the people I'll be working with on this story. Who will be helpful in giving me details? My editor loves details."

"Well, you just met Mary. Mary Wallace. She's in charge of our volunteer clerks. She's the daughter of one of the leading families in our Meeting."

Who thinks I'm too young. "Is she going on this trip?"

"Oh, no, she never goes on the Kindertransports. Her father won't allow it. Johann—Johann Klingler, Alice's fiancé—doesn't go to Germany either. They wouldn't let him out again."

"He's in trouble with the Nazis?"

Tom's head bobbed up and down. "They don't like people with religious principles."

"Who else is going on this trip?"

He handed me a typewritten list, with Alice's name scratched out and mine penciled in at the bottom.

"You'll meet them all when we leave for Berlin. Be at Liverpool Street station at six- thirty the morning after next."

I nodded.

He rose.

I looked up at him and said, "Alice is still a story all the papers are carrying. Do you know why she was in the East End the night she was killed?"

He dropped back into his chair hard enough that it wobbled and squealed. "Yes. Well, we all were. Everyone on the list. It could have been any of us."

"How awful for you." Any mention of her death seemed to rattle him.

He took a deep breath and continued. "We were checking on the homes of the families who will be taking in some of the children. Their relatives. Seeing if they had someplace to sleep. If they had room at their table."

"Were you all together?"

"Originally." He hesitated. "We did the actual visits in pairs."

"Who went with Alice?"

Tom started to shake. In a weak voice, he said, "I did."

Could the solution be this simple? Did Thomas Canterbury kill Alice Waterson? Would I be able to go back to work, unimpeded by Sir Malcolm's plots and plans? "What happened?"

"We were on our way to a German-Jewish family's flat when Alice said, 'You go ahead. I'll meet you at the Underground stop.' When I asked her why, she said something had come up."

"Did she give any hint as to why she was going off on her own at night in the East End? Did she have friends in the area?"

"No friends, no hints, nothing she said, but I saw a figure at a distance. I know she had seen the person, too."

"Could you tell who it was?"

"I'm not even certain it was male." He took off his glasses and polished them. When he put them back on, he said, "My eyesight is badly defective, particularly at a distance."

"So, you went off on your own to visit the family?"

"Yes. When Alice told me to do something, I did it. Disagreeing with her got you nowhere."

"Did you see which direction she went?"

He nodded. "She walked toward the figure. She didn't say anything and neither did the person who walked toward her. At least not that I could hear. I went around the corner and down the street to the flat where they were waiting for me."

"How long were you there?"

"Five or ten minutes." He cleared his throat. "It seemed a bit snug, but the family said they could take in the two little boys from the woman's sister. They're coming on the next Kindertransport, and we try to keep families together if at all possible."

"What did you do when you left the flat?"

"Do?" His elbow hit a stack of papers and he had to shove them back onto his desktop before they slid to the floor. "I went to the Underground station where we were all supposed to meet. We waited a quarter of an hour for Alice to appear, but she never showed up. Some of the people in our group, some of the women, were getting annoyed with Alice, and others wanted to go out looking for her."

"The men?" I asked.

"Yes."

It seemed to be a strange divide. Alice was not a femme fatale that I had ever noticed. "Had she wandered off on her own before?"

"Yes, twice. Once here, once in Berlin."

That sounded like it could have been by prearrangement. "Did she give any explanation as to why she left you waiting for her the other times?"

"None."

"Did anyone go looking for her after she was so late?"

"Yes, Charles and I split up and spent a quarter of an hour looking, starting at the point where I'd last seen her. We met up at our starting point when we had no luck and went back to the station, thinking she'd already traveled home."

"Did you check with her family to see if she'd returned?"

"No." He shook his head, widening his eyes slightly. "Alice would not have appreciated that. She believed in keeping her private life private."

"Even from her family?"

"Especially from her family." He gave me an earnest

gaze. "Alice was determined to do everything her way, and she didn't want people to try to dissuade her. That annoyed her."

A telephone rang. Tom ignored it and outside the closed door, I heard Mary murmur something into the receiver. "You never found out what she wanted to do that she had to keep secret?"

"Gosh, no. I gave up trying to figure out what Alice was up to a long time ago."

This was getting me nowhere. "How long have you known Alice?"

"Since university. We both went here in London. Her family was against her attending at first, but Alice was determined. Eventually, they gave in, just as everyone does sooner or later." The smile slid off his face. "Did. Everyone did sooner or later." The air seemed to leave his body. "I'm going to miss her."

Tom gave me the information I needed about our trip to Berlin and the Kindertransport on our return leg. He then excused himself, saying he had a meeting to attend, but told me that Mary could help me.

I lingered in the main office and watched Mary Wallace watch Tom with hunger in her dark eyes. While I felt sure he was at least thirty-five, she was probably several years younger. Her lack of ornamentation or cosmetics gave her an older, grayer appearance. She wore her dark hair in a bun at the nape of her neck and her dress was unfashionably long and plain.

A moment after the door shut behind him, I said, "Have you known Mr. Canterbury long?"

She jumped. Apparently, she had forgotten I was still in the office. Smoothing her skirts, she said, "I've known him most of my life. We attend the same Meeting."

"He's very good looking. Is he married? Engaged?"

"No." A glare accompanied her brief answer.

"He doesn't like girls?"

"No!" Shock showed in her voice. "He—he's just shy."

"And you. Are you married? Engaged?"

She didn't look me in the eye. "No. My parents feel I'm too young."

"But if you weren't, Tom would be courting you?"

At this point, she looked ready to explode, with a red face and I could imagine steam rising from her ears. "Why don't you mind your own business and write a good story about our work? That's the only reason you're here."

I wish you were right. I shrugged into my coat and walked out the door.

* * *

Next, I planned to question Johann, the suspicious fiancé. Lady Waterson had given me both his home and work addresses. Since it was during the work-day, I tried the solicitor's firm near the Inns of Court.

After climbing up from the Underground at the Chancery Lane station, I found my way to the offices where he worked. By now the rain had slacked off, making my journey slightly better. I didn't drip all over the wooden floors as I entered the front office of the law firm.

The clerk behind the desk asked me to state my name and business. I gave my name, but I only mentioned that I wanted to speak to Johann Klingler.

"I'm sorry," the man with gray liberally threaded through his brown hair told me. "Mr. Klingler has taken the afternoon off."

"Does this have anything to do with the death of his fiancée?"

He flinched as if I'd shown him her corpse. "I'm afraid so."

"Funeral arrangements? Interview with Scotland Yard?"

He snorted. "Nothing so useful. He's gone to pray for her."

I had a feeling the clerk was not a friend of Johann Klingler. "Where?" I expected to hear some Quaker meetinghouse or in a quiet stretch of parkland.

He raised his eyebrows practically to his hairline. "On the spot where they found his fiancée's body."

"Thank you."

As I turned to go, the man said, "You know where that is?" He sounded shocked that I would know something so unladylike.

"Yes." Then I decided to follow up, as long as I was here. "Have you found anything else he's done to be strange?"

He pursed his lips together. "Practically everything. His choice of foods, his unfamiliarity with our legal system, his running off in the middle of the day. We're used to our junior solicitors meeting a certain standard, and Mr. Klingler doesn't. And now his fiancée has been murdered. Scandalous."

The office clerk was against Mr. Klingler, his fiancé's family was against him, and the Nazis probably wanted to put him in prison. I couldn't wait to speak to Johann Klingler.

Anyone who had managed to make himself so unpopular should have a lot to tell me. If he was willing to speak.

Chapter Three

Fortunately, Sir Malcolm had given me the details of where Alice's body had been found by a constable long after midnight.

I took the Underground to Canning Town station, amazed when I reached street level at how different everything around me was from where I'd entered the system at Chancery Lane. Instead of formal stone and brick buildings with large windows and barristers dressed in black gowns and white wigs, these buildings looked as though they leaned on each other as they peered out through small windows along alleys, while the people who walked on the pavement looked frayed and scruffy.

A five-minute walk brought me to the entrance of an alley. A man stood a few buildings down the narrow space, his hands folded in front of him and his head bent. Guessing this was Johann Klingler, I walked down and silently joined him.

No wonder Canterbury couldn't find Alice. This area would have been very dark and desolate, and the alley would have been impenetrable at night without a torch. Had anyone in the group brought one?

We stood together in silence for perhaps five minutes before Johann glanced over at me. "Did you know her?" he asked with a noticeable German accent.

"No. I—"

"Then why are you here?" he snapped at me and bowed his head again.

"I've been tasked with finding Alice's killer. Opinion seems to be divided between those who think you'll hang for her murder and those who think you've suffered a great loss."

"Which side are you on?" His tone was aggressive.

I tried to match him. "The truth."

We stared at each other, neither breaking eye contact. Finally, he said in a calmer tone, "I didn't kill Alice. I had no reason to. If nothing else, she was my ticket to a new life in England, safe from the Nazis."

"Was that the only reason?"

"The only one that might convince you and the police."

I shook my head. "Did you love her?"

He glared at me. "Of course I loved her. What do you take me for?"

I made a decision to believe him until I had reason not to. "Someone who may suffer an even greater wrong." Curious, I asked, "Why do you pray here?"

"This is where her body was found." He looked down and sighed. Then he looked at me with great sadness in his eyes. "I didn't protect her. I offered to join her in meeting the families, but she said no. I let her have her way, and she died. I failed her. I need to ask her forgiveness."

One reason he might be carrying around guilt. Another was her murder. Either way, he looked ready to drop. "Let's head toward the City and find a tea shop.

You look like you haven't eaten in days."

I gave him a rueful smile and he nodded. "I have no appetite."

I gave him my arm and we left the alley. A few minutes later we found a coffee shop and went in to get a table near the back. He kept staring at the tabletop in silence, so I started asking questions. "How did you meet?"

"At the meetinghouse by Trafalgar Square. I was new to London then, and she was very helpful in introducing me to people who were able to find me employment and a place to live among our brethren. Whenever I went there, I always made it a point to speak to her. We became friends almost immediately."

"How long ago did you come to England?"

"It's been four years now." He tried to smile but his lips drooped immediately. "I can't even return with the Kindertransport. There is still a warrant out for my arrest and incarceration."

Our order, coffee for him, tea for me, and a couple of scones, arrived then, and he fell on the food eagerly. When he finished the scones, including mine, he thanked me.

"Would you like some more?" I asked.

"No. I've made quite a pig of myself. I was wrong when I said I had no appetite. But may I have more coffee?"

"Of course." I signaled our waitress and then asked, "Do you keep in touch with family or friends in Germany?"

"My sister and a few friends are still in Berlin. We exchange letters. My brother-in-law is a minor functionary in the Berlin government with loose ties to the Nazi party, so I'm sure my sister will be all right. I'm not so sure about my friends. They are solicitors and Quakers, as you call them. They are trying to get out."

"They are the ones who've warned you there is still an arrest warrant out for you?"

"Yes."

"How long had you and Alice been engaged?"

"Since the beginning of the year. She met my family on the first Kindertransport she traveled on and approved of them. Only then did she accept my offer of marriage."

"Did she carry messages between you and your family? Things you didn't want the censors to read?"

"Of course. Otherwise, some of our letters never get through, and others have words cut out so they are like—French cheese?"

"Swiss cheese."

"Ah."

"Did you meet many of Alice's friends?"

"Yes. We went to many parties at their homes and out to the theater with some of them. And, of course, we saw them at the meetinghouse for services and I helped at this end of the Kindertransport."

"Do any of them seem to be possible candidates for her murderer?"

He gave me a disgusted look. "Don't tell me you also believe Alice was killed deliberately and was not a random victim of robbery with violence."

"It's possible her killer was spotted that night talking to Alice."

"Alice talked to everyone." He smiled slightly, the first sign of someone who once must have been a happy man. "It was one of her many good qualities."

"She went out of her way to talk to this person, who seemed to be waiting for her."

Johann shook his head. "I can't believe it. Alice wasn't everyone's favorite person, but no one hated her. Not really."

I looked at him over the rim of my teacup. "Not really?"

"Well, Mary Wallace didn't like her, because she thought Alice was interested in Tom Canterbury. That was silly. They were friends who went on the Kindertransport together. Mary was jealous because she wants to marry Canterbury, who can't afford a wife."

So I kept hearing. "Anyone else?"

"Before I came along, Alice was briefly engaged to Charles Brooks, who is also involved in the Kindertransport. But they parted amicably." He set his coffee cup down with a clatter and glared at me. "This is ridiculous. No one wanted Alice dead."

"Someone did."

"No." He stared into his coffee cup. "It's unbelievable. It's impossible. It couldn't be anyone who knew her."

* * *

It was near the end of the workday, but I knew Sir

Malcolm Freemantle never went home early. There were too many plots to hatch. Or uncover. I went up to his office and once the guard had left, sat down in the chair across from his desk.

Sir Malcolm finally looked up and said, "Make yourself comfortable."

"I have." I didn't want to work for the spymaster, and it showed in my attitude. If I hadn't had to sign the Official Secrets Act to find out what had happened to my father the previous autumn, I wouldn't have been stuck working for Sir Malcolm again.

Then I realized that was ridiculous. He'd force anyone he wanted into working for him using any means necessary.

And he seemed to want to use me to find Nazi agents when they became killers.

Since Sir Henry paid my salary at the newspaper, I came wonderfully cheap.

He set down the papers he'd been reading, then lay down the pen, every movement slow and measured while he studied me. "What do you want?"

"I understand why you want me on the Kindertransport, so you can get me into Berlin to speak to someone at our embassy. But why do you want me to try to solve a local murder when Scotland Yard hasn't been able to figure it out?"

"We suspect certain Kindertransports are being used to send intelligence to Germany."

"So you said, but these people are pacifists. They are determined to save children's lives. You see spies under every table," I told him. I couldn't believe pacifists would actively try to undermine our country.

"Perhaps I do. Or perhaps we have Nazi infiltrators in every part of our society. What better way to get word past the censors than to send messages orally by way of a chaperone on the transport?" He tapped his pen on the desk.

Exactly what Johann Klingler told me he'd done to communicate with his family. I wouldn't tell Sir Malcolm that or he'd have Johann arrested immediately, and I had a feeling he wasn't the killer.

"This seems to be happening, but we've not been able to figure out how, or who, is receiving and then transmitting information to the Nazis." He set down the pen again. "By the way, your presence here saves me a call. The Quakers want you to attend a meeting about the next Kindertransport at the meetinghouse on St. Martin's Lane near Trafalgar Square. Be there tonight at eight."

"What am I supposed to tell these people when I just show up and ask a lot of questions?"

"Remember, you've been asked by the Refugee Children's Movement to write a newspaper article to drum up support and funding for the Kindertransports. Your assignment is to go along, work with them as one of the chaperones, and to write up the story when you get back. And try not to tie your work into Alice Waterson's murder."

"And you arranged it somehow so I'm slated to take Alice's place on the next transport to Berlin, leaving here the morning after next." I shook my head at how blatantly he was using me.

"Of course." He smiled at me broadly. "Make sure you report in to the British embassy in Berlin. You have the name of your contact there."

Douglas MacFerron. "And learn about my other assignment."

"Don't worry. It won't interfere with your work on the Kindertransport."

I shook my head in frustration. "Are you certain?"

"Of course. You have two important tasks to perform on this trip. Both must be carried out expertly. There are a lot of people counting on you."

Wonderful. I had no idea how to carry out two investigations I knew nothing about. I felt like I was drowning. "Have you told them I'm an untrained journalist, an untrained investigator, and an untrained spy?"

"Mrs. Denis, we don't have time to train anyone." Sir Malcolm looked as grim as I'd ever seen anyone. "We take the people who seem the best qualified and hope they can keep us safe until the government can figure out how to stop the invasion we all pray will never come."

"That's a lot to throw on people." I was scowling, even though I knew it would do me no good.

He shook his head. "Not as much as what may soon be thrown on all of us."

* * *

I had dinner and changed into one of my plainer

dresses, only to change my mind and put on a suit. They knew I wasn't one of them, so there was no reason to try to blend in. I reached the Quaker meetinghouse a minute late and found a group of more than twenty sitting at the far end of a large meeting room waiting for me.

By the looks on their faces, I knew they were not impressed.

"Now that you're here," a middle-aged man said as he rose, "perhaps you'll take a seat and we can begin."

I walked down the long middle aisle and took a seat as soon as I reached their group. I recognized Tom Canterbury and Mary Wallace. I didn't see Lady Waterson.

The man who appeared to be leading the meeting stood. He was middle-aged and wore a dark suit and tie, and what little hair he had was gray and circled his bald crown. "As you know, the Refugee Children's Movement has asked us to include Mrs. Denis on the next Kindertransport in the hopes of receiving good publicity from her newspaper, leading to increased funds and homes for the children. I thought it would be good for all of you to meet her."

A distinguished-looking gray-haired man in a well-tailored suit rose. "My daughter was to go on this trip when she was killed." I realized this had to be Lord Waterson. "Mrs. Denis has experience in avoiding danger while traveling back and forth to Germany. My hope is that she can prevent anyone else connected with the Kindertransport from dying."

When he resumed his seat, a middle-aged woman in a navy-blue dress with a tiny pattern in white stood and said, "What makes you think you can protect the chaperones on this Kindertransport when Scotland Yard has had no luck in finding Alice's killer?"

I stood and faced her. "I don't know that I can. But I am willing to try and prevent any attacks that may be aimed at the chaperones. I am going at the request of the Watersons and the Movement for the Care of Children from Germany, the parent organization for your efforts, to make sure the transport runs smoothly."

The woman continued. "That is a noble objective. Why should we believe you can accomplish it?"

"The Watersons are the ones who lost a daughter, and they want me to try." I emphasized "me." I stared at her as I said, "I have no intention of harming the transport or any member of your assembly, but I will stand against anyone trying to harm them or their work."

"Who put you in a position to judge?" The woman was relentless.

"I'm not judging anyone. I'm trying to protect people."

"Hmmph." The woman sat back down, her arms crossed.

The man sitting next to her rose. "Why should we let you travel with the Kindertransport? We know nothing of your moral character. We know nothing of your work ethic. You aren't one of us. You aren't Jewish, either. How do we know you won't cause problems for all the Kindertransports with the Germans? How do we know you're not a troublemaker?"

I looked around at a roomful of skeptical faces. How could I convince them I would be a help and not a hindrance?

And what problems would Sir Malcolm cause for me if they didn't allow me to go to Berlin?

Chapter Four

"I'm fluent in German, which should help in Berlin. I've traveled to that city twice in the past year and a half, helping the relatives of my boss, Sir Henry Benton of the *Daily Premier,* leave Germany. I also helped more than a dozen Jewish people get out of Vienna. None of them questioned my work ethic or my moral standing. They only wanted me to succeed in helping them escape the horror that is the Nazi government. And I did." I stared at the man standing across from me.

He was middle-aged, with a thin face, thin lips, and thin hair. He didn't appear impressed with my arguments.

"There's a danger you could be caught in Germany when the war begins. Are you ready to take that chance?" he asked me.

"I hope not, but I also hope the people from your congregation are not trapped behind enemy lines either."

"To us they are not enemies. We aren't called the Society of Friends for nothing," he said.

"The Nazis will treat us all as enemies if war begins. Quaker, Jew, and Church of England. Let's hope we all get out before the collapse of Czechoslovakia leads to war. Before the war reaches England's shores."

I saw a couple of heads nod when I finished.

"How did you get involved in rescuing these

people?" a woman in a large dull brown or rust-colored hat asked.

"It was all at the request of our newspaper publisher, Sir Henry Benton. He told me who I was to help and where to find them. I went under the cover of a newspaper assignment and the Nazis let me in as a journalist. Sir Henry knows I speak German and I've traveled there as a diplomat's daughter and as a diplomat's wife."

"What does your husband think of you running off to Germany without him?" the man asked, rising again.

I gave him a cold stare. "Nothing. He died over a year ago."

The man reddened and quickly sat.

"So, Sir Henry Benton will vouch for you?" the woman in the large hat asked.

"Yes, I believe he would."

"If there are no objections," the bald-headed man said, "we will accept Mrs. Denis as one of the chaperones on the Kindertransport leaving the day after tomorrow. We will now go on to discuss the operational details of the transports." The meeting then began to talk about a wide range of information that would be good to know for the article I needed to write.

The facts I needed were that I should be at Liverpool Street station the morning after next and to bring only one suitcase.

* * *

The next morning, I went over to Esther's house when I hoped baby John Henry Simon Powell, Esther's newborn son, would be awake. I rang the bell, and instead of the maid, the door was answered by Esther's grandmother, Mrs. Neugard.

"Don't ring the bell," she said in her thick German accent, "you'll wake my precious Simon."

The baby, named after his father's grandfather and two of his mother's grandfathers, was called Simon by Mrs. Neugard in honor of her late husband. Everyone else called him Johnny.

"Oh, I was hoping to see him awake. Is Esther available?"

"She is having her breakfast."

I peeled off my coat, hat, and gloves and immediately headed for the dining room, where I found Esther dressed in a ruffled, pink dressing gown having a full breakfast. "Oh, Livvy," she greeted me, "come join me."

"A cup of coffee wouldn't go amiss," I told her. "How are you doing?"

"He's feeding every three hours, so I'm not getting much sleep. Grandma has been a big help."

Knowing Mrs. Neugard to be a woman of strong and forceful opinions, I wondered how truthful Esther was being.

"He is growing fast like a piglet. So hungry. So greedy," Mrs. Neugard said.

I looked at Esther, ready to burst out laughing. Mrs. Neugard was a city dweller who kept a kosher home and had probably never seen a piglet in her life. Esther's stare silenced me immediately.

The maid brought me a cup of coffee and I sat down across from Esther. "Guess where I'm going tomorrow."

"Someplace warm? Lucky."

I shook my head. "Berlin. I'm going on a Kindertransport."

Esther set her fork down with a clank. "You're going back to Berlin? You are brave."

"To save all those babies," her grandmother said. "You are doing a good thing, Olivia."

"But what if war breaks out?" Esther asked.

"Then I'll see you after the war." When I saw her horrified expression, I waved a hand and said, "Since we're part of a humanitarian group, I suspect the Red Cross would find a way to get British citizens back to England. Sort of like diplomats."

"And the children? What about the children?" Mrs. Neugard asked.

I took a deep breath. I didn't want to think about it. "If we're in Germany when war breaks out, they won't get out."

The old woman shook her head. "That monster Hitler has a lot to answer for."

"At the meeting last night, I heard they are desperate for places to put all these children."

"We've been talking about taking in a small child," Esther told me. "It seems like a way we can help out."

We heard the cry of a hungry newborn come from upstairs.

"Come up with me and see the little one," Esther said with a proud smile.

I followed her up and spent a few minutes with an adorable, and very hungry, young man.

Then I headed to the *Daily Premier* building, carefully avoiding Miss Westcott and the office of the women's, home, and society pages on my way up to the top floor and Sir Henry's office.

His secretary ushered me right in, bypassing a delegation of printers as well as a reporter. Sir Henry looked up when she opened the door. "Olivia, come in."

I waited until I was across his huge desk from him and the door was shut before I said, "I just saw your grandson."

Sir Henry's face lit up. "Isn't he the most amazing child? So bright. So aware of everything already."

Johnny might be that someday, but right now, he was a newborn. He seemed to only eat and sleep. I nodded in reply before saying, "I'm off to Berlin in the morning. Is there anything you want me to particularly notice?"

"How people are faring in Berlin. How prepared they are for war. And of course, all the details of the Kindertransport."

Again, I nodded. "Do you have any friends who run schools in Britain?"

"Acquaintances, possibly. Why?"

"The people running the transports are speeding them up since the Nazis swallowed Czechoslovakia. They need more places to put the children. If some of the older ones could go to boarding schools, or if schools could expand their boarding facilities, that would help."

"I'll see." Sir Henry shook his head. "Another country with over one hundred thousand Jews overrun by the Nazis. More children will need to be rescued. You know Esther has asked James if they can take in a young child."

"She mentioned it, but doesn't she have enough on her hands at the moment?"

He raised his eyebrows. "She seems to be thrilled with motherhood and thinks she can help this way."

"That's Esther. She's a good person and loves to help. And Mrs. Neugard would probably love someone to speak German to. Someone else to mother."

"You think that's it? She wants to give her grandmother a purpose?"

"Absolutely." That's what I guessed Esther was thinking. "It could be good for both of them. And they have the room." And James might have a chance to get to know his son, something that I'd heard from Esther wasn't happening with Mrs. Neugard constantly hovering, telling them what they were doing was wrong. Then I thought of the poor child being over-watched by the old woman and cringed inwardly.

"I'm cleared to be gone for the next week or so?" I asked.

"I've spoken to Miss Westcott," Sir Henry said. "And now I'd better face the printers, or we won't have a paper going out in the morning." He rose on his platform behind his desk, making him appear several inches taller, and wished me safe travels as I left his office and the printers walked in.

After lunch, I went back to the Refugee Children's Movement office, supposedly to see if they had any last-minute requests for me. Really, I wanted to see if any of Alice's friends on Lady Waterson's list were there.

I found the office manned by Charles Brooks and Dorothy Young, two of the names on the list. We introduced ourselves, and then brown-haired, blue-eyed, delicately boned Dorothy said, "Have you been on one of these trips before?"

"No."

"They're frightful. We're watched constantly by the Gestapo to make sure we don't meet with any undesirables. Our luggage is searched before we leave so we don't smuggle anything for the children or their parents. The hotel we stay in is foul," Dorothy told me.

"It's cheap. We can't afford anything else. Every penny we raise has to go to transporting the children. Still, you think our money could run to a place with hot water," Charles told me.

When I looked surprised at the idea of no hot water, Dorothy said, "It never gets above luke-warm. Next summer it will be all right, but this winter it's been difficult."

"Do we stop in Amsterdam on the way?" I asked, hoping for a chance to rest in the middle of our lengthy travel.

"Only for a short stop, so be sure to wash your hair tonight," Dorothy said. She walked across the office with some paperwork and began to file, ignoring us.

"Anything special I should pack?" I asked Charles.

"Don't pack anything you'll miss if the Nazis steal it. Last time, they stole a cheap cigarette case from my luggage," Charles told me.

"I'll keep that in mind." I already knew about customs guards' love of petty theft. "I have to stop by the British embassy and see someone while we're there. Nobody should have a problem with that, will they?"

"No. In fact, you can do me a favor. Someone has to fill out the paperwork at the embassy for the Kindertransport and all the British citizens on it. It's my turn this time, but as long as you plan to go over there anyway..." Charles said. His face broke into a charming smile.

"I'll be glad to."

"Thank you," he said. He was no taller than Dorothy, although with lighter hair, with a handsome face and a cheery disposition.

"Charles hates paperwork," Dorothy told me when she returned to where we were standing and saw we'd accomplished nothing. "Actually, he hates all kinds of work."

He began to hum a tune and waltz around the office by himself. "I'm good at dancing and going to parties and enjoying myself. I'm no good at all at anything serious."

I smiled. "This isn't work, going on a train and herding lots of young children?"

"I just have to be there in case the little darlings try to kill each other. And as long as I'm doing this, my father doesn't make me work in the family business." He finished with a pirouette.

"Which is?"

"Making halfway decent furniture for people who want furniture that looks antique but don't want to spend a great deal for it." He gave me a smile and waltzed one more circuit around the office, this time with Dorothy in his arms. They looked very comfortable dancing together.

"I understand you and Alice Waterson were once engaged."

He laughed, not surprised that I had heard. "That was a long time ago. Before the earnest Johann came along."

"Who ended your engagement, you or Alice?"

"Alice, of course. No one walked away from Alice. She walked away from you. Once you know how the world is supposed to work, all was peaches and cream." He took hold of one of my hands and danced a few steps with me.

We weren't as practiced as he and Dorothy were. "You two knew her for a long time."

"Yes. Alice and I were in school together," Dorothy said once I extricated myself from Charles's embrace.

"That must have been a terrible shock. A random mugger killing her on an East End street. Unless it was someone who knew her."

"It was random," Charles said.

"Someone who knew her," Dorothy said at the same time.

"There seems to be a difference of opinion." What

did Dorothy know or guess? Alternatively, what was Charles trying to hide?

"Dorothy finds us all a bit suspect," Charles said. "Especially Wil."

"Wil who? And why him?" I asked.

"Wil Taylor. And you'd have to ask him why." Charles gave me a big smile that didn't take in the rest of his face.

"Pay no attention to him. When it comes to who murdered Alice, you men are all alike. Isn't she wonderful? Isn't she brilliant? She had you all fooled." Dorothy pulled on her dark wool coat and a dark wool cloche and strode out of the office, banging the door behind her.

I'd have to talk to her more during this trip.

Chapter Five

"What now?" Charles demanded in a petulant tone. "She's left me with all the filing. I don't know how to file."

I was about to ask if he knew his alphabet when we heard, "Just wait a minute, and Maggie and I will help you." I turned to see a woman in her late thirties speak as she took off her coat.

"I've been rescued," Charles said. "This filing was about to destroy my brain, or what little is left of it. May I present Mrs. Olivia Denis, our savior from the newspaper who will write a piece that will get us more funding. This is Betsy Taylor," he gestured at the older of the two women, "and Maggie Faircastle. They're sisters," he added.

It was a good thing he told me. Maggie was under thirty, a pretty brunette with big dark eyes. Betsy had her coloring but none of the beauty. She was a solidly built, no-nonsense sort of woman who immediately came over to shake my hand. "My husband Wil and I will be on this transport with you. Maggie is staying behind to watch our children."

I faced Maggie. "Another important job."

She smiled. There was no snobbishness in her voice when she replied, "I know."

As she walked over to begin work on the filing, Betsy said, "What upset Dorothy? She ran past us without a word of greeting."

"I mentioned that Alice Waterson could have been killed by a random stranger or someone who knew her who had a grievance," I told her. "She and Charles disagreed. The idea seemed to anger her."

"I'm sure she said someone who knew Alice well."

"She did. But why would the suggestion annoy her so? Was she close friends with Alice Waterson?" I asked.

"She was," Betsy told me, "until the two had a falling out. For once it wasn't over a young man. Dorothy had been chosen to lead this Kindertransport by the committee in charge. They try to rotate the leadership among the younger members to give them experience."

She shook her head, more in sorrow than in anger. "Alice had accepted that the leadership chosen for the first two trips were because they were men. But she tried to completely take over the lead this time in place of Dorothy. Undermining her every decision. Ignoring her directions. Dorothy was so upset she was about to resign when Alice was killed."

"And then what did she do?"

"She still wanted to quit. We all encouraged her to stay on, so she finally agreed. Told her it was good experience for her." Betsy began to sort a stack of papers.

Was Dorothy upset because she was a killer, or because she gained at another's death? I'd have to find out. In the meantime, I wanted to know how these two felt. "What do you think?"

"Someone who knew her," Betsy said with a

determined set to her shoulders. Maggie looked over at me and nodded.

I glanced over at Charles who was sitting on a table making no pretense of filing and glaring at Betsy. "Charles seems to disagree with you," I said. "Why is that?"

"Dorothy wouldn't kill Alice. She might resign, but she wouldn't kill anyone. We're pacifists," Charles declared.

"Nobody's accusing Dorothy. But to know Alice, if one had a brain," Betsy said, glancing over at Charles, who made a face at her, "was to know she attracted men like insects to a streetlamp. It didn't matter who the man was, whether he was single or not, and whether he was eight or eighty. It annoyed any woman in the man's life."

"Did she break up any marriages or engagements?" I could see that being a reason for murder.

"Not for long, although some of her flirtations caused bad feelings at the time. Then Alice would flit over to a new favorite. Most of the time, the men would quickly realize what good fortune they'd had to be dropped as Alice's current favorite." Betsy looked at Charles. "Of course, the young, single, foolish boys were heartbroken."

He made a face at her and left the room, putting on his coat and scarf as he departed.

Now I hoped the sisters would speak openly. "Were all of these men members of your Meeting?"

"Most of them, but there were a few who weren't

even Friends."

It took me a moment to realize she was referring to Quakers. "How did her parents react to all of this? Did it cause bad feelings between her parents and others in the congregation?"

"Never," Betsy said in a scoffing voice. "Alice could do no wrong in her parents' eyes. A few people tried to say something when she was barely out of her teens, and her parents, her mother especially, made it clear that Alice was not at fault."

"In Alice's defense, everyone, male and female, did Alice's bidding. She was a natural leader," Maggie said.

"There was a lot of coercion applied on anyone who wanted to do something other than Alice's assigned role for them," Betsy replied.

"Coercion by Alice or by the group?"

"Oh, by Alice. She didn't need anyone's help in making someone toe the line when it came to her wishes. She would just wear people down," Betsy explained. "Or ignore them as she walked over them."

"Was anyone, male or female, part of her closest circle of friends for long?" I asked. I could guess the answer to that question, but I wanted confirmation.

Betsy and Maggie looked at each other. "Not really," Maggie finally said. "Sooner or later, everyone wanted to do something other than Alice's way, and there'd be— not a falling out, exactly, more of a parting of the ways."

"That never applied to her parents," Betsy said. "They always wanted to do everything Alice's way. She was their only child, you see. They worshipped her."

"I'm surprised they allowed her to go on the Kindertransport since she was their only child. There is a danger of war breaking out or Kindertransport chaperones running into difficulties with the Nazis."

"Alice wanted to go. And her parents had been well trained, so that if Alice wanted to do something, she was permitted to do it," Betsy told me.

"That's not fair," Maggie said. "You make Alice sound like a monster. She wasn't. We all liked her—well, most of the time."

"That's true," Betsy said with a sigh. "Most of the time, we really didn't notice or mind Alice's manipulations. She was fun to be around. She was hard-working, energetic, and frequently kind. And she was intelligent and tried to be fair."

"Was there anyone she'd annoyed lately? Anyone's husband she'd favored recently?"

Betsy and Maggie exchanged a look. "No. No one," Betsy said.

Somehow, I didn't quite believe her.

* * *

The next morning, I wrote Adam a note while I drank a cup of coffee. I left it on the kitchen table where I was sure he'd see it if he came to London on leave from the British army before I returned from Berlin. We were engaged, and liable to remain in that state for the foreseeable future.

I couldn't see getting married to a man I wasn't likely to see for weeks and months on end, especially if being wed meant I'd no longer be free to work outside the home. The war would change that. I was sure then, like during the Great War, women would be allowed to take the place of men in the workforce.

I'd promised Adam I'd marry him on the day when war was declared.

I had already called my father the night before to tell him I'd be out of town for a few days and wouldn't be able to see him for Sunday dinner. We had the habit of meeting at some upscale restaurant at midday on Sundays and ignoring each other the rest of the week. Other than asking how Adam was, and if we'd set a date yet, he hadn't appeared interested in what I was doing. He didn't ask where I was going, and I certainly wasn't going to tell him and listen to that lecture.

I headed to the Liverpool Street station, arriving a few minutes early. The rest of the group was already assembled. Dorothy was checking off names on her list.

She put a mark by my name as she said, "Charles, you're to inform the British embassy of our arrival and give them this list."

Apparently, Dorothy hadn't heard me talking to Charles in the office. "Dorothy, I have to go to the British embassy when we get in anyway. Would you like me to take the list over to register us at the same time? I know where the embassy is, and I'm sure Charles will be of more assistance since he knows how the Kindertransport works. Otherwise, I'll have to tag along with him since I have to show up in person."

I'd heard how much Alice had upset her and I didn't want her to think I was trying to usurp her leadership.

Her expression changed from indecisive to mulish. "Why do you have to go there as soon as we get in?"

"My boss requires it." I didn't mention which boss. "My duties to him shouldn't interfere with my duties to you and the transport, but I do have to report into the embassy at least once, and probably more. I thought in this case I could do you a favor." I shrugged and stood with my feet planted, waiting.

"Fine. Mrs. Denis, you'll be our liaison with the embassy." She handed me the list of names and turned to board the train car.

We all shuffled on after her, lugging our suitcases.

The train to Harwich stopped at what felt like every station in the east of England. Our group of passengers read, knitted, worked crossword puzzles in the morning paper, and slept.

Previously, I'd flown to Germany and taken the train on the return journey when I had helped Sir Henry's late wife's family escape with their valuables. It had been necessary to use two different routes to avoid the interest of any guards who might remember me, so I could smuggle out furs and jewels that I claimed as mine. Luxury goods I didn't have when I entered the country.

On this trip, I watched the city fall away and the scene outside my window become all farmland, relieved that I'd be myself from the beginning to the end of the journey. When I grew bored, I began to read the *Daily Premier.*

The train took us to the end of the line at the edge of

the ferry docks, and then it was a short, brisk walk in a cold wind to reach the ferry building where Dorothy handed in our group ticket. Then we hurried up the ramp and found our cabins to drop off our luggage.

I found I was in a tiny cabin with two berths pressed up against the walls, with a woman I hadn't met before. "Gwen Endicott," she told me when I gave her my name. "You must be the woman who's supposed to write articles to help us raise funds for the Kindertransports and is fascinated by Alice's murder."

"I'm a reporter. I'm always interested in a story. Are you in the group that believes she was murdered by someone who knew her or believes it was a random case of violence?"

"Someone who knew her, and since we're all raised to abhor violence, it must be someone she knew who isn't a member of the Society of Friends."

"Did she know many people who aren't members of your church?"

"Of course. People from university, children of peers, people she's met through our work with the transport. All of them about our age." Gwen appeared to be thirty, as I knew from the records that Alice had been. Since I was only twenty-six, I wasn't flattered to be grouped in with them.

"Anyone in particular she'd mentioned lately? Either in a good or a bad way?" I hoped someone I spoke to on this trip would hold the key to the murder.

"Not to me. We knew a lot of the same people, but after I told her several times that I didn't like gossip, she stopped talking to me. Which suited me just fine."

"It sounds like Alice Waterson didn't have any female friends." And from the times I'd seen her at parties a few years ago, I hadn't liked her either.

"She preferred the company of men to women." Gwen shrugged. "Some women are like that."

"Have you traveled to Berlin before?" I asked. "What is your usual task on the Kindertransport?"

"I've gone twice. I'll be in a train carriage with older girls on the way back. While we're there, I'll help with the paperwork, getting the lists ready for someone, you I hope, to turn into the British embassy."

"I know someone there, and some of the embassy people probably know my father or knew my husband. It'll make dealing with the embassy easier." I gave her a smile.

"In the normal way of things, you'd be the one to turn in the list to the German government, too. I don't know if Dorothy will have you do that or not. That'll depend on how much she trusts you by the time we leave Berlin." She smiled in return, but I didn't see any warmth in her expression.

"Where do we turn in the list to the Germans?"

"At the station, to the customs guards when they search our luggage. The Gestapo always already have the list. Somehow."

"Oh, goody. The guards really are swine." I'd had trouble with the ones at the Vienna rail station that I really didn't want to repeat. And this time I wouldn't have Oberst Wilhelm Bernhard of the German army to help me. Although he could be in Berlin. I wondered if I'd see him again.

As unlikely as it was, I would like to. We'd developed a sort of cautious friendship, and to me, he represented the best of Germany as our countries marched toward war.

"Are you fluent in German?" Gwen asked, breaking into my thoughts.

"Yes."

"Better you deal with them than me," Gwen said. "Are you coming up to the café? You can see us all in action, then, and start working on your story for the paper."

It appeared Gwen wasn't concerned with me or my task. I wondered how many others weren't either.

Chapter Six

Most of the crew for the Kindertransport ate in silence, reading or otherwise ignoring me. I sat with Betsy Taylor and her husband, Wil. I learned Wil was short for Wilbur and he was a plumber. They had two children, a five-year-old boy and a seven-year-old girl, that they both adored.

Wil and Betsy were evenly matched, average height and stocky, but I noticed now both had lovely brown eyes. They were people you had to search to find their outward beauty. Their inward beauty I found obvious by their presence here rescuing children.

I was surprised to see that Wil appeared several years younger than Betsy, but no one else seemed to notice or care.

Betsy told me over a sandwich and coffee, "We couldn't bear to send our children away to strangers, and I'm sure the parents of the children we're taking out of Germany feel the same way. If they had any other choice, they wouldn't be sending their children off with strangers." She shook her head. "Those poor parents."

"We try to give the children a little no-nonsense security on the trip. Make them feel like the world isn't coming to an end," Wil said with a rueful smile. "The world might be in the middle of unraveling, but some things aren't changing."

Wil's stockiness I now noticed was most evident in

his broad shoulders. He almost heated up the café with his rock-hard body, but none of the other women in our group seemed to notice. They must be used to him. He made me miss Adam.

"You sound like ideal parents. Loving, but realistic."

"Thank you, Olivia," Betsy said, not looking toward her husband. "What were your parents like?"

"My mother died when I was six. My father tried, but he had to travel for his position at the Foreign Office. There was a series of housekeepers until I was old enough for boarding school. I envy your children. Two sensible, loving parents who are there day in and day out."

They looked at each other, and then away. Betsy began to tell me about their daughter's schooling. My comments made them uncomfortable, but I couldn't figure out why.

The sea was rough, but not frighteningly so. I wandered the deck for a while after dark before returning to the cabin. Gwen was already asleep. I managed to get some sleep before we reached the Dutch port of the Hook of Holland in the early morning darkness and trudged from the dock to the train that would take us to Germany.

The sun soon rose over the winter-blighted landscape of fields and canals, followed by a brief stop in downtown Amsterdam. Then we were rushing toward the German border at Bentheim, the train wheels clacking off the miles. We'd been a quiet group before, reading and knitting. Now we were completely silent.

The tension in our carriage grew by the mile. Shoulders hunched. No one seemed to breathe. I glanced around, but couldn't get anyone to look at me.

My stomach clenched and my chest hurt. I told myself it was ridiculous. I'd left Germany before without much difficulty, but what if the war started? What if the Nazis found out whatever it was Sir Malcolm wanted me to do?

And then we stopped at Bentheim and the Nazi border guards came onto the train. I found it hard to breathe. My fellow passengers paled.

They examined Charles Brooks's passport first. Dorothy held our group visa for this trip. She tried to show it to the border guards, but they ignored her.

The head guard snapped out a command about the visa in Austrian-accented German. Great. Austrian officials were more difficult to deal with than the Germans. Charles and Dorothy were both stumped by his thick accent.

"It's a group visa. Approved at the highest levels of the Third Reich," I told him in German. I hoped I wasn't lying. Earlier, I had learned that guards on the border didn't want to check with Berlin because it made their workday longer. I hoped that still held true.

"Where did you learn German?" the guard snapped at me.

"While attending school and on many trips to your beautiful country," I told him.

"Jewish?"

"None of us are. We will be removing Jewish children from your country on our return journey." I hoped that would make him speed us on our way.

"Kindertransport," he sneered.

"You'd rather we left them in Germany?"

He called us some foul names, tossed Charles's passport back at him, and stalked out of the train carriage, leaving Dorothy holding the visa he hadn't given a glance.

"What was that about?" Wil asked.

"We're good to go to Berlin," I said with a shrug.

Dorothy stared at me, but she didn't say a word. She kept watching me after she sat and we waited for the train to move.

Once the train was underway, she rose again and gestured for Gwen, who was sitting next to me, to move. Gwen looked at me, raised her eyebrows, and moved to Dorothy's former seat. Dorothy sat next to me and leaned closer. "You're fluent in German."

"Yes."

"How did you get so familiar with the language that you could understand that guard?"

"I recognized his accent. He's from the hills in western Austria. I studied German in school and then traveled here frequently, first with my father and then with my husband. Both were with the Foreign Office's German desk at one time or another."

"I think I'm going to be glad you came on this transport with us." Dorothy gave me a hint of a smile before she turned back to her book.

The tension eased in the carriage and I felt my muscles relaxing. Maybe the trip wouldn't be too dangerous after all.

We arrived in Berlin and walked the cold distance from the station to our hotel. Like all travelers' hotels near train stations, it was threadbare, with lumpy beds and, ordinarily, hottish water.

As soon as I dropped my suitcase off in my room, I found Dorothy, told her I was going to register us, and left for the British embassy. Knowing Sir Malcolm would reimburse me, I took a taxi.

When the wind blew me through the front entrance, I showed my British passport to the guard at the door. Then I asked for Douglas MacFerron. He looked a little surprised, but he waved one of his fellow guards over to escort me.

MacFerron's office was on the second floor off a nondescript corridor and behind an unmarked door. My escort knocked on the door and then opened it, gesturing me in.

Inside were three men of similar size and dress sitting at dark wooden desks on three of the four chairs in the office. All three shoved any papers on their desktops into drawers as they stood in unison.

"Douglas MacFerron?" I asked.

The three men looked at each other. Then the one at the middle desk said, "Yes?"

"I'm Olivia Denis. Sir Malcolm Freemantle should have told you to expect me."

"Of course." MacFerron, tall, thin, and balding, came

around his desk to move the fourth chair directly in front of where he had sat. The smile he greeted me with didn't reach his eyes. "Please, sit. Would you care for tea?"

Tea at the British embassy had to be better than any I'd get at our miserable hotel. "Thank you."

As I sat, one of the other two men—also tall, thin, but with a thick head of hair—left the room.

"How much has Sir Malcolm said about this little task he has for you?"

"Practically nothing. He said you would tell me."

"I'll wait until my associate returns with the tea." MacFerron leaned back in his chair. "Did you have a pleasant journey?"

"It was long, but the sea wasn't rough. Good preparation for traveling back with all those children." I shuddered a little. I wasn't ready to spend two days surrounded by frightened children.

"Ah, yes. Sir Malcolm mentioned that you are taking a murder victim's place on the Kindertransport in an effort to find clues to a killer. How is that going?"

"Slowly." Rather like the way this man was dragging out our conversation. "I have the list of British subjects on the transport that I'm supposed to turn into someone here. Do you know which of your colleagues I should see?"

"You have the list?" A smile crossed his face. "That could be useful. Very useful."

"Useful for what?" I was getting tired of his cryptic comments.

"Just a—ah, here he is," MacFerron said as his colleague came in with the tea tray. MacFerron's desk was used to prepare our cups as the chairs were pulled over to form a circle around the desk. "You must be hungry and tired."

"Yes."

Once we were settled, MacFerron looked at his colleagues. When they nodded, he said, "There is a German dissident who had a well-placed position in the German government until a few days ago. He had been secretly informing us on German military buildup. Very hush-hush information. Very valuable for the British army and air force. Then he was taken to Sachsenhausen."

When I looked at him blankly, he said, "Sachsenhausen is a prison just outside of Berlin. Horrible place. Run by the SS. It's where they send the dissidents. Rumor has it they don't last very long there."

"Sir Malcolm wants me to get him out?" If so, Sir Malcolm was insane.

"Impossible. But our man wants us to get his wife and sons out. And it has to be soon. He can't hold out for long, and he has told us if we don't, he will let the Nazis know all the information he's given us."

"You want his sons to leave on the Kindertransport." No wonder Sir Malcolm wanted me to take Alice Waterson's place.

"And his wife."

"The boys I can get out fairly easily. Put their names on the list and give them numbered tags for them and their suitcase and rucksack. Then someone just needs to bring them to the assembly point at the correct time. But his wife? How am I supposed to do that?"

Instead of answering, he said, "And they have to go out under assumed names, with forged papers."

MacFerron kept adding problems to this assignment. Did they think I was a miracle worker? I didn't have the contacts to pull this off. "I hope you can forge German papers. I definitely can't."

"I know someone who can forge the boys' papers, but you'll have to approach him. We'd draw too much attention and endanger him."

"And you need to pay him." My voice was flat. I didn't have that sort of money. If I did, I wouldn't be staying in that awful hotel.

"Yes. We have Reichsmarks for just such cases. And we can produce a British passport, under a different name, for his wife. We just have to add her name to the visa lists."

"We'll have to hurry. We leave the morning after tomorrow. Thirty-six hours." I doubted we could manage it.

All three men nodded. "We know. We can do it, with your help," MacFerron said.

They'd thought of everything. I'd just have to pull all the pieces together.

And therein lay the danger.

"The boys' Christian names are Gerhard and Heinrich. Nice, common names. Now we just need a nice common surname."

"Schmidt," one of the other men said.

"That'll work. Can you get 'Gerhard and Heinrich Schmidt' added to your list of children?"

"I'll have to, won't I?" I felt as if I was being pushed along by a current, allowed no will of my own. I was annoyed. If it hadn't been for a good cause, I would have been really annoyed.

"The mother's Christian name is Agathe. That should work on an English passport if we anglicize the spelling. And the last name?" He tapped his pencil on the desk. "How about 'Manchester'? That should work. Change the birth date slightly."

"Got it," one of the other men said. "We'll get to work on it right away."

"Good. Now, Mrs. Denis, let's go see that German forger."

I gulped down the last of my tea and rose, pulling my dull brown coat, so sensible for long travels, back on. The third man in the office, who was slightly shorter and blonder, opened the safe and, glancing through several envelopes inside, chose one and handed it to me. When he told me how much money was in there in Reichsmarks, I gasped.

"That's how much two sets of children's papers cost, plus a bonus for fast work," he told me.

"What about their photos?"

"Use the ones in their current papers. You'll need to take the photos out before you meet the boys at the train station and glue them into the new papers. That means you'll need to meet with the boys sometime before going to catch the train."

"And the mother's passport photograph?"

"We've taken care of that already," MacFerron said. "If you'll come with me, I'll show you where the forger is."

"What's his name? I can't just call him the 'forger.'"

"Then call him the 'shoemaker.'" MacFerron grinned at me as he held the door open for me to go first.

We went out the main entrance of the embassy building and down the street, walking quickly and holding onto our hats. If the Gestapo was trying to see our faces, they'd have difficulty in this wind and the darkness as night fell. We hopped onto a tram and rode it for a distance before getting off and walking.

MacFerron appeared interested in what was on display in all the shop windows. We walked a distance, turning several times, until I was lost. My stomach grumbled.

Then he smiled and said, "Good. We're not being followed any longer."

"Were we?" I felt my empty stomach churn as it sank to my knees.

"Of course. Welcome to Berlin."

Chapter Seven

"I don't think I like it," I murmured to him. "This is too dangerous. How can I accomplish anything if I'm being followed all the time? Does Sir Malcolm think we can do this under the watchful gaze of the Gestapo?"

MacFerron glanced around before whispering in my ear as we walked. "Sir M wants this done. To do this requires risks. If we don't, the prisoner will tell what he knows and all England pays. The babies, the grandparents, your family and mine."

"He was that well-placed?" No wonder the Nazis put him in a prison camp. And there would not have been a trial under the present German government. He would just disappear.

MacFerron gave me a dry look. "Until the Gestapo became suspicious and pulled him in, he was England's best-placed source. We don't know who tipped off the Gestapo."

I began to suspect why the embassy was working so hard to rescue his family. "There's a leak at the embassy?"

"Possibly." He shrugged. "We don't know."

"Why do you have the mother's photo?"

"Our contact was demanding we move them out of the country. We were starting to when the Gestapo put a freeze on their passports." He glanced around, then at me. "Again, we don't know if we have a leak or if they have nosy neighbors or if someone in the defense ministry became suspicious."

I was certain of one thing. "I need to meet the family before we travel away from their home. And at some point, I'll need to get the boys' photos to paste onto their new papers."

"Not at the embassy."

I nodded my understanding.

"Don't turn your head, but across the street is Schumacher's Bookshop."

I froze, stopping my instinct to look at the last moment.

"Mr. Schumacher is the man you need to talk to. If there's anyone else in the shop, just tell him you're browsing. He says he doesn't trust anyone, not even his old friends. Fortunately, he's seldom busy. You can come and go safely."

"Do I mention your name to him?"

"No, just ask for a book on flowers."

That must be their prearranged signal. "May I leave you here and speak to him if he's free?" I might as well get this started. We didn't have much time, and apparently the need to get the informer's family to safety was critical.

"I'll get a coffee in this café. Meet me when you finish." He gave me a kiss on the cheek so anyone watching would think we were friends out shopping, and went inside the small restaurant.

I crossed the street and walked into the bookshop, the movement of the door making the bell overhead jingle loudly. Beyond the shelves of Nazi propaganda, the shop was crowded with shelves carrying books on every possible subject. A portly, middle-aged man wearing thick glasses was assisting a customer at the counter. I wondered how someone wearing such thick lenses could do fine forgery work.

I wished them a good morning in German and began to search the spines of the books for a title that mentioned flowers.

When the customer left, the man walked over to me. "Are you Herr Schumacher?" I asked.

"Ja. How may I help you, mein Frau?"

"I hear you have excellent books on flowers."

"They're back here. You just didn't go far enough to find them." He led the way along a bookcase that stood parallel to the front door and bent down. The books were on the next to the bottom shelf.

I crouched down also to look at the copies as he murmured, "What do you really want?"

"Two children's identification papers and passports. Here are their names and birth dates." I slipped him a scrap of paper. "I need them by tomorrow night. And I'm willing to pay above the going rate."

"I can't do it. It takes time to age the documents."

"They're young boys going on the next Kindertransport. And they're not Jews. How aged do their papers need to be?"

He nodded. "Not particularly. Not with the Kindertransport. Do you have photographs?"

"I'm to glue them in when I remove them from the old papers."

"Use a very thin blade to cut the photographs out, and be sure to burn the old passports to destroy them." He gave me a quick lesson in removing and reattaching photos, one ear constantly cocked as he listened for anyone entering his shop.

I nodded and then pulled out the envelope with the Reichsmarks.

"Come back tomorrow afternoon at five. Plan on buying another book. Say nothing to anyone."

A moment later, the bell over the door clanged, signaling another customer. I sucked in my breath and hoped they couldn't hear my heart as it began to pound.

Herr Schumacher pulled two books on flowers off of the shelf and put the envelope with the Reichsmarks inside one that was hollowed out in the center. "I would think one of these two will do well for you."

"Danke."

We both rose and I followed him to the counter as he called out to the customer, "I'll be with you in a moment. Ah, good evening, mein Frau."

I nodded to the woman. She stared at me through narrowed eyes. All I could think was that she was an informer for the Gestapo and I was about to be arrested.

"Have you decided which book you want?" Herr Schumacher asked.

"Yes. I'll take this one," I said, pointing to the book that didn't contain the embassy's money in the hollowed-out center. He slipped the other book under the counter.

He told me the price and I paid it with some spare

Reichsmarks MacFerron had given me at the embassy. Shaking, I bobbled my change.

"Shall I wrap it for you?" he asked.

"There's no need. I'll just take it," I said with a smile, taking a deep breath to try to settle my nerves. As he handed me the book, I said, "Thank you for your help." Then I gave the middle-aged woman a smile and left the store.

I tried not to run as I reached the pavement and crossed the street to the café.

MacFerron looked at me over his newspaper. "Did you get your book?"

"Yes, it should prove to be very helpful. I'd like a cup of coffee," I added.

MacFerron signaled the waitress who wordlessly brought a cup and filled it with coffee. I put in a little supposed sugar and tasted it. It was so bitter I didn't think I could swallow a sip, let alone drink the whole cup as I knew I would if I were a German.

He went back to his newspaper and I browsed the book on flowers, enjoying, if that was the proper word, our coffee in silence. Finally, he paid our check and we left, walking back to the tram.

I tried to memorize the route, but we seemed to turn at nearly every corner. Finally, I said, "I don't think I can find my way back to the shop."

"I thought you knew Berlin."

"Not this part."

He grumbled, but he finally said, "When do you have to be there?"

"At five tomorrow afternoon."

"Come to the embassy at four. And wear business clothes. Don't plan on wearing an evening gown on this trip."

"Good." I grinned at him. "I didn't bring one."

"Are you coming back to the embassy now?"

"Yes. I need to officially present the list of British chaperones on the transport, including Agatha Manchester, and then take the list back with me."

He studied me for a moment. "Will you be able to convince the Quaker chaperones to keep quiet about the extra woman in their group?"

"I'll tell the woman in charge and hope she'll agree. I'd rather keep this away from the other members of the group until the last minute."

"Why?" He looked puzzled.

"Alice Waterson, the woman who was murdered, could have been killed for one of three reasons. One, it was a random robbery gone wrong. This is favored by the police, but something I learned makes that unlikely. Two, one of these pacifist Quakers lost their minds and killed her over a personal quarrel. This is favored by the women who knew her."

"And the third?"

"Three, Alice found out that one of the group was aiding the Germans. Alice is from a pacifist family, but her father worked as an ambulance driver in the Great War. They are loyal to Britain. She might have confronted this unknown person and been killed."

"Yes, I can see why you don't want to risk letting

everyone know about the extra passengers." He raised his eyebrows, and we continued to the embassy in silence.

I found that one of MacFerron's colleagues had retyped the list exactly as it had been, with one addition. I took the new list to the clerk who kept track of British citizens traveling to Germany with group visas. He stamped it and made a copy for their files, returning the original to me.

I went back to the hotel to find the group in the lobby getting organized. Betsy, Helen, Dorothy, and Gwen had the few chairs, while Wil, Tom, and Charles leaned against the faded wallpaper of large pinkish flowers with greenish leaves and a background browned with smoke and age. "What took so long? I thought we'd have to go to dinner without you," Dorothy said.

I made a gesture of puzzlement, shrugging my shoulders and shaking my head, while I wondered what they had done while I was involved with my other assignment. Had I missed a handoff of British secrets? "Paperwork always takes forever."

"Did you get our visa filed with the embassy?"

"Yes."

"What about the German border officers?"

That surprised me. Why would the Germans be interested in us before we left the country? "The embassy said the Nazis aren't interested in us until we board the train."

"Alice Waterson always said she presented our

visas to the main border enforcement office in Berlin," Dorothy told me.

"Why did she do that?" I asked. "No one ever wanted to see mine except when I climbed aboard the train or when we stopped at the border. And the embassy said there is no reason to."

"I don't know, but there must be some reason," Dorothy said, sounding flustered.

And then I had a fourth reason why Alice might have been killed. She was a Nazi agent, or she and Johann together were helping the Germans, and someone found out and stopped her. "Was the list stamped when she returned?"

"I..." Dorothy frowned. "I don't know." She looked around the small area. "Does anyone know if our list was stamped after Alice returned from the border security office?"

One by one, the group members shook their heads or shrugged.

Tom said, "I took the list on our first trip. The Germans had no interest in Britishers who were only in the country for a couple of days to take Jews out. They told me not to bother them."

"Could she have been doing something she didn't want to tell you about?" I asked.

"You mean was she visiting Johann's family?" Gwen asked. "I think that's very likely. I know she wanted to get to know them before she agreed to marry Johann. That was why she went on her first transport with the Refugee Children's Movement."

"They were engaged shortly after she returned," Dorothy said.

"Why wouldn't she have told you that's what she was doing?" I asked.

"Alice liked to keep her business to herself," Charles said.

"Usually because she was up to no good," Betsy muttered to herself.

Not quite quietly enough. "That's not fair," Charles said, moving away from leaning on the wall to stand over her. "She wanted to keep her private business private. Even if what she did had no importance."

"You know as well as I do that she did anything that popped into her brain, whether it was kind or cruel," Betsy retorted. "And often enough, she did things she didn't want others to take notice of."

"She did care about people. Really. She did." Charles sounded a little desperate, as if he was pleading for us to believe Alice was a kind person. I'd only met her a few times, but I didn't see her as considerate.

"If they were male. We females didn't see much kindness from her," Betsy said, standing to stare Charles in the eye.

His chin jutted out as he leaned toward Betsy. "Not every woman had the same problem with her that you had."

"Betsy," Wil said in a warning voice, reaching out with one hand to touch her arm. She speared him with a glare and he dropped his hand.

Betsy turned back to Charles. They were nearly

nose to nose. "Sooner or later every married woman did."

"No, only you and others who couldn't keep their cheating husbands happy. Your ex-criminal husband."

Chapter Eight

Someone gasped, and then the room fell silent.

Ex-criminal? I looked around. Did his crime have anything to do with Alice's death? Hopefully, someone would tell me what Charles was talking about.

"Charles, that's gossip. Apologize to the Taylors," Gwen said.

"I can't believe you said something so malicious," Dorothy snapped at him.

Charles looked around the room. Defiance leaked out of him as his shoulders sagged. He dropped down to sit on his heels. "I'm sorry. I miss Alice so much. She had such a joyous laugh." He glanced up at the Taylors. "I'm taking it out on everyone. You just happened to be in the line of fire this time. I didn't mean anything by it. I'm sorry, because you didn't deserve that."

"Apology accepted," Betsy said gruffly with a quick nod.

"Watch what you say next time," Wil said as he took Betsy's hand. "Keep it up and someone who's not a pacifist might knock your block off."

Charles hung his head. "Yes, sir."

Gwen walked over to me and said so no one else would hear, "That's why I think Alice was killed by someone outside of our faith. We can be perfectly beastly, but we are all encouraged to forgive. And if Wil and Betsy can forgive Charles's words and let it go, the rest of us certainly will."

I gave her a skeptical look. I couldn't believe all Quakers were so innocent. "Why Wil? And why 'ex-criminal'?"

"It's not my story to tell." Gwen looked at me, a bland expression on her face. She was the one who gave Charles a hand up from his position on the floor as we headed for the front door.

No one seemed inclined to talk to me or acknowledge my existence as anything but an outsider. In fairness, that's what I was.

We walked a short distance through the darkening streets, the wind cutting us from every direction, until we reached a small restaurant across the road from the train station. We found a few empty tables together, with green striped cloths and heavy wooden chairs.

It was quickly apparent that the place was familiar to several of our party when I was repeatedly told in English, "The sauerbraten isn't much, but the sausages are delicious." When it was my turn, I took their advice and ordered sausages and warm potato salad with sauerkraut.

I glanced around and realized half the patrons were in German army uniforms. Until that moment, I had ignored my memories of Oberst Wilhelm Bernhard. Now I realized I had been unconsciously looking around every corner, hoping to see him again.

That was silly. He was a soldier for a country everyone said we would have to fight sooner or later. He had helped me every time I'd been to Germany, but I shouldn't need his help this time. I was leaving in little more than a day with a Kindertransport.

With three people who hadn't been scheduled to be on our train.

Three people with forged papers. Two sets of which I needed to pick up tomorrow afternoon, transfer the photographs, and destroy the old papers before giving the forgeries to the boys.

No wonder I hoped the oberst would appear. He had provided me protection before. The only problem was he was a German soldier, and I didn't think he'd deliberately go against the laws of his country.

Forgery, I felt certain, was illegal in every country.

My thoughts were dragged away from forgery by Helen Miller, a slightly stocky brunette sitting across from me. "What do you think of us so far?"

"You're a hard-working group, obviously dedicated to rescuing these children." Why was she asking?

"You aren't going to write anything to upset the Watersons, are you?"

"I hope not." My surprise showed in my voice. "Why do you think I would?"

"It seems more than coincidental that you show up to write this article just after Alice dies. The Watersons have been good to me, to all of us, and they're upset over losing their only child. We want to be as considerate of them as we can." Helen stared at me as the other conversations faded away. "They are our friends."

"I certainly don't want to do anything to upset them

further. I'm sure they'd be happy for me to write an article that would bring in more funding for the Kindertransport."

"Make sure that's all you do." Helen then turned her attention to her dinner.

* * *

The next morning, after a breakfast of undrinkable coffee and rock-hard rolls at our hotel, we gathered in the parlor used as a breakfast room and began matching the lists of children who'd go with us with the numbered tags that would go on them and on their little suitcases and rucksacks.

The lists were hand printed. I entered "Gerhard Schmidt" and "Heinrich Schmidt" on the bottom of one of the pages from an orphanage. I figured if their father was in a prison camp and their mother was about to disappear, they were orphans.

I copied Gerhard's details in a fair copy of the handwriting on the sheet but was only halfway through Heinrich's details when Dorothy said, "How many do you have on that list, Olivia?"

I quickly counted down.

"What have you been doing? You were supposed to do that already," she told me.

"I'm sorry," I said. "Thirty-two."

She gave me the next thirty-two numbers to write on the list, along with the tags. I finished Heinrich's information and then wrote the numbers down the side of the list.

I slipped the tags for their numbers into my bag

when no one was watching me and hoped the rest of the rescue went as easily as getting the boys a place on the Kindertransport.

All of the paperwork was finished by noon. Then we had lunch and spent an hour or two going to various places, informing the people in charge that the children on our lists should be delivered very early the next morning to an area near the train station to say good-bye to their parents.

I wondered if this was how British secrets were passed to German hands. These people were supposed to be helping children escape, but perhaps someone hoped to keep themselves safe by passing on British secrets.

I wished I could be in a half-dozen places at once.

"The German government won't allow the parents on the platform," Dorothy told me, unaware of my thoughts. "Both the parents and the children are too emotional for the Nazis' liking. They are afraid if the people see these crying children being taken from their parents, the German people will object to the government programs that force parents to send their children away. Then they'll want all sorts of changes to their laws that the Nazis don't want and can't handle."

"Even Nazis don't enjoy appearing cruel," I replied. "And I believe they want their citizens to remain docile."

"I've not seen any sign of the German people speaking out against their government," she said.

"There are a few," I told her in a low voice, even though there was no one on the pavement with us to overhear. "And I'll need you to remain quiet about a woman and her children who will join us on the ride back to Britain."

"This woman spoke out?" she whispered.

"Her husband did. Now he's been taken away. Who knows how long a person can withstand torture? We need to get the family out now, before he breaks."

"Do they have papers to go with us?" Dorothy stared at me.

"They will by tomorrow morning."

"You're using us," she hissed.

"I'm sorry. There's no other way to save their lives. And I will do a terrific job on the article for the newspaper on your great rescue work."

"If they do anything to disrupt our saving the rest of the transport, I'll turn them in myself."

"Dorothy, it will be all right." I put a hand on her arm and fervently hoped this would end well. "I have to leave the hotel soon. Please don't mention our extra passengers to anyone."

She shook her head. "I wish you'd left me in ignorance."

"Being a leader can be difficult."

We strolled in silence the rest of the way to the hotel, where we ran into Charles and Helen. "Can we have the rest of the afternoon off?" Helen asked. "We want to see some of the town while we still can."

"Don't get into any trouble," Dorothy said.

"What could go wrong?" Charles said as they walked off.

"What, indeed?" Dorothy asked as we entered the hotel. "We'll go to dinner at seven, with or without you."

"I understand." I wished I could follow Helen and Charles, but I had to pick up the forged papers. I said hello to the Taylors as they entered the hotel and then headed to the British embassy. I was escorted to Douglas MacFerron's office again, where he gave me the passport for Agatha Manchester. It would have fooled me, probably because it was a genuine British passport. I hoped the Germans believed it.

I slipped it into my bag.

We traveled by tram and then crossed the crowded city streets as people wearily walked home from work, children proudly ran past in their Hitler Youth uniforms, and soldiers in German army uniforms strode with fierce expressions. It seemed that the entire city was out in the early spring chill as the sun set.

When we got close to Schumacher's Bookshop, MacFerron said, "You can take it from here. I'll go to the confectioner's shop over on that corner."

I nodded, smiling through stiff lips as my knees shook. Everyone around us looked like a Gestapo informant, shifty-eyed and sneaky. MacFerron strolled away from me and I knew I was on my own. I was completely alone.

My breath came in short gasps and I deliberately slowed my breathing before I fainted. I lifted my chin and strode forward, pretending I was acting the part of a wealthy German hausfrau shopping.

It worked until I reached the next block and opened

the door to the bookshop. Standing at the counter across from Herr Schumacher was Oberst Wilhelm Bernhard.

I could not imagine how I could collect fake papers with a German army colonel watching, let alone one who knew I was no hausfrau. And I'd had it impressed on me that England's safety depended in part on smuggling these two boys out of Germany.

The oberst glanced over at me, did a double take, and said, "Frau Denis?" as if he couldn't believe his eyes.

"Oberst Bernhard," I said, smiling widely, "what brings you here?" Trite, but I thought the last time I saw him was the last time I would ever see him.

"Herr Schumacher special-orders books for me. I enjoy reading history, particularly military history. What are you doing here?" He spoke in German to me as he slipped his change into his pocket, but his book was still on the counter and he showed no interest in leaving.

Blast.

"I've been looking for a specific printing of German nursery stories, and when I couldn't find it, someone said to come to Herr Schumacher." I hoped that sounded convincing.

He smiled. "No, I meant what brings you here to Berlin again."

"There's a Kindertransport leaving the Bahnhof Zoo station tomorrow morning. I'm one of the chaperones." Well, that was truthful.

"I'm hurt. How long had you planned to come here

without even a word to me?" The oberst made it sound like we were in constant communication.

"Not long. A young English Quaker woman who was supposed to be on this Kindertransport died in London. I'm a last-minute replacement." Well, it was close to the truth.

"When does your train leave?"

This was beginning to sound like an interrogation. "Very early in the morning. I'm sorry I didn't know you were in Berlin, or I would have made a special effort to say hello to you." I hope that sounded sincere. I enjoyed his balanced outlook on life and his quiet, cultured company.

"I'm afraid I won't be able to order a book for you if you are leaving tomorrow. Let us hope it is something I have in stock," Herr Schumacher broke in to say to me.

I hoped we'd find something I could afford that he could slip the boys' papers into.

"What is it called?" Oberst asked me.

"The Children's...? No, the Book of Children's...? No. Oh, dear. Well, I'll know it when I see it." I gave him a smile. "Where do you keep your children's books, Herr Schumacher?"

"Over here." He came out from behind his counter and led me to some short shelves across the shop. "I hope it is here, Frau."

"I hope so, too." I knelt and started to check for fables written for a nursery. Mrs. Neugard could read them to Esther's Johnny.

The oberst bent down and plucked one of the books

from the shelf. "I used to read this to my children." He flipped through the pages, lost in his memories. Then he snapped it shut. "It seems like a long time ago."

"How old are your children now?" I asked.

"Katia is thirteen, and Rolf is ten."

"I remember when I was thirteen," I told him. "I wish you luck."

He grinned. "Thanks. My sister deals with her much better than I do. But then, what do fathers know?"

I had to smile at that. "I was sent to boarding school. And my father knew very little. He was better off that way."

"Have you found the book you seek?" he asked me.

"No, but perhaps another one will do. What do you think of that one?" I pointed at the one he had been examining. "Is it good for a very young boy?"

"Oh, if the child is very young, you might like this one," Herr Schumacher said. He took another book off the shelf and showed it to me.

"The drawings are charming," I said, delighted with the whimsical animals on the pages. "How much is it?"

The shop owner told me. I could barely afford it in Reichsmarks, but it was for Esther's baby. I knew both she and the baby's great-grandmother would love it. "I'll take it."

Herr Schumacher carried the book to the counter, while I engaged the oberst in chatter. "I'm sorry I won't be able to go to the symphony with you on this trip."

"Perhaps we could have dinner?"

"An early one. I don't have any clothes appropriate

for anything the least bit nice. In fact, this is as nice as it gets."

"There's a small family restaurant a few streets away. Perhaps you'd like to have dinner with me when we leave here."

"Am I dressed all right?"

"You look perfect." He gave me a smile, and I led the way to the counter, basking in his possibly sincere compliment.

Herr Schumacher had my book ready for me, wrapped in brown paper. The oberst picked up his book and I was looking through my purse for enough money when the bell over the door jingled.

I glanced over and froze as two men in SS uniforms walked in carrying rifles. Behind them was an oily little man in a trench coat and a man in an SS officer's uniform wearing what appeared to be a very large revolver in a holster on his belt. "Him," the oily little man said, pointing a finger at Herr Schumacher. "He's the one dealing in forgeries."

I felt the blood rush from my head. I was the only one actually wanting forged papers at that very moment. And I was sure they were in my wrapped parcel.

Would they demand I unwrap the book if I picked it up now? And would they immediately drag me off to prison, British citizen or not?

Chapter Nine

"There must be some mistake," Herr Schumacher cried out. "I am an honest shopkeeper. A member of the Party." He pressed his hands together in supplication.

"Save it," the SS officer said as one of the soldiers pointed his rifle at the shop owner. "These are serious charges." He turned toward the oberst. "What are you doing here?" he demanded.

"Captain," the oberst said in a quiet voice laced with annoyance, "I am Oberst Wilhelm Bernhard of the Fifth Panzer Division."

They heiled each other, right arms raised from the elbow.

It was chilling to see the oberst acting like a perfect Nazi party member. I tried to breathe deeply to keep from shaking.

"The lady and I are in here buying books," the oberst continued. "And Herr Schumacher has been supplying books on military history for me for quite some time."

The oberst included me in his statement, in a way throwing the protection of the Fifth Panzer Division over me. I began to feel as if there might be a way out of this situation that didn't involve a German prison.

"What book?" the SS officer asked, tapping the oberst's brown paper-wrapped package with one finger.

"*Tactics and Practices in the War of the Spanish Succession.*"

"Useful?"

"It may prove to be." The oberst's tone was dry.

"And you, mein Frau?"

I prayed my voice wouldn't shake as I said, "I bought a book of children's stories to give to a friend who just had a baby boy."

"What is his name?"

"Johann." Esther would never know of my translation of her son's name.

"A strapping boy, Oberst?"

"I've not seen him. I've been busy."

"No doubt too busy for my questions. Very well, you may leave. Good day, mein Frau."

"Good day." I lay my payment on the counter, picked up my wrapped book, and strode out ahead of the oberst.

We were almost a block down the pavement when I spotted MacFerron. I shook my head slightly once and turned to the oberst as I said, "Do you go to this restaurant often?"

"Yes. The food is good. And I can't have you collapsing on the street from nerves."

I saw MacFerron turn away and disappear down the next street. "I'm not likely to collapse. I was just thinking of that poor man. What will they do to him?"

"Very little, since they won't find any forgeries. Will they, Frau?"

"How... How would I know?" I tried to sound indignant and failed miserably.

"I suspect they're inside your book." He sounded

mildly amused.

I was terrified. Had he changed? He'd told me before he was a loyal German soldier, but he was apolitical. I thought of him as the closest thing I could have to a friend in Germany. "Why would you think that?"

"If I thought you were a spy, I would turn you in." I must have paled, because he quickly continued. "Don't worry. I know your activities are directed toward helping people leave who don't want to be here."

"How did you know about the papers?" I asked in a whisper after a minute's silence.

"It seemed like the logical conclusion from what I know of you and the bookseller."

The oberst was too observant to make me comfortable. "And Herr Schumacher?"

"He's playing every side against each other. He bought out Jewish bookshops at very little cost. That's how he can sell me hard-to-obtain military history books I want, and at very high prices. He creates forgeries for those who can afford them. If he can convince the SS he's innocent, he should come out of this current situation a wealthy man."

"And you?"

"I am a loyal German army officer. My job is to win wars. Not to worry about details of policy." His face brightened. "Here we are. You'll enjoy this, Frau Denis."

We entered a small, crowded neighborhood restaurant and were shown to a small table covered with a red-checked cloth. We were handed small menus with an even smaller list of dishes. I chose sausages and hot potato salad, which this time included mixed beans in an herb sauce. It seemed to be the safest choice.

There was a piano near the bar area, and a man in an enlisted soldier's uniform was playing a love ballad from the Great War as three of his companions sang along.

"This song takes me back," the oberst said after we ordered.

"Surely you weren't old enough to have been in the war," I said.

"In a way. I was in the training school for officers at the end of the war, but I was much too young to be of any use." He gave me a brief smile.

"So, you've trained for this your entire life." I found that a depressing thought. Adam had gone to university before joining the military, which didn't seem quite so narrow a choice.

"Yes. It's odd, but those of us who have spent our lives studying war are the last people to want it." He glanced left and right, and then said, "What time do you leave in the morning?"

"The train pulls out at six."

"You'll be busy until then. Thank you for taking the time to eat with me." He sounded dispirited.

I gave him a smile and rested my hand over his. "If I'd realized you were in Berlin, I would have contacted you. I'm only interested in writing a newspaper article on the Kindertransport for my editor, so I wouldn't have caused any problems for you."

A faint smile crossed his lips. "Which doesn't explain the papers."

I shook my head. "That's a long story."

"I'm glad I had a chance to see you again. I've been working hard, so a chance to have dinner with a charming lady is a special treat." He raised his voice to a normal level and squeezed my hand as our dinners arrived.

He put mustard on his, and when he finished, I reached for the small dish and its tiny spoon.

"Careful. It's very hot."

"Isn't it always?"

"They make theirs here exceptionally hot." He glanced toward the window and said, "They don't have Schumacher with them, so that's a good sign."

I resisted the urge to turn around and look out the window. "They weren't there very long."

"That might mean nothing."

"Or?" I had no idea what SS interrogations were like.

He stared at me with a look that was as hard as granite.

My dinner lost its appeal.

"How are things at the embassy?" He ate a bite as he waited for me to answer.

"Not nearly as many parties," I told him, thinking of when I'd first met him at a German embassy party in London. I had been looking for my husband, Reggie's, killer at the time.

He swallowed. "I meant your embassy," he said as I took a bite of potato salad. "I know about MacFerron."

I swallowed and nearly choked. "You're watching him?"

"Not I." He continued to eat his dinner hungrily. Much like Adam. I decided armies don't feed their soldiers enough.

I toyed with mine. The piano player was now banging out a rollicking tune and his mates were singing along, mostly off-key.

"Any advice on how to talk to my daughter? My son is easy. We talk sports and mechanical gadgets. But my daughter? I'm lost." He sighed.

"It's not so much what you talk about. The main thing is to listen to her. And pay attention. Don't pretend to listen like my father did."

"When did you two finally start talking to each other?"

I grinned. "I'm still waiting for that."

We finished the meal talking of our childhoods and our families. The oberst paid for my dinner, and when we rose to leave, he picked up my book as well as his own.

My heart missed a beat. Was he going to turn me in? He knew my secret, or at least part of what I was trying to hide.

"Your book, mein Frau," he said, handing it to me.

"Danke," came out as an audible sigh.

He grinned and put an arm around my shoulders as he ushered me to the door. Once outside, he said, "Where are you going?"

"The embassy."

"I'll call you a cab, shall I?"

I nodded. I didn't know this part of town, MacFerron wasn't here to lead me, and the oberst shouldn't take me there for both his safety and mine.

"Thank you for a lovely dinner. You're always wonderful company," I told him and smiled. He was a kind man, and he'd been helpful in the past. Not something I felt safe to say in Nazi Germany.

"I'm always glad to see you, Frau." A taxi came past and the oberst signaled it for me. As it pulled up, I impulsively kissed him on the cheek.

As I did, he whispered, "Watch MacFerron."

My eyes widened. The oberst gave me a smile and opened the door for me. My heart racing, I climbed into the immaculate vehicle and waved as the cab drove off.

When I arrived at the embassy, MacFerron was waiting for me behind his desk. He greeted me with, "Do you have the papers?"

I hoped so. I'd not seen Herr Schumacher put them inside my package. I unwrapped the book and then flipped through the pages. Gerhard was on page ten and Heinrich on page fourteen. MacFerron rewrapped the book while I put the papers in my bag.

"Here," MacFerron said, handing me a small pot of glue. Then he said, "Do you still have the British passport?"

"I haven't lost it," I replied in a snippy tone. I was still feeling uneasy over the oberst's warning to watch MacFerron. The oberst had never given me bad advice.

"I don't know what to think when I see you with a

German officer." MacFerron wore an expression that said he wouldn't believe anything I told him.

"He got me out of the bookshop with the forgeries when the SS raided the store."

MacFerron leaped from his seat. "What happened to Schumacher?"

"I don't know. The SS were only there for fifteen or twenty minutes. And they left without him."

"We'll have to check on him, but that's not your concern." He gave a wave of his hand. "We need to get the papers to Agathe and her sons."

"And give her their directions for where they should be in the morning at the train station." I wondered if she trusted us enough to leave her boys alone in the hall while she went to the train. She didn't know me. "How well does she know you?"

"Well enough to trust me to get them out of Germany. Shall we go?"

MacFerron led the way down a corridor and some stairs to exit by a side door. Then we traveled by tram to an older neighborhood of stately four- and five-story buildings of ornate stonework. After we walked around a few corners, we entered one of the buildings and climbed to the second floor, where we knocked on a door.

After a minute, I heard a chain slide and then part of a face peeked out. The door shut. We waited in silence until it opened a moment later.

The woman who hurried us inside was fair-haired and probably in her thirties. She must have been pretty once, but now she only looked thin with fear. She led us into the drawing room, which was as poorly lit as the stairwell.

Two boys sat on the faded sofa looking as if they were afraid to speak.

"What have you heard from Konrad, Douglas?" the woman asked, grabbing MacFerron's arm.

"He's still alive."

She sighed and smiled.

"He sends his love and says to get out of Germany. This is Frau Denis. Olivia. She's with the Kindertransport. That's how you're getting out. Early tomorrow morning."

"But how?" She sounded nearly in tears. At the end of her strength.

"Come and sit down, Agathe," MacFerron said. We sat facing each other and then he nodded to me.

I opened my purse. "Do you speak English?"

"Some."

"Good. Here is your new passport in the name of Agatha Manchester. You are going to be one of the chaperones returning to England with the kinder. Leave your old passport here or burn it, if possible. Here are the boys' new papers. I need their photographs from their current papers to put in these."

She nodded.

"Also, here are their numbers to wear around their necks and to put on their suitcases and rucksacks. They can each take their own. They are to go with a party from an orphanage, so it won't be strange that they are there without family to see them off. When you take them to the area where the children are to assemble, get them to the group and leave them there. Then come to the train platform and meet the group speaking English."

"Leave my sons there?" she gasped. If she'd found her voice, she would have shrieked loud enough to wake the dead.

"Yes. If you want to get yourself and your children out of Germany, you have to follow our directions," I told her. "There will be people from the Refugee Children's Movement in the area by the station where you'll take the boys. Just drop them off and have them carry their suitcase and rucksack by themselves. They'll have to haul their belongings from the hall to the train. All the children will."

"No good-bye? Nothing? You're as bad as the Nazis." She folded her arms and turned her face away from me.

I was getting very tired of this ungrateful woman.

"You'll see them aboard the train. You'll have to be circumspect, especially until we reach the Netherlands, and you'll have to help out with all the children in your train carriage. And the boys can't call you Mutti or act as if they know you until you are all safely out of the country."

"What if something goes wrong? What if they don't get on the train? What if I'm on the train and they are left in the station? Who will look after my babies?" Her voice rose in hysteria as she wrung her hands.

Good grief. Were her sons really that helpless?

I feared this assignment would fail because the woman who wanted to escape didn't trust me or her sons or the people who wanted to help her. And that lack of trust would kill them.

Her attitude was making me feel both helpless and annoyed. The success I had been so sure of earlier now seemed to slip through my fingers as the woman whined and moaned over her children's fate.

Chapter Ten

I took a deep breath and decided to try another tactic. "I'll be there to make sure they get on the train." I looked at the boys. "Gerhard, Heinrich, will you remember my face in a few hours when we meet at the train station?"

Both boys nodded with serious faces. They were cute, the younger missing a baby tooth.

"Of course you will." I gave them an encouraging smile. "There will be perhaps two hundred children there, few of them will know more than perhaps one or two of the other children, and none will know us. You're lucky, you already know two of the chaperones. Your Mutti. And me."

They kept their solemn expressions. Who knew what they'd been through already to be so still and quiet?

"You'll be taken in groups, everyone lining up, to walk from the yard to the station and onto the train. You each have to carry your own luggage, so don't overload it."

"No one will help my boys. They might fall. They might get hurt. They'll be left behind." Their mother was sobbing loudly.

I hoped the neighbors couldn't hear her. "No, they won't. There will be three- and four-year-olds going without their parents and they have to carry their own cases. Who knows when they'll see their parents again? You'll be on the same train with the boys, and maybe in the same carriage. Count your blessings." I'd about had it with her as I thought of what the other parents were going through.

MacFerron signaled me to keep my voice down and my thoughts to myself.

She must have read my mind. "I don't care about the other families. I only care about mine," she said in a haughty tone.

I glared in response, sorry to dump such a selfish creature on the Quakers, who genuinely cared for the children on the Kindertransport train.

The older boy, Gerhard, moved to sit by his mother. "I'll make sure Heinrich and I get on the train. Don't worry."

"Be sure to label your suitcases and rucksacks with these tags, and to wear these cards around your neck." I gave him a smile. "Now, please get me your and your brother's passports so I can take your photos out to put in your new papers. You need to take the new papers with you. It gives you boys a new last name. Schmidt."

"Why?" their mother cried out. She glared at me through red-rimmed eyes.

"We don't know if we can get you or the boys out using your real names. We've used the same first names. If anyone asks, just use your first name." It would be easier to remember in the chaos at the train station.

Gerhard rose and left the room, returning in a few minutes with their papers. MacFerron lent me his pocket knife and I gingerly loosened the photographs.

I wasn't certain why Agathe or MacFerron trusted me with this delicate task. I'd never tried it before. I breathed deeply in an effort to keep my hands from shaking as I gently lifted the photos free of their old papers.

Somehow, I managed to remember Schumacher's suggestions for setting the photos. Taking the pot of glue out of my purse, I cautiously followed his directions as I attached the now- separated photographs to the fake documents, noticing that Herr Schumacher had taken great care to slightly age the papers.

I took a deep breath when the second set of papers were complete. "Leave the new papers closed for a while. And we need to burn the old documents."

Agathe looked away, her nose in the air. She appeared to want nothing to do with me or my efforts on her behalf. MacFerron shrugged before he burned the papers in the fireplace. Only then did Agathe lock gazes with MacFerron and say, "I guess now we'll have to go."

"Be at the yard at five in the morning. Try to eat a normal breakfast before then," I suggested.

"Really? How will anything be normal again?" She gave me a fierce look.

I stared back at her. "I doubt anything has been normal here for a long time."

She looked away, her displeasure with me evident in the stiffness in her back.

"Pack each of the boys a lunch and put it in their

rucksacks. We'll be locked in the carriages without a chance to get food or water until we reach either the Netherlands or the ferry." I looked at the family. Agathe ignored me. The boys both appeared to listen intently.

"I'm sure to be back in London soon. I'll look for you then," MacFerron said.

"Oh, Douglas. A strange country. Strange foods. Strange language. How will we ever survive?" She looked at him, her lower lip quivering. "Konrad promised he'd take care of me, and he's in prison. For helping you."

"Konrad Dietrich sent me, and I've brought Olivia and with her, a way out for you three." MacFerron put his hands on her upper arms. "Trust me. It'll work out."

"And when we get to England? Where will we live? How can we eat?" She gave him a piteous look.

Everything she had said was true, but... I suspected her words were designed to get the very best given to them. While I knew her worries were genuine, I had the sudden thought that this performance was an act to try to coerce the British government to take care of her in the comfortable style she was accustomed to and not in the manner that refugees were normally treated.

"Don't worry," I said as a satisfying thought sprang into my head, "I know exactly who to take you to. He'll know what to do." Sir Malcolm always did.

"Who?" Agathe asked, sounding considerably less sniffly.

"I can't say anything here. The walls might have ears."

MacFerron and Agathe glanced around, worry spreading across their faces. The boys looked around with curious expressions, the younger one no doubt in hope of seeing actual ears.

We made certain they knew the time and place, and I warned them not to be late. Gerhard listened more closely than his mother. I thought the boys would do well on this escape.

"Will you be there, Douglas?" Agathe asked. She wore the helpless damsel expression I'd seen on the faces of more than a few debutantes while I was in the marriage mart. I thought it worked better for a girl of eighteen than a woman of nearly forty. "Please, Douglas."

He looked at me, annoyance written on his face for a moment, and then nodded. "All right. Yes. On the train platform."

After we left the gloom of the flat and the stairwell for the darkness of the streets, I whispered, "You're sure this won't cause any difficulties?"

MacFerron looked at me. "I'm beginning to think it's liable to stop more difficulties than it will start."

"Has she always been this... emotional?"

"I've only known her since her husband was looking for a way out, but apparently, she was a much-loved, much-cared-for only child. So, the answer is yes." He blew on his hands. "Unfortunately, we didn't get all the pieces together for his removal in time. Decent chap. I'm sorry we're not getting him out, too."

"Will you be safe meeting us tomorrow?"

"There's good reason for the embassy to have a presence with so many British citizens in one place."

"Thank you."

"Who are you going to hand their case off to?" He sounded puzzled.

I smiled. "Sir Malcolm. He'll be able to arrange things."

"Sir—?" He appeared to choke. "What makes you think—?"

"He enjoys disrupting my life. I'd like to return the favor."

I saw a ghost of a smile as we passed under a streetlamp. "You know him well, I take it."

We hurried back to my hotel. MacFerron asked me questions about the German officer he'd seen me with when I left the bookshop, which I shrugged off with uninformative answers until he dropped me off at the front door of the hotel. Since Oberst Bernhard had warned me about MacFerron, I thought I'd better protect his identity.

No one from our group was in the lobby and I didn't run into anyone in the corridors or the shared toilet facilities. I got undressed and climbed into bed, wishing I'd fall asleep.

Instead, I tossed on the hard mattress and shivered under the thin blanket. If a hotel was this bad, what were their prisons like?

I didn't want to find out. I shook in a way that had nothing to do with the cold. The train departure couldn't come soon enough as long as I was in one of the carriages.

I drifted in and out of sleep for I had no idea how long when I heard footsteps on the stairs. Whoever it was sounded as if they were tiptoeing as they walked down the hall away from the stairs. It took me a moment to gather my courage and rise, peeking out into the hall to find out who had come back to the hotel later than me.

By the time I opened the door, I heard whoever it was enter one of the other rooms and shut the door before I stuck my head out. I was still wondering who had walked down the hall when I fell asleep.

Morning came far too soon. I was awakened in the dark by a loud rapping on my door and Dorothy calling out, "Time to get going. We have a train to load up and leave on."

"All right," I called out and quickly dressed, hurried on by the cold as well as my fear. Would the Gestapo be waiting for me on the train platform? Would they be waiting for the wife and sons of the man they considered a traitor?

I brushed and pinned up my hair, put on some lipstick, and carried my suitcase down to the lobby. Charles was just returning from a bakery down the street with rolls and honey. Along with coffee someone had already brought in, we had our breakfast.

"Don't forget," Dorothy said, "this will be the last food you'll see until Holland."

Someone groaned. I wanted to. Of course, arriving in Holland would make everything right. We might be hungry, but we'd be free.

"I heard someone in the hall in the middle of the night," I said. "They were walking away from the stairs, nowhere near the loo, and must have entered someone's room."

The responses I received were either shrugs or "Not me." Gwen said, "We don't monitor each other's movements."

"And you're only here to report on our work. Everything else is off-limits," Helen added. Her dark eyes flashed although the rest of her expression was bland, making me wonder if she was hiding something. Was she having an affair with one of her fellow chaperones?

No one owned up to wandering around in the middle of the night. I wondered if I'd heard the hotel proprietor or the Gestapo spying on us. But then, where did they go? Whose room did they enter? Was the Gestapo being aided by one of the Quakers?

Everyone was in the lobby now with their cases. If it were the Gestapo, they hadn't hauled anyone in our group away. But could it be possible someone in our group was working with them? Giving them British secrets in the dead of night? If so, and Alice had found out, that presented a frightening reason for her murder.

Chapter Eleven

We trudged through the cold, dark streets, tired, still hungry, and in my case, grumpy. I had to admire the Quakers for putting up with such terrible conditions for the sake of saving any extra money to use to help the children they were rescuing.

I couldn't see any of these kind people as murderers.

We reached the train platform at two minutes before five and Dorothy began handing out assignments from her checklist. Two border guards searched our luggage one piece at a time, looking for anything being smuggled or anything of value to steal before returning it for us to load it into our carriages.

As soon as they finished with us, the SS border guards walked away to check the children's luggage.

"Most of the children have their suitcases checked at home and then wired shut. Makes less work for the inspectors," Dorothy said. "They want to make sure nothing of value is smuggled out by the children."

"If the children try to take anything of worth, the border guards will steal it," I replied.

The Taylors, Gwen, and Charles left for the storage yard behind the station where we could hear the children assembling. The sobbing and wailing reached us on the wind. No wonder the Nazis wouldn't let the parents come into the station with their children.

Dorothy told me to check the first car we would be

using to make sure no one was lurking inside and that all the windows were closed. Helen was sent to check the second carriage.

I gave the platform one last glance to see if Agathe had arrived. She hadn't. I wondered if she would.

The train car was third class and dirty, with worn seats. I shut the few open windows as I made sure no one was hiding in the chilly carriage. The toilet stank and the window above it wouldn't open, but it would have to suffice. The doors at both ends, leading to the next cars, were locked.

I went back out, not willing to spend any more time in the enclosed space, with its lingering odor of unwashed bodies and rotting vegetables. I spotted Agathe coming slowly toward us on the platform, looking around and hesitating so much I feared someone would become suspicious and call the Gestapo.

I hurried over to her and took her arm, murmuring, "I'll introduce you to our leader, Dorothy, and then put you in the first rail car with me."

She began to pull out of my grip. "The boys…"

"Will be fine. Our people over there haven't lost anyone yet. Look. The first group is being led over here now."

It was a young group for the most part that were having their names checked off the master list by Tom and then marched over to the first carriage led by Charles. He glanced at Agathe and took a second look. "What? More help? Terrific." He beamed. "Get this lot on board, will you?"

Agathe stared at him, speechless. I wondered how good her English really was.

Charles sauntered off, ruffling the hair of a boy and playfully pulling a girl's braid.

Dorothy came over as Agathe set her suitcase down. I said, "This is the woman I told you about. Agatha Manchester. She'll help in the first carriage with me."

With a sharp look, Dorothy said, "Are your papers in order?"

Agathe nodded and pulled her English passport out of the pocket of her heavy, blue coat.

Dorothy looked it over and handed it back. "Very well," she said, looking at me, "but if anything goes wrong, I'll make sure you go to a German prison, not the rest of us." With a final glare, she stalked off.

"Do you want to get them seated or keep order out here?"

"Out here." Agathe handed me her suitcase to put on board.

She probably was waiting to see her sons. The second group was already making their way, single file, to the second car.

"All right. Let's go." I climbed up the two steps into the carriage and walked to the end, the first child following me. It was an easy job to get the children seated and their luggage stored in the shelves above their heads or under their seats. I could see we had room for another group in the other half of the carriage.

I put Agathe's suitcase next to mine in the overhead shelves.

Going back to the open carriage door, I stood on the first step and looked out. The second group of children, mostly boys, was already filing into the next carriage and a third group was headed toward us.

"I must go there. My sons are there." Agathe began to walk away.

"Don't be a fool," I snapped. Keeping my voice low, I said, "Call attention to yourself and you and your sons will all die. Wait until Holland to be reunited." I was running out of patience with her.

She walked back past me to Douglas MacFerron, who'd just reached our part of the platform. "I am frightened, Douglas. I'm sure I've been recognized by the Gestapo. You must get us out of here."

He gave her a big smile as he walked her back to the entrance to our carriage. "The safest thing you can do is get on the train. You'll be out of Germany in a few hours. Tonight, at the latest. You must be strong, Agathe, for your sons."

"But I know who—"

"It'll be all right," MacFerron said, cutting her off. He was probably as tired of her as I was.

She grabbed his arm. "They know. They'll stop us."

"Get on the train and seat the children," he said, sounding like he was running out of patience.

"Douglas, please. We'll die on this train."

He nodded to me as well as Charles and Helen, who'd led the next group of children to the entrance to our carriage, helped Agathe onto the train, and stepped out of the way.

"All right, young ladies and gentlemen, onto the train one at a time. And behave yourselves." Charles gave some girls a wink and strolled over to Dorothy.

I glanced inside. With the addition of this group, the carriage was almost at capacity. I came back out to see another group heading toward the next carriage.

"I wish you a quiet journey," MacFerron said.

"With all these children?" I asked and smiled.

"You can never be certain with the Germans," he said, adjusting his hat, "but I hope you get into Holland without the border guards getting too intrusive."

"I hope so. I worry more about Agathe screaming at the border guards and getting us both thrown into prison."

"I wouldn't worry about that. I doubt she'll be much help with the children, though."

"I've suspected as much." We shared a grin. "Good luck at the embassy and thank you for your help."

"You did the hard work. Speaking of which, I need to get to the office. Thank you, Mrs. Denis."

I could hear the train engines rumbling, anxious to leave. Steam shot out in clouds in the cold air around MacFerron as he strode off.

Dorothy appeared, her lists in hand. "You'll have the Taylors and me in this carriage with you and your friend." Her tone soured on her last words.

I decided to try to cheer her up. "You've done a good job, Dorothy. The Refugee Children's Movement should be proud of you. This trip is going off without a snag."

She gave me a sharp look. "That's because we

haven't reached the border yet. And Helen and Tom and Charles have all been trying to undermine me."

"I don't know why they'd want to."

She gave me a loud hmmpf that didn't tell me a thing.

The Taylors came on board with their suitcases. "There's no one left in the field or on the path to the station," Wil told Dorothy. "We waited as long as we could, but no one else came."

"Then we're short two, and it will have to stay that way."

"Short two? Who are they?" I stopped Dorothy before she could exit the train. I'd promised Agathe her children would be on this train. I almost jumped off in a panic, my heart pounding.

"A boy and a girl, both five years old. Perhaps their parents decided not to send them after all. It happens sometimes. I can't blame the parents for changing their minds." Dorothy pulled away from me and climbed down the stairs, her lists gripped in one hand.

I loosened a sigh of relief. The boys were definitely on the train.

Betsy Taylor gave me a puzzled look before she said, "Wil and I usually sit in the center of the carriage. If you and Dorothy take the two ends, we should be able to spot any problems and take care of them."

"Sounds good to me."

"And the woman down there? Who is she?" Betsy nodded with her chin toward the far end of the car, where Agathe was seated.

"An Englishwoman heading back to London who offered to help us on this trip." I'd already decided on that story, knowing the question would arise. It said little, making any future lies easier.

I was certain there would be more lies. I just had no idea why.

Dorothy climbed aboard the other end of our carriage and called out, "We're good to go," before settling in her seat.

After what felt like too long a time, the carriage doors were shut and locked from the outside. I had known it would happen, but I still felt a moment of unease, knowing we were locked in until we reached Holland. The sound of the lock turning had a finality about it, as if there was no escape.

The train jerked and shuddered, steam hiding the station, as we began to move. I felt the sensation of movement, slowly at first and then more quickly as the clouds of steam blew past and disappeared into the air.

And then the younger children started to wail, more or less in unison.

Leaving Wil to watch the older children and to break up any fights, Betsy and I went to the end of the carriage to help Dorothy deal with the cluster of the youngest children. Agathe glared at the children and they avoided her, shrinking away to lean on us or each other.

By giving hugs and balancing the youngsters on our knees and comforting three or four children at once, we managed to get the wailing below an ear-splitting level.

I worried more about the children who watched us silently through wide eyes leaking tears.

Dorothy glared over a little boy's head. "Think you could comfort at least one child?" she demanded of Agathe.

Agathe's response was to rise and stride over to the door that led to the toilet and the locked passage door to the next carriage. She stood looking out the small window toward the next carriage where her sons were, her arms crossed over her chest.

With the windows shut and the shades down per Nazi directions, the air was stuffy. Mixing that with the rhythmic clatter of the train wheels made the younger children gradually grow sleepy. We encouraged them to be as comfortable as we could before Betsy and I went back to the other side of the car so as not to disturb them. Agathe remained where she was by the door to the toilet. Dorothy took a seat two rows away, stiffly looking away with her back to Agathe.

One boy, about twelve years old, pulled out his violin and began to play for us. A slightly younger girl took out her flute and joined him in the songs she knew. I was glad to see Agathe, at the other end of the carriage, finally take a seat in the first row, even if it was facing away from the rest of us.

It was well past what would have been lunch time when the older boys became rowdy. We were all tired, bored, hungry, and stiff from sitting in the train for hours. We'd been shunted off to a siding twice, adding to our journey time and the children's increasing impatience. A game of catch with a small, battered ball one of the boys had smuggled on board led to an argument between two lads who were perhaps fourteen years of age.

Suddenly, insults were shouted, fists flew, and a dozen boys entered into the fight. Dorothy stayed with a huddle of the younger children while Wil, Betsy, and I waded in to break up the melee.

When we finally pulled them apart, Wil asked in English, "What started that?"

The boys looked at him blankly.

"What started that?" I repeated in German.

A half-dozen boys answered me in Yiddish, a German dialect.

I'd heard Esther and Sir Henry's relatives speak it when I'd helped them get out of Germany and German-controlled Austria. I could understand about every other word.

"In German," I said, "unless one of you can speak English."

Betsy patted her husband's arm and went down to help Dorothy.

Among much shouting and one shoving match that Wil quickly broke up, I managed to piece together the grievance. On one side, the boys came from strictly religious homes with a great deal of learning and little money. On the other were boys from wealthier families, children of doctors, lawyers, and businessmen, many of whom were not as observant of religious laws. Both sides felt they should have precedence in escaping the horror their country had become.

"If it weren't for these…" one of the boys said, using a phrase I wasn't familiar with but could tell could start another fight, "my little brother could have had a spot and traveled with me."

"I'm sure there are children on the opposite side of this argument who feel the same way," I told him. "We're doing the best we can to get as many children out as possible. Don't make us sorry we rescued you."

The boys fell silent, and I felt ashamed at my words. They were just reacting to the upheavals in their lives caused by adults such as myself. I hoped the Quakers didn't hear my words, or if they did, didn't understand them. I'd been unnecessarily cruel.

"We'll be in the Netherlands soon. And when we are…" I said.

The boys trudged back to their seats, heads down. None of them looked at me. Peace was restored, but I wasn't proud of the price.

Dorothy and Betsy rejoined us and Dorothy asked, "What was that about?"

"The wealthy boys versus the religious ones. Trying to figure out their importance in a world gone mad. How soon until we get to the Netherlands?" I asked.

"It can't be much longer."

"Was that woman any help?" Wil asked his wife.

"Never moved a muscle to help. She's your friend, Olivia. Speak to her about helping us."

"I thought she was asleep," Dorothy said, "although I can't imagine sleeping through that racket."

I felt the train slow.

"I think we're at the border," Dorothy said and began readying her lists.

Agathe still didn't move. Something was wrong.

Chapter Twelve

I rose and hurried down the aisle of the third-class car. When I reached Agathe, her head was slumped over and she leaned a little from her seat onto the side of the carriage. I shook her shoulder to awaken her, and then jumped back as she nearly pitched over onto my shoes.

Dorothy arrived at that moment. "What's going on?"

"I think she's dead." I spoke in English, which the children didn't understand, but I still murmured.

"Dead?" she shrieked. She lowered her voice. "Dead? How?"

"I don't know."

"Well, do something. We're about to face the German border guards and if they find someone dead, they'll stop us indefinitely. And I'll let them know it's all your fault."

I felt Agathe's cheek. "Still warm. This just happened a short time ago. During the fight?"

"Maybe." Dorothy nodded, then shrugged. "Yes. No. I don't know."

"Do the border guards come the whole way through the carriage?" They did for individuals, but this was a large group of children, enough to frighten any man.

"No, just part way through the carriage until they choose a child and its luggage to examine. They also want to speak to one of us for each carriage." Dorothy frowned at me and said, "Take our passports and the papers for the children. You speak to them."

The train came to a halt. The children stared at us in silence.

We were in Bentheim. The German border. The boy who'd been playing his violin put it away in its case, set it in his rucksack, and slipped it under the seat.

I set Agathe up so she appeared to be sleeping. "Not a word of this to anyone. Not until we reach the port in Holland. That way, most of us can get on the ferry to England before we'll be stopped."

Dorothy nodded, but she looked dubious.

I took Agathe's passport out of her pocket and then Dorothy and I went to the other end of the carriage where I gathered all the documents I would need to face the German border guards. And the Gestapo.

Despite the chill on the train, sweat slid down my back and under my arms as I went to the door and waited. It didn't take long. I hadn't stopped trembling before the door in front of me was unlocked and I found myself facing a young German soldier carrying a rifle with a bayonet.

I shrank back as the soldier stepped aside and a black-uniformed officer moved forward followed by a border guard. "Papers," the border guard snapped in German.

"These are the children's papers with the list on top," I replied in German, "and these are the passports of the British subjects who are chaperoning the children to England."

The SS officer handed the children's papers to the border guard and looked through the passports himself.

"How can so few adults handle so many children? Who else is in there?"

"No one. It's not long and the children are well behaved." I gave him a small smile. "I admit I'll be tired by the time we reach the end of our journey in London, but there will be others to take over then."

He gave me a gruff stare and gestured me out of his way. I saw at once as he climbed the steps that his left knee was completely stiff.

As I moved aside, I said, "Is it a war wound? Your knee?"

"Ja."

"I'm sorry."

He was level with me standing in the aisle of the carriage and he stared into my eyes. I tried to look sympathetic while I thought of Oberst Bernhard and Captain Adam Redmond and worried. Then he looked over the carriage. The children either stared back or crouched down, hiding. Wil nodded to the officer, Betsy gave him a shaky smile, and Dorothy stared at him defiantly. Agathe sat with her back to us, apparently asleep.

The officer, followed by the border guard and soldier, walked down the center aisle of the carriage. It was all I could do to keep breathing. What would happen when he reached Agathe?

He looked between the seats, seeing if there were any hideaways. I glanced at Dorothy, who seemed on the verge of speaking. I glared at her to be quiet. He wasn't looking for corpses.

About halfway down, he waved one hand at a boy about nine years old sitting on the aisle. "You. Get your suitcase and come with me."

The boy turned white. I could see his suitcase shake as he rose and lifted it to follow the officer.

The soldier hurried out of the carriage as if afraid of the children. The border guard handed me the stack of papers, took the list sheets from the top, and left. The officer handed me the passports and, with a dismissive click of his tongue, exited the train after the boy.

I followed the boy out onto the platform.

"I didn't tell you to come along, Frau."

"You didn't say not to, so I thought I'd see if I could be of assistance."

"Well, you can't."

"All right." I remained motionless on the platform while the soldier took the boy's suitcase to a table, opened it, and searched it. The SS officer stared at me until the soldier said, "Nothing here."

The officer gave one sharp nod. The boy closed his suitcase and nearly sprinted past me. I followed him on board.

A moment later, they locked the exit door.

I collapsed into a seat by the door before I fainted from fear and relief. Dorothy and Betsy took the documents from my numb fingers. The children, the chaperones, and I sat in silence waiting for the train to move. Willing it to move. Holland was now so close.

After what seemed too long, making us fear we'd be stuck in Germany forever, we jerked into motion. I could hear the exhales of the more than one hundred people in our carriage daring to hope. The engine chugged slowly along for a surprisingly long distance before spitting out steam as it creaked to a stop.

Some of the teenaged boys raised the shades and opened the windows before we gave the word, but nobody complained. Betsy and Wil helped the younger children with their windows.

Here we found civilians on the platform, handing in cocoa, apples, and zwieback to the children, who gobbled them as fast as they could. No one had eaten in over twelve hours except for what food parents had packed for their children. We were all hungry. Someone handed in some pastries for the adults and I managed to grab a cheese pastry and wolfed it down.

Nothing had ever tasted so good.

I turned, my mouth still full of pastry, to find a pair of Dutch border guards in our train carriage.

I was still trying to swallow a huge mouthful when Dorothy tried to speak to the guards in English as she waved the paperwork in front of her. They looked puzzled and spoke German to her.

Waving a hand, I finally swallowed the rest of the cheese treat and got out in German, "These are our passports and the papers for the children. We're in transit to the coast to board a ferry bound for England."

The older guard looked around and saw the younger children at the far end of the carriage along with Agathe's body. "They are a handful."

"Yes, they are."

"They've worn out one of your number already."

He'd seen Agathe, but believed she was resting. I hoped he wouldn't go down to that end of the carriage. "Yes. We've been taking turns resting. They keep us busy, but now we're halfway there."

"You'll be in England in the morning?" the younger guard asked.

"Late morning."

"Have a pleasant trip," the older guard said and handed all the paperwork back to me with a nod.

"Thank you." I gave the paperwork back to Dorothy as the guards exited our carriage and went on to the next one.

This time, the doors remained unlocked. After the children drank their cocoa, they handed the cups back to the Dutch women through the windows.

Dorothy and I looked at each other and sagged with relief.

Betsy stepped next to me and whispered, "What are we going to do with her? And who is she?"

I looked into Betsy's wide eyes. "She's a British citizen married to a German who's been sent to a German prison camp. Their two young sons are in the next carriage. We need to get her body back to England so an autopsy can be performed."

"An autopsy?" Dorothy gasped. "Why?"

"She was healthy when she climbed onto the train this morning." It felt like murder to me.

"There are no obvious wounds," Betsy said.

"We're members of the Society of Friends. We don't

kill people," Dorothy said.

"I've heard the same thing about Alice's killer. Perhaps one of you isn't as much of a Friend as you thought."

Dorothy and Betsy exchanged glances. I probably shouldn't have said that, and I couldn't guess what thoughts passed between them.

I needed their help. I couldn't afford to alienate them. "I'm sorry. That wasn't fair of me. Perhaps she was poisoned before she joined us."

Always the practical one, Betsy asked, "How do you plan to get her body off the train and onto the ferry? The Dutch officials might not approve, and we are leaving on that ship, with or without you."

"I'll think of something." I had to. Sir Malcolm and two little boys were counting on me.

"You'd better."

I spent the ride through the Dutch countryside trying to devise a plan that would get us all, including Agathe, onto the ferry. By the time we left Amsterdam on our way to the coast, I thought I had a way to accomplish my goal of getting Agathe's body back to England for autopsy. I hoped the darkness and the late hour would help.

I walked halfway down the train carriage to Wil and Betsy and sat down across from them. "When we get to the ferry, I'm going to tell the border guards that we have a seriously ill chaperone and I'd like to have her carried onto the ferry on a stretcher. If Betsy and Dorothy can get the children on board, I'd like you, Wil, to act as my assistant."

He hunched his shoulders and shook his head. "I don't speak German or Dutch."

"That's fine. I just want you standing there looking somber. Once we have her on the stretcher and on her way to the ship, you can go join the other chaperones."

As Wil nodded, Betsy asked, "Why?" She was definitely the suspicious one in the family.

"I want the Dutch border guards to organize a group to carry Agathe on board. They'll be more likely to do that if they think a man is in charge and wants their help."

Betsy smiled at that. "Men are the same the world over. Do it, Wil. I'm sure her family would appreciate it. But for heaven's sake, don't tell Dorothy. She's sensitive enough about her authority as it is."

I nodded. The only family I was sure Agathe had was her two sons, and I was sure some day they'd appreciate it if their mother's killer was apprehended. I doubted their father would survive Sachsenhausen, and the Nazis might never be held accountable for their brutality.

I looked from Betsy to Wil. "You two make a great team. I appreciate your help."

They looked at each other. Finally, Wil said, "Tell her. It's not like everyone else here doesn't already know. And with that woman dead, too..."

I waited in silence.

"We all know it wasn't you, Wil," Betsy said.

"We might, but the police won't, when we get to

England." He sounded resigned to being dragged away in irons.

"What is it?" I asked very quietly.

"I was in jail. Malicious wounding."

Betsy rushed to finish the story Wil began. "I was a prison visitor and met him there while working with the Friends Committee. This was before he learned to control his temper. Before he became a member of the Society of Friends. Before he learned a trade and developed self-control."

I stared at Wil. "How did you wound this person?"

"Stabbed him. Fortunately, with a short-blade knife. If it had been any longer, I would have killed him." He looked at me levelly. "I wanted to. He cheated at cards. I lost money I couldn't afford because he cheated and I wanted him dead."

"Had you ever met Agathe before today?"

"No." He swiped at his sweaty forehead with his sleeve. "I have to live with my anger and my stupidity every day for the rest of my life. After that experience, I can't even think of taking a life. But still the police will think it was me. They always prefer an ex-prisoner to blame. Who else could it have been, they'll ask?"

In a way I was relieved. I didn't want it to be Wil. Agathe's death was the opposite of what he had done. There were no obvious marks on her body. "I don't know who did it yet, but this was done in stealth, unlike what you did. Don't worry."

Dorothy joined us. "What's going on?"

I told her my plan to get Agathe on board the ferry.

"You think that's going to work?"

"She hasn't been dead too long, and it's dark out. I hope so."

When we reached the port, I asked the first border guard to reach our carriage for a stretcher and bearers to carry a very ill member of our group on board the ferry and to a cabin. He looked at Wil, who nodded somberly, and hurried off.

Betsy marched the older children in our carriage off toward the ferry, with Dorothy behind lining up the little ones and shooting me dirty looks. I don't think she believed I could pull this off.

Honestly, neither did I. But I had to try.

The border guard returned with two of his colleagues, both young, strong-looking men, and with Wil assisting, loaded a still relatively limber Agathe onto the stretcher and covered her with a clean white sheet. I opened up the door close by Agathe from our train carriage to the outside and the men carefully maneuvered her down the stairs and out. I picked up Agathe's suitcase and mine and our handbags before leaving the carriage.

Hurrying with the suitcases banging against my knees as I trotted along, I soon caught up with the men. I was glad to see all the children were already boarding or on board the ferry, so they were less likely to see our procession and be upset.

"Wil," I said in English, "would you please check both of our train carriages to make sure no one left anything behind."

He nodded and loped off.

"Did she have a communicable disease?" the older border guard asked me.

"No. She was healthy when we left Berlin."

"Healthy young women don't just suddenly collapse. Any coughing, shortness of breath, rash, fever, chills..."

"No, nothing like that. In Berlin, there is danger of poisoning for people who help Jewish children escape," I said, remembering something I had read. "We must get her back to England as quickly as possible."

The older guard, obviously in charge, nodded and said something in Dutch to the other two guards.

The two younger men were more interested in carrying the stretcher properly and not tripping on loose rocks in the shadows than they were in their passenger or her condition. The older man walking alongside glanced down as we passed under a particularly bright light and I saw his brow furrow.

We were no more than ten feet from the bottom of the ramp into the ship. "Officer," I said to him in German, "if we could take her straight down to her cabin, we won't have to bother your men any longer."

He gave me a long sideways stare. "I don't think it matters anymore."

He knew.

"It matters a great deal. Her young sons are on the ferry with the other children. She is an Englishwoman and her family is waiting for them in Harwich." I gave him a beseeching look. I'd beg if I had to.

He stopped, and the stretcher bearers hesitated. My

heartbeat stumbled. I had to get her body back to England. I needed Scotland Yard to order an autopsy on her. She couldn't have just died in the middle of our journey. Not when I was already looking for a killer.

Chapter Thirteen

It was less than ten feet from where I stood until we reached the long, sloping walkway to the passenger entrance to the ferry. *Keep moving,* I silently begged. The younger guards looked puzzled.

"How old are the boys?" the older border guard asked.

"Ten and six."

"Youngsters." The guard nodded to himself. "It is a shame. So far from home." Then he looked at me. "Is this a case of influenza or disease?"

"No. I'm certain it is not. She was fine a few hours ago. We don't know what happened."

After a long pause, he nodded. "The paperwork would take all night. Not pleasant for any of us. Look after those boys until you get them to their family."

"I will. Thank you."

He signaled to the two tall blond guards. "Go on to the ship. We'll find out which cabin is hers."

We slowly walked up the ramp where a ship's officer hurried to meet us. A quick perusal of the papers on his clipboard and he led the way downstairs to one of the cabins.

Once freed of their burden, the two younger guards nearly ran off the ship with their stretcher. The older guard turned to me. "I suppose I won't find out what happened."

I shook my head. "You sound suspicious."

"You have my men carry a body disguised as a sick passenger from Dutch soil to an English ferry. I have every right to be suspicious."

"You can be certain your people and your country played no part in creating this—unfortunate situation. And," I added, "you can ask Scotland Yard for their report in a day or two."

"If they will release it. We are glad to support the work of the English Quakers in rescuing children, but this had better not happen again. Next time we will not be so lenient." He looked stern as he nodded to me and walked off.

I left the cabin, shutting and locking the door behind me with Agathe's and my luggage inside. Then I went in search of Dorothy.

By the time I found her, the ferry was rocking as we sailed out of the harbor. Dorothy was in the small lounge on the upper level of the ship organizing a dinner of bread, cheese, and juice for the older children as they walked past the long table, receiving a single roll and a piece of cheese on their plates. The younger children were seated and the other chaperones were bringing them their dinners.

"That's all sorted," I told her. "What can I do to help?"

"You got her on board under the noses of the Dutch authorities." Dorothy shook her head as the line paused, waiting to be served. "Amazing. But why?"

"For an autopsy. If it was murder, this may give them a clue to Alice's death," I murmured to her.

"And if it was natural causes?"

I met her glare with a faint smile. "Then we will all breathe a big sigh of relief."

She nodded and then pointed to the platter next to her. "Put one roll on each plate for the children. Only one. That's all we can provide."

"You're doing great work with very little money," I said for only her to hear as the children began to file past again.

"Most of what we raise goes to the Germans for exit visas and train carriage rental and unexplained fees. Then there's passage on the ferry and through the Netherlands and our train tickets to Germany and lodging in that miserable hotel. All that leaves us with little to feed the children." She continued to hand out cheese while she spoke. "And who's going to pay for the cabin for your friend?"

"The British government. This was their idea." Actually, Sir Malcolm's, and I was very happy to make him pay.

"Sounds like she was important."

"Oh, my, yes." Gerhard came up to me at that moment, and as I gave him a roll, I gave him a smile. The ten-year-old gave me a serious stare in return.

Had he seen his mother carried on board? Did he realize she was the person on the stretcher? Did he wonder where she was?

After all the children had been fed, Dorothy and I

took what remained to a table in the corner, where our colleagues were waiting with cups of watered-down beer.

The cheese, a good Dutch variety, was the only food with any taste. The leftover bread was so stale it must have been baked the day before.

For once, Charles kept his voice down as he asked, "What happened? We've been hearing about your friend collapsing on the train?"

"That's not quite accurate," I replied.

"What happened to her? Was she poisoned?" He continued with ghoulish fascination written on his expression.

"Charles! Ooh," Dorothy said.

"Don't be morbid," Helen added.

"Why would you think that?" I tried to give him a quelling expression, but I should have known from our waltz around the Refugee Children's Movement office that he was quite unstoppable.

"He watches too many movies," Gwen said as she rose. "I'm going to try to read to the younger children. Anyone want to give me a hand?"

Betsy volunteered and the two women walked off.

"Charles has a point," Dorothy said. "If we look through her things, we might find poison. Or medicine. Perhaps she had a bad heart. We should at least check."

Helen screwed up her face, deep in thought. "Perhaps we'd better," she finally said. "If this woman was murdered, too, and we can be sure it wasn't the children, then it might be the person who killed Alice.

And we owe it to Alice to learn who killed her. If it was one of us."

"I just pray it was natural causes," Wil said.

"Sweet on Alice, were you, Wil?" Charles asked with a smirk.

"It was nothing like that. I admired Alice. She was determined. In charge. Like my Betsy."

"I wouldn't say that around Betsy if I were you," Dorothy said as she rose to clear plates.

I stood to give her a hand and then looked down at Wil. He was bright red the whole way to the tops of his ears. I glanced around. No one was paying us any attention, since Charles was arguing with Helen and Tom about how the Kindertransport should be run to allow them better accommodation in Berlin.

"Wil, calm down. It's all over, isn't it?"

His head jerked as he looked up at me. "She was nothing to me." Then he sighed. "Not really. Alice was refined. Passionate. Totally out of reach for an ugly workingman like me. I think I just wished that I were different."

"Nothing happened?"

He shook his head. "Of course not. I'm the man you see in front of you. Not the man I wished I was when I was around her. Shy. Tongue-tied. And very much in love with my wife. I'd never hurt Betsy."

"But you did hurt Betsy, didn't you? She saw Alice flirting with you." I wondered how blind some men could be. Thank goodness Adam wasn't like that.

"Yes, and it made her wish she was different than

she is. Pretty like her sister. But then we'd never have married if one of us had been different. It was all my fault."

My stomach did a flip unrelated to the churning sea. "Wil, did you...?"

"No. Of course not. Once Alice went on to someone else, we talked, and Betsy forgave me."

"Before Alice died?"

"A week before."

I nodded to Wil and walked off, not certain if I believed him about being forgiven a week before the murder. An affair Wil wanted to keep from his wife could be a powerful motive for murder, whether or not a knife was his choice of weapon. But why would he kill Agathe?

Or for that matter, why would Betsy kill Agathe? I could understand her hatred of Alice. They'd known each other forever. Perhaps there was even a motive beyond trying to steal Betsy's husband.

And the Taylors, like all of the others on this Kindertransport, were in the East End the night Alice was killed.

Gathering up a huge pile of plates, I followed Dorothy to the ship's galley.

"Set them down there, will you?" she said, not looking my way.

"I've gathered up the rest." I waited a moment, and when she didn't look my way, I added, "You've done a terrific job on this trip."

"No thanks to you." I saw her shoulders heave and

then she turned to face me. "No, you've done a good job. You're getting that woman's body back to England past the Germans and the Dutch. I guess you took care of whatever it was you were to do in Berlin and you got out again. And most important, you didn't slow down the Kindertransport."

All that was true. "Now if Agathe's death can help them figure out what happened to Alice, it would be a relief."

"I hope it doesn't."

I gave her a sharp look. "Why would you not want justice for your friend?"

Dorothy propped her hip against the counter and watched me. "I never held Alice in high esteem. I'm afraid, though, when they learn the truth, it will mean someone I admire will hang."

The depth of her fear came through in her voice. "You think you know who killed her."

"I have a suspicion. And don't ask me who. My guess is only that, a guess, based on nothing."

I was about to press her on her guess when Charles came in. "Things are pretty quiet out there. Most of the children have gone to their bunks in the cabins. This would be a good time to check the woman's things. See if we can find a cause of death."

"Shouldn't we leave that for the police? We'll be in England in the morning," I said.

"She might not have been murdered. She might have something pointing to a wonky ticker or suicide or something. I think we should check," Charles said.

"Not me," Dorothy said. "Take Betsy or Gwen. They can stomach searching through a dead woman's things. I can't."

"And a dead woman," I added.

"Do you have any medical training?" Dorothy asked.

"No." I sounded a little sheepish as I admitted my lack.

"We'll take Gwen," Charles cheerily said as if we were off to a party. "She's a nurse."

Charles left and returned a few minutes later with an unhappy-looking Gwen. "You realize I have little experience with the dead," she said. "My work at St. Timothy's Hospital is aimed at keeping my patients alive."

"Just see if she had any medicines with her that might explain her death," Dorothy said.

"Or any not-so-obvious injuries," I added.

All three of them turned to stare at me, but no one said a word. The only sounds were the rumble of the engines down below and the murmur of the galley staff while they worked.

"Well, let's get to it," Gwen said as Charles and I followed her down the central stairs, gripping the railing. The sea was getting rougher. I was glad they'd convinced most of the children to lie down. I hoped it would keep them from falling or getting seasick.

Once down below, I led the way to the cabin where Agathe lay and unlocked the door.

I don't know what I expected, but she lay on top of the sheets, still and pale, and her suitcase and bag sat on the floor next to mine by the bed where I had left them.

Charles picked up her bag and emptied the contents onto the bed next to the dead woman before Gwen and I could stop him. "Lipstick. Nice red color..."

"Not your shade," Gwen said. "Passport, wallet, comb, change purse, handkerchief. Nothing unusual here. No medicine."

Charles saw an envelope and picked it up. "Photographs." He carried it to the table along one side of the cabin and spread them out.

I stood next to him and glanced over the snapshots, hanging on as the ship hit a particularly high wave.

"So that's what she looked like alive. Striking," Charles said.

I was more interested in the photo below it. I slid it to the side. I didn't recognize the shorter of the two men, but the taller one was Douglas MacFerron. Another was a photo of Agathe and MacFerron. While he looked at the camera, she looked at him with a mixture of anger and adoration. Why, I wondered.

I wondered what Agathe's husband thought of them as he remained in the horrid confines of Sachsenhausen.

Gwen came over and pulled out a photo of Agathe, the shorter man, and the two boys I knew as Gerhard and Heinrich when they were a little younger. "Nice-looking family. I wonder where the rest of the family is."

"The boys are upstairs with the rest of the Kindertransport." As soon as the words came out of my mouth, I wondered if I had erred. Would the same fate that befell Agathe visit the boys, too?

"Do they know about their mother?" Gwen asked.

"I haven't told them. I doubt anyone else has."

"Shall we check her suitcase?" Charles asked. Before anyone could respond, he had the case on the table and had it opened. I wondered if he thought this was some sort of game.

Gwen gathered up all the photographs and returned them to Agathe's handbag, along with the rest of the contents. "I don't know what you expect to find. The Nazis have already pawed through her things, same as they did to us."

But they hadn't. At least I hadn't seen them check her suitcase in the Berlin bahnhof. The guards had walked off before she arrived. What had she sneaked past them?

I watched as Charles pawed through her things. I couldn't tell what he was looking for, but he was certainly enthusiastic about his search. He wrinkled and mussed everything as badly as the German border guards.

"Found anything not quite right?" I asked.

Charles shook his head. "No medicine. No suicide note. Nothing to explain her death."

A tap on the door made us all turn our heads. I opened it to find Helen in the hall. "I heard about this from Dorothy. Shouldn't we wait for the police in Harwich?"

"What if she died of natural causes? Won't we feel silly dragging the police in?" Charles called from behind me.

"The police will have to be called in anyway. We're bringing in a body from outside the country," Helen told him. "And we've got a jailbird with us."

I gave her a sharp look as another high wave had us all grabbing for something anchored.

Gwen stood beside the bed, moving the dead woman's limbs and then checking her eyes and mouth.

"Something wrong?" I asked.

She swiveled Agathe's head around on her neck. "That's not right." With wide eyes, Gwen looked at us. "I think she's had her neck broken. We definitely need to contact the police."

Chapter Fourteen

We stared back at Gwen, the only sound the rumble of the engines fighting the North Sea waves. "Are you sure?" Charles finally murmured.

"No. I'm a nurse, not a doctor. But there's something wrong with her neck. With her spine. We'll need the police in Harwich."

"Was Dorothy aware this woman was joining us?" Helen asked, sounding annoyed at this extra distraction.

"I asked her to look the other way," I told her. "She told me if there was any trouble with the border guards, I'd have to answer for it and the Kindertransport would continue without us."

"Quite rightly. Was she in your train carriage? When did she die?" Helen asked.

"Before we reached the German border. We're not sure when," I told her.

"Someone had their neck wrung like a chicken and no one noticed?" Charles's voice rose in volume and pitch. "How could that be?"

When could this have happened? I thought back. "The boys were getting bored and two of them got into a fight. Others joined in, and it took three of us to break it up. Everyone's attention was on the fight. Agathe was at the other end of the carriage. That had to be when."

"But who could have done this?" Charles looked from one of us to another as if he thought we held the answers.

"No one was near her but the youngest of the children. It's impossible. They couldn't have. They wouldn't have." We didn't hit a bad patch on the tracks that could have thrown her across the carriage. She didn't move from her seat.

"She didn't have a hard fall or take a hard blow, did she?" Gwen asked, echoing my thoughts.

"No. She was in her seat, alive, and the next thing we know, she's in the same seat, dead." I raised my hands. I couldn't explain it. I wasn't prepared for it. I felt like I failed in the task Sir Malcolm had given me, and as a result, a woman died.

"If someone killed her, it stands to reason someone wanted her dead. Why was she traveling with us? Was she on the run?" Helen's expression said she wanted the whole story from me.

At this point, I knew I didn't have much choice. "Her husband is in prison—"

"He's a spy?" Charles asked, eagerness in his tone.

"He's a political dissident." That sounded good. I wouldn't admit anything I didn't have to.

"It just gets better," Helen said. "Go on."

"We were helping her and her two sons get to England—"

"You used us." Helen sounded ready to explode. "Do you know how many children are in danger of dying at the hands of the Nazis? And you took up places—"

"Do you think those two children were safe in Germany, with their father in a prison camp? Now their mother has possibly been murdered."

Helen and I glared at each other until she finally looked down and nodded. "You're right. Those children need our help. But we don't have any extra sponsors."

"I'll think of something." Such as dropping this on Sir Malcolm. Their father helped the spymaster. Now he could help the children.

"You'll have to," Gwen said. "You have a responsibility to them."

A responsibility that meant leaving them with Sir Malcolm wasn't enough. "Come on, let's put everything back and lock up until we get to port. Charles, will you go with me to speak to her sons?"

He paled. "I'm not very good with things like that."

Gwen said, "I'll talk to them with you."

"Thank you." In truth, I wasn't very good with things like this, either. Being an only child didn't give me much experience with children.

Charles shoved Agathe's things back into her suitcase and shut it before leaving the cabin with Helen leading the way. Gwen and I tidied up her bag and locked the door on our way out.

We found the older boy, Gerhard, on deck sitting with his arms around his little brother. Heinrich seemed to be half asleep. Gerhard straightened when he saw me, jolting his brother awake. "Where's Mutti?" he asked in German.

"Do you speak English?" Gwen asked, also in German.

"No. My parents said it wouldn't be safe for us to

learn it. They both spoke English, but they hid it. From us, the neighbors, everyone."

If she spoke English, Agathe could have spoken to any of the chaperones. Any of them could have known her from before this trip. Anyone could have killed her.

Gwen looked at me. I knew her German wasn't as fluent as mine. "Gerhard, Heinrich," I began, "I'm sorry, but something bad has happened to your mother."

"As bad as when they took Papa away?"

There was no way to sugarcoat this. "Yes."

"Dead?" Gerhard whispered.

I nodded.

A tear slid down Gerhard's face. "Mutti said the Nazis would kill her, too. She knew some of Papa's work, and she said they would come for her next. She knew secrets. Some she said even Papa didn't know."

"Do you know the secrets?" How much danger were the boys in?

"No. Mutti said it wouldn't be safe for us to know. The bad men would come and lock us up, too," Heinrich said and then began to cry. The two boys clung together, with Gwen rubbing their backs.

Chances were good a Nazi agent was on board with us. One of these upstanding, Quaker good Samaritans was a killer. A second thought made me cold. Did Alice and Agathe hold the same secret?

I would have to keep these boys close until we left the ship in Harwich and then I'd have to spirit them away. The question was where?

"Gwen, will you stay with the boys until I get back? I

need to speak to the captain."

She nodded, still rubbing their backs.

I wandered down a few back hallways and asked for directions until I reached the bridge.

"Hey, you can't be in here," the first man who noticed me shouted.

"Who's in charge?"

"I am," an older man in uniform said. "Captain O'Leary."

"Captain, I need to get a message to London. To Sir Malcolm Freemantle at the Foreign Office in Whitehall."

"Whitehall?" The captain looked suspicious. "Should I be letting the Home Office know?"

"You can. They won't mind you sending a message from me to Sir Malcolm. They may be very glad you assisted in this way." I watched him, trying to look as calm and self-assured as I wished I was at that moment.

"Meahan, send a message to Whitehall for the lady," the captain called out and walked back to the middle of the bridge.

A short, dark-haired man waved me over to a room where he took the seat in front of a shortwave radio and other gear I didn't recognize. He held a stub of a pencil in one large hand and said, "What do you want to say?"

What did I want to say that wouldn't alarm the sailors? "Sir Malcolm Freemantle, Foreign Office, Whitehall. Meet the ferry in the morning in Harwich. Package arrived for coroner. Signed, Olivia Denis."

Meahan's bushy eyebrows rose to his hairline, and he glanced through the doorway at his boss. The captain gave a nod and the radioman sent the message as I said it.

Thanking the men, I found my way back to where Gwen sat with the boys. Tom was with them. As soon as I appeared, he excused himself and led me over to the railing. "I've checked my lists. We don't have housing for all the children we've brought on this trip, let alone two more you slipped in. You're going to have to find them a home." He gave a sigh. "And what are we going to do about the dead woman?"

"Their mother," I corrected, brushing my hair out of my eyes as the wind whipped it across my face.

He nodded, looking out into the dark sea. "Their mother. How is this going to affect your article in the paper?"

"Don't worry about that." The salt in the air stung my eyes as I added, "I've sent a message to Whitehall to meet the ferry and bring a coroner. And I will take the boys with me to London."

"But where will you take them?" He sounded genuinely concerned.

"I don't know. My father's house, perhaps. Or Sir Malcolm may have some ideas. Or..." Esther and her grandmother, Mrs. Neugard, popped into my mind. Mrs. Neugard had only raised girls, but both women spoke German. Was it possible?

"You have an idea?" Hope rose in Tom's voice.

"Maybe. We'll find out." I gave him a smile. "Don't worry."

I walked back to the boys, rolling my walk to the

sway of the ship, and sat down facing them. "When we get to port, you're going to come with me to London."

"Are we going to stay with you?" Heinrich asked, his wet eyes shining in the bright deck lights.

"I'm hoping you can stay with a friend of mine. Her grandmother lives with her and only speaks German. It might make being introduced to living in England easier for you."

"Will we go back to school?" Gerhard asked. His serious expression didn't include tears, but I suspected the scars on his heart and his mind would be long-lasting. Like the other children on this voyage. Hitler had so much to answer for.

"I'm sure you will. You'll have to have remedial lessons in English, but you're both smart boys. You'll be up to the mark in no time."

He nodded solemnly.

Charles came out on the deck. "Aren't you cold?"

"Frozen," Gwen replied. "Let's see if we can get more of the children inside." She rose from the metal bench and went to talk to some of the teenagers, ushering them indoors.

"How about you two?" Charles asked.

Heinrich looked at Gerhard, who shook his head.

Charles shrugged and walked off to talk to some other boys.

I sat down on the cold, hard bench to take Gwen's place. Heinrich snuggled into my side. Gerhard huddled next to him without touching his brother or me.

A while later, one of the seamen brought out some

rough wool blankets to those few of us left on the deck. I wrapped one around the three of us so the boys were covered and only my head and feet were exposed. The blanket warmed me up, but my ears were icy despite my hat.

Heinrich's eyes were drooping shut no matter how hard he tried to stay awake, but Gerhard stared into the distance, thinking.

"Try not to worry, Gerhard," I told him.

"How can I not?" he said, sounding miserable. "Mutti is dead. Papa is locked away in prison. How will I keep Heinrich safe?"

"I have some ideas of where you can stay in England. Where you can be safe."

"Do not let them separate us."

"I won't."

"Promise." His voice was fierce. Commanding. I looked over and saw him stare at me with anger and defiance. His fair hair was ruffled by the wind, but he seemed impervious to the chill in the air.

"I promise." How could I not? Gerhard was determined to stay with his brother, who now leaned against me sound asleep, exhausted, warmed by the wool blanket as he nestled between Gerhard and me. How was I going to keep that promise?

At least for our first night onshore, I could count on my father and his next-door neighbors, the Oswalds, if I had to. But after that? I had no idea.

* * *

As the sun rose high in the sky behind us, we

watched the port at Harwich grow closer. The children, having breakfasted on a roll and coffee, spilled out on deck to watch their new homeland appear.

Betsy came up to us. "We need to get all the children, and their luggage, into the smaller indoor hall. They can watch us dock from the windows in there."

"All right." I gently shook Heinrich. "We need to go inside. We're docking."

"We're in England?" he asked with a yawn.

"Yes, and you're going to have to carry your case to the hall where we had dinner."

"Will Herr MacFerron be waiting for us?" the youngster asked.

"No, he's back in Berlin."

"I hoped we could tell him about Mutti. And get news of Papa."

"Afraid not, Heinrich." Gerhard rose and shook himself. "Get your stuff." Then he turned to me. "What about Mutti's case?"

"It's downstairs with mine. I'll bring them both up."

He nodded gravely.

"I have to round everyone up. If we get separated, meet me on the dock and I'll take you to London," I told them.

They nodded.

"I mean it. Try to stay with me in the hall. Otherwise, we meet on the dock. And stay together."

I must have sounded cross, because Gerhard said, "Don't worry. We will."

I wondered if I sounded like his mother, who'd been

frantic about getting her sons on board the train.

We had everyone accounted for in the indoor hall by the time the ferry docked. I slipped away to unlock the cabin where Agathe's body was, retrieved both suitcases and bags, and was back on deck before anyone left the hall.

We waited for the other passengers to disembark before we lined up the children and began to march them off the ship.

I caught up with Dorothy. "I need two of the boys' papers. They're going with me."

We looked through the stack of papers. We searched through more slowly a second time. We counted the number of passports against the number of children in our care. Two were missing. Gerhard and Heinrich's.

They'd never be allowed to land in England without their papers. Even Sir Malcolm couldn't solve that problem in the time we had to get the boys on shore.

There was no one and nothing for them in Germany, if they could even get back in. And there was no place for their papers to have gone, unless someone tossed them into the sea. That thought made my throat instantly dry. Done perhaps by the someone on this trip who had already committed murder.

My heart was pounding. I'd brought their mother's body to England, but I was out of ideas. I didn't know what to do if we couldn't find their papers.

Chapter Fifteen

"Who's been carrying the children's papers?" I asked.

"I have," Dorothy told me. "I don't know how two sets of papers could be missing. They must be here somewhere." She set down all the papers on a table and began to sort them in a hunt for the passports I needed.

Tom came up to us. "We're running behind. What's the holdup?"

"We're missing two sets of papers."

"Did we ever have them?" Tom gave me a hard stare.

"Yes. They were with the others when we left Berlin," I told him.

"Well, we can't slow the rest of the children disembarking. They need to get on the train. Dorothy, get the next batch off. I'll help with this," Tom said.

The room rapidly emptied. I started to breathe like I had run a race. I had, but this one wasn't over yet. Tom walked along the benches, checking behind and under each one, and I assisted, not understanding why this would help. The two boys stood with their rucksacks at their sides, looking bewildered.

Tom suddenly held up the papers. "They were under the cushions on this bench. Charles knocked over a whole stack last night. We thought we found them all, but I guess we were wrong." He handed them to me.

I glanced inside. These were the papers the boys needed, carefully forged by Herr Schumacher. I put them in my bag. "Why didn't Dorothy search here?"

"I don't think she knew about it. She was dealing with the children with seasickness. Charles was holding the papers and we hit a wave and everything went flying." Tom shrugged. "Helen and Charles and I picked up all of them from where they landed, I thought. Guess I was wrong."

"Thank you. All right, boys, let's get off and go through customs."

"Mutti's suitcase?" Gerhard said, glancing around.

"I have her things here with mine." I was getting good at carrying two pieces of luggage and two handbags.

We walked down the ramp carrying all our baggage to find Sir Malcolm and some other men waiting for us. He motioned us over as someone opened a car door.

"We need to go through customs," I greeted him.

He took my papers as well as the two youngsters' and nodded to one of the men, who took them and walked off. "We'll get you sorted through customs."

"And the coroner?"

"On board already." He glanced at the boys and then stared hard at me. "What is going on?"

"All three got on the train in Berlin. The boys in one carriage and the mother in the other. She collapsed shortly before we reached Holland. She was dead. I was in the carriage with her, and I have no idea how anyone could have done it. Poison from before we boarded? One of the chaperones, a nurse, said something was wrong with her neck. Could it have been snapped like Alice's?"

"Possibly."

"Now what?" I glared at Sir Malcolm, who looked slightly amused.

"What do you plan to do with the boys?" he asked.

"Isn't that what you should handle?"

"I root out spies and learn secrets to save our country. I don't have time to be a nursemaid." His tone was dry, and his words sounded final.

"Their parents are both out of the picture." I knew the boys didn't speak English, but I was trying to be discreet just in case.

"That's what orphanages are for."

"That's heartless." I was certain my face showed what I thought of Sir Malcolm's suggestion.

"Then you do something, Mrs. Denis. But remember, you have two murders to solve now, and a newspaper job to carry out." He turned away to speak to a man carrying a doctor's bag. After a minute of hushed conversation, the man walked off and Sir Malcolm said, "Do you want a ride to London?"

"Yes." I switched to German. "Come on, boys."

We piled into the back seat, Heinrich on my lap and Gerhard between Sir Malcolm and me. All our suitcases, Agathe's case and bag, and the boys' rucksacks were tossed into the boot. With a driver and an underling of Sir Malcolm's in the front seat, we started down the road to London.

Heinrich, who'd managed a fair amount of sleep on

the ferry, sat wide-eyed, looking at the countryside around him. Gerhard, who'd been awake worrying all night, finally collapsed and fell asleep immediately.

"What made you suspect murder?" Sir Malcolm asked.

"She died so suddenly, and then when Gwen, one of the chaperones who's a nurse, examined her, she said there was something wrong with her neck."

"She was right. Her neck was snapped."

"But it's impossible!" When Sir Malcolm looked at me after my exclamation, I explained, "We were locked into our individual carriages, and she was sitting with only very young children around her."

"Are you certain the doors to the next carriages were locked?"

"Yes. I checked before we left."

"And after you found her dead?"

Blast. I hadn't thought of that.

"Who was in your carriage?" Sir Malcolm continued, no doubt correctly reading my guilty expression.

"Four adults beside her. Me, Betsy and Wil Taylor, a married couple, and Dorothy Young, the leader of the expedition. A group of older boys, some slightly younger boys and girls, and a group of very young children, boys and girls."

"And the other carriage?"

"Four more adults. Gwen Endicott, the nurse, Helen Miller, Charles Brooks, and Tom Canterbury, who's the head of the Quaker rescue efforts and manager of the Refugee Children's Movement office."

He asked a host of questions, which I answered, but nothing that shed any light onto the problem of who killed a woman none of us had met before. If only I could be sure that was true.

I told him what I'd learned of Wil Taylor's prison sentence, but Sir Malcolm agreed the two murders didn't sound like his previous crime. However, no one knew what skills he might have learned in prison. Including breaking necks.

Finally, I asked, "How much do you know about Agathe?"

"Her mother was English, her father German. He was a successful industrialist. She was an only child, educated in the best schools. Married to Konrad Dietrich for twelve years, two children. And she spoke excellent English." He stared out the window until I was certain he wouldn't add anything.

"Does she have any living relatives in England?" And would they take the boys in?

He shook his head. Then he said, "Konrad Dietrich was brave and clever. We don't know how he got caught."

"You said 'was.'"

"We got word to him that his family was out safely before we knew about—this."

"How?" It wasn't as if the SS let anyone wander in and out of their prisons.

"MacFerron pays one of the guards to pass messages back and forth. The guard later reported that when the prisoners were called to line up, Dietrich ran toward the fence. He knew what would happen."

"How awful." The image in my mind sickened me. How would I tell the boys their father was dead now, too?

"His secrets, and ours, are safe now."

I looked at Sir Malcolm, amazed at his callousness.

He glanced over at me. "You really have no idea how terrible these Nazis are. Torture to them is as routine as your morning cup of tea. His secrets are safe because they are no longer crushing his body to learn what he may have passed on to us." His tone was as dry as toast.

It was my turn to stare out the window, feeling vaguely nauseated.

"When we knew Frau Dietrich and the boys had to escape, we looked for relatives," Sir Malcolm finally told me. "There's no one. If you want to keep the boys together, you're going to have to find a way to do it. I don't have the time or resources to deal with two little children."

I gave him what I hoped was a firm expression. "I promised them."

"Fine. Keep your word. But you also need to find a killer, who could be sharing our secrets in Berlin."

"If we assume both women were killed by the same person, there are only seven possibilities. If we think they were murdered by different people, then the number is almost infinite."

"Is there any evidence leading us in either direction?"

"Nothing other than it would be a huge coincidence

if I went on this trip to look for one murderer and found myself facing a second one." I could no longer stifle a huge yawn. "I'm sorry. I'm too tired to think."

"And you have domestic responsibilities at the moment." He nodded at the boys. "We'll drop you off at your flat and I'll see you tomorrow after you take care of appeasing Sir Henry."

My boss, Sir Henry Benton, would want an article for the *Daily Premier* newspaper, which I knew wouldn't go out under my byline. He kept promising, but after a year I'd almost given up. Since he paid my salary, even when I was working for Sir Malcolm, I was willing to play by his rules.

Before I could satisfy Sir Henry or Sir Malcolm, I needed to find at least a temporary answer to the question of what to do with the boys.

With that thought in mind, I must have fallen asleep. I woke up to find us stopped in front of my building. The boys and I piled out while Sir Malcolm's underling retrieved our luggage from the boot and set it on the pavement. Gerhard rubbed the sleep from his eyes as Heinrich looked around, a look of awe on his face.

"Tomorrow afternoon at one," Sir Malcolm called out before his assistant climbed in and the car rolled away.

"This way," I told the boys in German and waved to Sutton, our building doorman. He helped us carry in all our luggage, and then squeezed it and us into the tiny elevator. Only then did I realize Sir Malcolm's assistant had left us with Agathe's suitcase and bag.

I unlocked the door to my flat and entered with a sigh. While I was glad to be home, I'd returned with more problems than I'd left with. Not the least of which was two ravenously hungry children.

I told them to sit while I picked up the phone and dialed a familiar number. When I glanced over as the other end of the line rang, I found the boys had squeezed in together in one chair. I couldn't split apart those two terrified boys.

When Esther answered the phone, I told her about the boys and their need for a home.

I heard a sigh over the line. "I'd love to, and it would probably be wonderful for my grandmother, but James has dealt with as much German and extra people in this house as he can stand."

Blast. "I can understand how he'd feel that way—"

"Please don't ask me, Livvy. Things have been difficult."

I thought I heard a sniff over the line and felt like a cad. Esther was a new mother with a baby to take care of, a husband who was just learning to be a father, and a grandmother who was constantly interfering. "I'm sorry, Esther. I thought I had a solution to your problem, but instead it would cause more trouble. Forget I asked."

"What will you do?"

Typical of Esther to worry about others instead of herself. "I'll think of something. Starting with taking two hungry young men out to lunch. I have a present for the baby. I'll get it over to you in a few days."

"Oh, Livvy—"

"Don't worry, Esther. Every problem has a solution."

She laughed. "You sound like my father."

"Where do you think I learned it? Sir Henry."

When I hung up the phone, I told the boys, "There's nothing to eat here. Let's go out and have lunch."

"In a restaurant?" Heinrich jumped out of the chair.

"Why not?" I was stalling, but I really had no idea what to do next. I couldn't keep the boys in my flat. There was no room, no food, and I was working for two bosses, which left no time for two children who'd just lost their home and both their parents.

They needed the attention of someone who could make them feel welcome in their new country and teach them English.

We went out to get something to eat. I wracked my brain to remember what I considered a treat when I was young and eating out. Then it came to me. "I have a London treat for you," I told them. And then said in English, "Fish and chips."

They looked at each other and followed me to a small shop that smelled of salt and fish and frying oil. We took our newspaper-wrapped packages and walked to a nearby park. Fortunately, although it was cool, it was dry, and we sat together on a bench and ate our greasy treat with our fingers.

"Fish," I said and pointed to my batter-covered cod, "and chips," pointing to my strips of deep-fried potato.

The boys immediately had their first words of English.

After we ate, we walked around the park. It was a

small park, and chilly, and I was soon trying to think of something else to entertain them while I thought of someone to take them in.

My late husband, Reggie, had never gone in for sports, so there weren't any balls or toys or anything of the sort in the flat. My father had tossed out my childhood toys from his house when he redecorated. My flat had barely enough room for two adults, and certainly not enough space for two growing boys. They'd be bored, and I had to work if I wanted to afford the flat.

What was I going to do? I needed inspiration, but I was too tired to think, and time was running out. I had to solve this problem before the start of work tomorrow.

Chapter Sixteen

The gardens in the park reminded me of Summersby House. A manor house with a garden and farm animals and Sir John and Abby's sons' outgrown toys. And then I realized I had the perfect place to take them.

If only Abby and Sir John agreed.

"Come on," I said in German, "I need to go back to the flat and make a phone call."

I rushed from my front door to the telephone in the hall and asked the operator for a trunk call. Gerhard and Heinrich followed me in and again sat together in one of the two stuffed chairs in the drawing room, looking around in an effort not to be bored. It took a minute before I heard a maid come on the line. Almost immediately after, I heard Abby's voice.

After I explained the basic story about the boys, Abby said, "Just a moment. Let me talk to John."

I strained to hear their conversation, but the hum on the line meant I couldn't make out a single word. I looked again into the drawing room, knowing I had to find a way to keep my promise.

Abby finally came back onto the line and I sent up another prayer. "Well, why don't we try it out for a week or two and see if we suit each other." She sounded not the least bit hesitant, as if she expected a good outcome with her new lodgers. "What train do you think you'll be on? I suppose the five o'clock. I'll meet you at the station. And you will stay the night? John is going to want to hear all about this."

"Official secrets and all that."

Using her no-nonsense voice, Abby said, "Oh, we've been through that already, Livvy. We just want to know what we're facing."

"I hope you won't be facing anything but two delightful boys who need to learn English and how to help you around the garden." But their mother had been murdered, and I suspected an English person was the killer.

"Any time two little boys are the subject of official secrets, there has to be more to the story."

"I'll tell you and Sir John what I can."

"Good. I'll see you at the station."

When we hung up, I walked into the drawing room and sat on the sofa. "I'm taking you to the countryside to stay with my cousin and her husband. Have you ever lived in the countryside before?" I asked in German.

Heinrich shook his head.

"Will they take both of us?" Gerhard asked.

"Of course. They have two sons of their own. They're older and away at school, but you'll meet them on school holidays. They're great fun and play football and cricket. And I'm sure they must have a bicycle or two that would fit you."

"A bicycle?" For the first time, Gerhard had a gleam in his eyes.

"Animals?" Heinrich asked.

"A bicycle and horses and cows and pigs." I thought so, but I had never paid any attention. "At least around the estate. And a kitchen garden."

Now Heinrich showed a spark of interest. "What is a kitchen garden?"

"That's where you grow your vegetables for the kitchen. For meals."

"Don't they go to the market?" He was more openly inquisitive than his older brother.

"Some, but not for everything. Where do you think the vegetables in the market come from?"

Heinrich's face glowed when he thought of the answer. "The farm."

"Yes, and that's where Sir John and Lady Abby live. On a farm. And you're going to live with them."

"What about you?" Gerhard asked.

"What about me?"

"Will we see you anymore?"

"Of course. Abby's my cousin. She doesn't live that far away. I visit her frequently on weekends at Summersby House."

"Summersby House?"

"That's the name of their house, which is on the Summersby home farm." I saw the puzzled looks on their faces. "Don't worry. Soon it will all make sense. You'll be speaking English and helping around the farm and meeting the other children in the district."

Heinrich nodded, looking as if he welcomed the adventure. Gerhard scrunched up his face. "We'll not go back to Germany, will we?"

I shook my head.

"But what if they release Papa? He won't know where we are."

I didn't want to have to tell him. He'd just lost his mother the day before. But I had to. "I'm sorry, Gerhard. I've been told the Nazis killed your father in Sachsenhausen."

The boy wiggled back into the chair as far as he could and turned away from me.

Heinrich looked down, fat tears falling on his short trousers.

I remained on the couch watching them. Trying to think of something to say. Finally, I said, "Your Mutti and Papa can't be here with you anymore. They're in heaven, but I think they'd approve of Sir John and Lady Abby. They'll do a good job of taking care of you."

And then the three of us sat in silence.

* * *

We arrived at the station shortly after five in the afternoon to find Abby waiting for us. She greeted me with a kiss on the cheek and then turned to the boys. "Gracious. From the way Livvy talked, I expected little boys. You're half-grown men. Now, who is who?"

When they remained silent, I said, "I believe they only speak German."

Abby gamely repeated herself in stumbling German.

The older held out his hand and said, "I am Gerhard," then he looked at me, "Schmidt?"

I nodded.

Heinrich then imitated him.

The porter put our cases in the boot and we piled in, the boys in back and I in the front seat with Abby. "How was the trip down?"

"Quiet. I had to tell them their father died. Their mother died yesterday during our travel. None of us have had much sleep."

"I can imagine." Then in a more cheerful voice, she said in halting German, asking me for an occasional word, "We'll be home for tea in just a few minutes. There are two meanings for tea in England. One is the drink. The other is a small meal held at five in the afternoon after we've worked up an appetite since luncheon. Then dinner is between seven and eight."

Turned around in my seat, I could see Heinrich was interested when she mentioned food. Gerhard looked gloomy.

When we arrived at Summersby House, the boys climbed out of the car and stared at the manor house. I had seen it so often, I never noticed it anymore. Now I saw what they saw; a three-story, long Georgian mansion perhaps half the size of their block of flats in Berlin. They looked awestruck, and I could understand why.

The maids took our luggage from the car, and Abby led the way inside. "Livvy, you're in your usual guest room. Gerhard, Heinrich, we have a big room you two can take over together. Will that do?"

"We want to stay together," Gerhard said in a decisive tone.

"Come this way, then."

As soon as I saw she was leading them to the nursery, I marveled once again in how sensible Abby was not to call it the nursery in front of these two sensitive, frightened children.

I glanced into the guest room where my suitcase was being unpacked and walked down the hall toward Abby's voice. "I know the wallpaper is too juvenile for two older lads like you, but we can quickly fix that. How does the room suit otherwise?"

Heinrich rushed over and hopped onto the twin bed by the window overlooking the side of the house. "I want this bed. Look, there's a tree outside the window."

"No climbing down it," Abby said in mock seriousness.

Heinrich peered out the window. "And I can see a field with horses and another field with even lines drawn on it."

"It's been plowed and seeds have been planted that will grow into crops."

"What's 'crops'?" Heinrich seemed to be coming into his own.

"Beans, or hay, or potatoes, or grain. We'll have to wait until it comes up to figure out what has been planted there," Abby told him, her German coming back to her quickly with practice.

We all turned toward Gerhard.

"I like this bed with a view out the window toward the road," Gerhard said in a polite, disinterested voice. Then he took his mother's case from the maid and slid it under his bed to the back against the wall.

Abby and the maid exchanged a look. "I think the boys will want to unpack their own cases," Abby said. "I hope you like it here, Gerhard."

The boy nodded, staring at the floor.

"If you want to clean up, the facilities are behind the door there." The nursery area took up the whole end of the house. The rooms with the plumbing fixtures had once been a nursemaid's room and were also spacious. "And then come downstairs and we'll have tea."

"Yay, tea," Heinrich said. He was definitely starting to fit in.

We were all in the small drawing room a few minutes later to find Abby had thought of everything. Lemonade as well as tea, thick cut bread, cold leftover slices of roast, slices of cheese, early lettuce, and early berries with cream. "I wasn't sure, after you said no one had slept last night, if anyone would be awake for dinner," Abby said.

Sir John came in and introductions were made as an older, shaggy, brown-haired dog with floppy ears came in to sniff everyone. After being warned away from the table with the food, Rufus used his long tongue to wash Heinrich's face, which made the boy laugh, and he hugged the dog in return. Gerhard managed a small smile.

Sir John's German was better than Abby's because of his work during the war. He promised the boys, at Heinrich's insistence, for a walk to see the horses the next morning. He warned them that life on the farm began when the sun rose. He asked about their schools in Berlin and their knowledge of caring for animals. As we finished eating, he asked if they wanted to see if any of the bikes in the barn fit them.

For the first time since we arrived, Gerhard showed some interest.

Sir John and the boys hurried outside to see the barn and the marvels it contained while I went into the flower garden with Abby. "Can you stay awake after the boys go to bed? John and I have a lot of questions."

"I'm sure you do. But in fair warning, there are things I haven't learned that I'd like to know. I am grateful to you and Sir John for taking them in, if only for a short time if that's what you want."

"It wasn't so long ago our two were this age. And they seem well-mannered. Their parents must have done a good job raising them." She looked me in the eyes. "Is there no family at all?"

"Sir Malcolm says not."

"And Sir Malcolm looked into their family?" She raised her eyebrows.

"It was their parents, or rather their father, that interested Sir Malcolm, although he told me the mother had British roots. He said there wasn't anyone left to take the boys in."

"What about their schooling?"

"Once they learn English, they should be able to go to the village school, shouldn't they?" I hadn't thought that far.

"Does Sir Malcolm have any interest in their schooling?"

"I don't know. It's not something I've considered."

"Oh, Livvy. You're so impractical. Shouldn't Sir Malcolm at least sign papers that show we can keep the boys here? Two German-speaking boys suddenly dropped into an English farming community in 1939? In an area near the coast? People will be suspicious. I would be, particularly since Germany took over the rest of Czechoslovakia and now we're all expecting a war any day. We're looking for spies everywhere."

I wanted to argue, but I couldn't. I knew, deep down, she was right. "I'll speak to Sir Malcolm tomorrow afternoon. I'm sure he'll want to make the situation regular. It saves him having to think about it. And maybe, if I'm very persuasive, I'll be able to talk him into putting aside money for the boys' schooling when they're older."

"Sir Malcolm? I doubt it." She'd met him, and as with most people, meeting Sir Malcolm didn't leave them assured of his underlying kindness. "But it's good of you to try, Livvy. When is the funeral?"

"The funeral?" I asked blankly, stifling a yawn.

"For their mother. I imagine they'll want to attend."

I'd lost my own mother when I was nearly Heinrich's age. I should have thought of learning about Agathe's funeral. Since I hadn't, I suspected I was trying to avoid thinking about the pain of losing my mother in the influenza epidemic. "I'll find out the place and time."

"Good. Now, along this border..." Abby proceeded to tell me in great detail all the flowers she planned to grow. Then she walked me over to the kitchen garden, where work was already under way and the first plants were just peeking up out of the ground.

We cleaned up and dressed for dinner. Abby checked the boys' hands and face for cleanliness and helped them pick out nicer clothes for dinner before we met downstairs.

The change in Gerhard was amazing. Sir John quickly explained it by telling us how much the older boy liked bicycles and how much he already knew about tinkering with them.

While Gerhard told us about the bicycles in the barn, Heinrich added what he'd learned about the animals. He asked if Rufus could sleep in their room. Sir John assured him Rufus was happy with his spot in the kitchen hall.

Their enthusiasm was wonderful to see.

Abby told them about her two sons, who would be coming home in three days when the term ended. Matthew, the older, had one more year before he'd attend university, while Mark was three years younger. Sir John promised them there would be lots of time for sports with four lads in the house.

By the end of the meal, both boys could hardly keep their eyes open. Sir John excused them from the table and told them to go up and put on their pajamas. We'd come up and check on them in a few minutes.

We listened to them go upstairs before Abby said, "I think we'll wait on coffee until after we check on the boys. I expect they'll be asleep as soon as their heads hit the pillow."

"They seemed to have a wonderful time in the barn. City boys, but willing to learn about life in the country. And Gerhard is quite mechanically inclined. Make a fine engineer someday." Sir John had a broad smile on his face. I suspected he'd enjoyed his time in the barn as well.

By the time we reached their room, their clothes had been neatly folded, they claimed to have brushed their teeth, and Heinrich was already lying down, three-quarters asleep. Gerhard gave a mighty yawn as he climbed under the covers.

"Windows open or closed?" Abby asked.

"Open a little, please," Gerhard said.

The windows were adjusted, we said good night, and we tiptoed out. When I glanced back, Gerhard appeared to have gone limp with sleep.

When we reached the ground floor, Abby said, "Coffee in the study, please," to the maid as she led the way.

Once we each had a cup of coffee in Abby's delicate china cups, Sir John said, "Now, Livvy, we need to know the whole story. Starting with why you're involved."

"There are things I haven't been told. Things I'm not sure I can repeat. Official secrets and all that," I said.

Sir John shook his head. "I don't need to know official secrets. I need to know about two young lads under my roof."

This was going to be difficult. "I don't know how to separate them from the secrets."

Sir John glowered. Abby said, "Try."

Chapter Seventeen

I rested my head against the back of my high-backed wing chair and thought before I told them everything I could, including Gerhard having to be responsible for himself and his younger brother at a young age since his mother tended toward hysteria. I saw Abby and Sir John exchange looks at various points, but neither spoke until I finished.

"John and I have talked," Abby said, "and I don't think any of our neighbors are Jewish. I could ask around to find the closest synagogue—"

"They're not Jewish," I interrupted.

"But they came on the Kindertransport. We've been led to believe that most of those children are escaping the Nazis precisely because they are Jewish."

"I used the Kindertransport as cover to move them and their mother out of Germany." I was going to have to tell them more. "Until a few days ago, their father apparently was in a position of trust within the central German government while he secretly aided the British government. I suspect, although I don't know, he belonged to the Nazi party, although he obviously wasn't an enthusiastic member. He couldn't have joined if either he or his wife were Jewish."

"That raises two questions," Sir John said as he endeavored to light his pipe. "Why were they escaping?" A cloud of smoke went upward. "And why were you on the Kindertransport?"

"The father was denounced and died in Sachsenhausen within the last couple of days. I suspect the family would have been next. As to your second question, that I'm free to answer fully."

"Go on." Abby leaned forward in her chair.

I told them everything I knew or had heard about Alice Waterson and finished with Sir Malcolm's role in my traveling on the Kindertransport to learn all the details of the rescue efforts so I could write up a long article for the newspaper.

"At least you've accomplished one goal," Abby said.

"But the mother was killed the same way as Alice, and the only adults around were Alice's friends. We were sealed into the train rolling across Germany when she died."

"You think both women were killed by the same person?" Sir John asked.

"They had nothing in common. They didn't know each other. There doesn't seem to be a motive that would apply to both. But yes, I believe they were killed by the same hand. The manner of death was identical, and it's an unusual method."

"So, you're looking for someone with military training," Sir John said.

"For strangulation?" Abby asked.

"They had their necks snapped." Sir John pulled on his pipe and added, "Find a death that way and you're looking for a man with military training."

"Would a woman be strong enough to do this?" I

asked.

"If she were young, strong, and had been trained."

That fit all of the women on the Kindertransport. "Would a woman have received that sort of training?"

"Not during the war, and not in this country. Who knows what the Nazis are training women for these days?" His displeasure left him in a cloud of smoke.

"But the whole group on this Kindertransport are Quakers. Pacifists."

"Even a pacifist can snap and kill someone," Abby, always the practical one, told me.

"Possibly," I agreed, "but where would pacifists have received military training?"

* * *

That question plagued me the next morning as I said good-bye to Sir John, Abby, and the boys, who were busy practicing rudimentary English. I noticed most of it revolved around food.

At least they were eating and appeared cheerful and curious about their surroundings. They rode with Abby on the trip to the station. After I promised to come down on Friday if I could, I waved before I went in to buy my ticket.

As I was lost in thought, my ride to London and then to the Underground station seemed to go quickly. I walked to my building, said hello to Sutton, our porter, and went up in the lift.

Then I unlocked my door, kicked off one shoe and stopped, foot in the air, and stared at the hallway. We'd left the flat tidy. Now there was a sofa cushion and a couple of books in the hall.

I left the door open as I walked forward, shouting, "Hello?"

No one answered as I walked from room to room. The wardrobe doors were ajar, sugar had been spilled around the canister, and the book shelves were rearranged. At least I hadn't caught anyone inside my home.

I strode back to the telephone. My first call was to the police. My second was to Sir Malcolm.

When he came on the line, I asked, "Why was my flat searched?"

"How would I know?"

"Well, I'm glad to hear it wasn't our government breaking in and taking my flat apart. So, who was it? The only thing different was having had the two boys here. What don't I know about them?"

"Where are they?"

"With friends of mine. Are they in danger?"

"I wouldn't think so." Sir Malcolm didn't sound certain.

"You don't know. Wonderful. I don't want them hurt. I don't want my friends hurt. I'll be at your office this afternoon, and I'll want answers."

"Livvy, you can't—"

I hung up on him, and none too gently. Perhaps it wasn't a sensible reaction, but it felt good.

A constable arrived and took a report, but since there didn't appear to be anything missing, he didn't spend much time taking notes and left as quickly as possible.

I had the drawing room straightened when I heard a knock on the front door. I opened it and shrieked. "Adam."

After a kiss that left me breathless, my fiancé, Captain Adam Redmond, said in my ear, "I was afraid you'd be at work."

"I would have been, if I hadn't come back and discovered I'd been burgled."

"You sound frightened rather than angry. What's going on, Liv?"

I gave him the bare outlines of the two murders, the trip to Germany with the Kindertransport, Sir Malcolm's role, the two boys, everything. He grumbled at Sir Malcolm, congratulated me on my work with the Kindertransport, and was grateful Abby and Sir John could take in the boys.

"But you're frightened," he finished. "That's not like you when there wasn't any damage done or anything taken and they'd left before you returned. They didn't leave a threatening note, did they?"

I shook my head. "There was no reason for anyone to break in and not take anything. All the papers from the Kindertransport are kept in the Refugee Children's Movement office. The children are now dispersed all over the country. No one gave me anything to bring back to Sir Malcolm except the woman and her two sons, and the woman is dead."

"Could this woman have been bringing back something for Sir Malcolm?"

"I suppose it's possible, but she didn't seem like the type to carry out espionage. She seemed more like the type of woman to expect everyone to do everything for her. Besides, a couple of the Quakers went with me to the cabin on the ferry where we put her body. After Gwen—she's a nurse—told us she thought the woman's neck was broken, just like the first murder, we went through her suitcase and handbag."

"And?" Adam sounded impatient.

"Nothing. Just clothes and a few German marks, a handkerchief and her papers in her purse. Oh, and a few photos of her with her husband and children."

He shrugged. "Maybe this had nothing to do with the two murders or your trip to Germany for Sir Malcolm."

"Why else would anyone break in here?" I was both annoyed and shaken. This made no sense. I had no idea where the threat was coming from, and I was scared. I was very glad Adam was here and clung to him. "How long will you be in London?"

"I don't know. A few weeks, I hope."

My smile matched his. "Are you staying here?"

"Officially, I'm staying at the Transient Officers' Quarters, where no one holds a bed check like they did at my public school." He lifted my chin and added, "Of course, we could get married."

"Not until they declare war and married women will be free to work again." I'd told him of my determination to continue working as long as he was traveling and carrying out secret missions. He understood and was willing to wait, but not patiently.

"Since Czechoslovakia has fallen, it won't be long now." He sounded grim. With the information he gathered in his job, I suspected he had every reason to be somber.

The entire country was preparing for war. Gas masks were being issued, employers were told to build bomb shelters, and trenches had been dug in the largest of London's parks for some protection against bombs. Sandbags were beginning to be stacked around government buildings. All of London appeared to be waiting for war.

I was glad the boys were in the countryside with Abby and Sir John, but the fear that plagued me when I thought of the coming days left me cold. I hugged Adam as closely as I could.

He kissed the top of my head and said, "I have to return to work, but I have time for a quick bite first. Where would you like to eat?"

"Here, but there's nothing to eat in the flat." I gave him a big smile.

"I haven't had a bite to eat all day, and all I can think of is food. Come on."

We went to a nearby pub for a ploughman's lunch and then went our separate ways, promising to meet at my flat after work.

I took the Underground to Fleet Street and walked to the *Daily Premier* building. When I reached Sir Henry's office, I was told he was at a meeting at the Home Office. I decided the next best thing was to report in to Mr. Colinswood, who gave me special assignments for the paper when Sir Henry wasn't available.

If anything, his office was smokier than before. I knocked on the door frame. He signaled me to come in with one hand while taking notes with the other and cradling the telephone receiver against his shoulder. I walked in and sat while I waited for him to finish.

Once he hung up, he said, "Welcome back, Mrs. Denis. Sir Henry tells me you've been on a Kindertransport. I'd like for you to write up your notes to put in the paper for the article Sir Henry asked for." Then he grinned and added, "At least the ones you can reveal."

"Sir Henry told you I was sent on someone else's orders?"

He nodded. "We're relieved to have you back. There's plenty for you to do here." His tone changed. "The government is doing a great job of getting us safe and ready for this next war, and we get to tell our readers all about it."

I recognized sarcasm when I heard it. "That bad?"

"Have you heard about the latest accident? They were doing a recruiting drive for barrage balloon operators in Sheffield and sent one up in a gale. In a gale, of all times. The balloon broke free, floated around, and became a danger to air travel."

I laughed at the image of a huge barrage balloon flying overhead, sending people out of their homes and pointing skyward.

Mr. Colinswood grinned. "Of course, it could be a

good way to bring down German planes without risking any of our own."

Using Great War language, I said as I imagined it, "A barrage balloon recorded five kills today."

"Wouldn't that be nice." Then Mr. Colinswood's eyes took on a faraway glaze, and I remembered he'd been in the Great War as a young man.

I was afraid I was causing him pain by bringing up horrible memories. "I'll just borrow an empty desk and type up my recollections of the Kindertransport and Berlin."

There was no need to write them up properly. I knew I wouldn't get a byline. It annoyed me, but there was no changing the chances to get my name beneath the headline.

In less than an hour, I was finished. I turned in the yellow scrap sheets of paper and waved good-bye. Mr. Colinswood was on the telephone again.

It was getting to be late in the workday by the time I fought my way through the people crowding the London pavement to arrive at Sir Malcolm's building. The uniformed soldier at the door hit a button and a minute later, another soldier arrived to take me upstairs to Sir Malcolm's office.

He knocked and, when we heard Sir Malcolm's familiar growl "Come," opened the door. As I walked in and the soldier closed the door, the spymaster waved me into a chair.

"Your assignment was quite a bust. When I said I wanted three people brought to England, I thought they'd arrive alive. Imagine my surprise when the one I really needed to speak to, the one who might have the information we need, arrived with her neck broken."

"With the train in motion, I thought we'd be safe. Her death during travel wasn't what I expected, either. And I didn't know you were waiting for a message from her."

"In our last message from Konrad Dietrich, he indicated he had something important for us. So important he used a secondary channel outside the embassy to contact us. Then he was arrested. We had hoped he got whatever it was home and gave it to his wife to bring to us. Or told her. It might have been an oral message. It wasn't sewn into her dress or her coat. We checked her clothes."

Sir Malcolm leaned forward in his chair. "You failed, Olivia. And you weren't even on time for our meeting."

Chapter Eighteen

His complaints hurt my pride. "One o'clock wasn't convenient and I didn't ask for this. I haven't been trained. All I can do is my best and hope I succeed." I clamped my mouth shut in a tight line.

"You're very capable, Olivia. Your best is success. Remember that."

I stared past him out the window. The bare branches of the tree outside, finally freed of the unseasonable snow and freezing temperatures that had blanketed London a week or two ago, were showing the first brushstrokes of green. I concentrated on them until I had my temper under control.

When I looked at Sir Malcolm again, he said, "I need you to talk to the boys. See if their mother gave them a message to hand off to me. And where are her things?"

"Under Gerhard's bed."

"Search them."

I'd seen how Gerhard had guarded her belongings. "He won't like it. It's the one thing he can hang on to of his parents."

"If we don't get that message, a lot more parents will die. Children, too."

I knew where my duty lay. "I'll try this weekend."

"Good. Now, what progress have you made in finding the traitor or Alice Waterson's killer?"

I told him what I had learned and what I'd guessed.

It didn't take long.

"I agree that two deaths associated with the Quaker Kindertransport is suspicious. Leave it with me for the time being, since this group won't be returning to Berlin to trade more British secrets for a few weeks. Meanwhile, you need to either find me that message or have the boys repeat it for you."

"You're certain this secret exists? That Agathe had it or knew it?"

"I certainly hope so. If she didn't, grabbing Dietrich when they did is a triumph for the Nazis."

"And he passed his last message to you by a different route? A route bypassing the embassy?"

"Yes."

I found that highly suspicious. "Who didn't he trust at the embassy, and why?"

"I don't think it was a lack of trust. I think it was a lack of time. If the Gestapo was circling around, he may have only had a few minutes to hand off this important secret and get a message to us saying the information was on its way."

That made sense. "In exchange for finding this information, I need two things. No, three things."

"You do?" Amusement colored his voice.

"Some sort of official writ for the Summersbys to act as the boys' guardians, and money, probably promised to their father, to be put in trust for the boys' education. And at least a graveside ceremony for Agathe's interment with the place and time so the boys can attend."

"Is that all?" He sounded both surprised and relieved. "I'll take care of it. Now, you need to find the secret Dietrich died for."

I suspected Sir Malcolm had already begun the paperwork for my requests before I'd even asked.

* * *

The next few days dragged by. Of all the new spring colors that designers could have chosen, black and apricot tan were perhaps the most depressing combination imaginable. The news from overseas dampened our spirits even more. All air service to Prague had been canceled, Jewish-owned shops in Czechoslovakia were being destroyed, and another hundred thousand people were trying to escape Hitler's grasp.

I didn't want to read the news, and I worked for a newspaper. I couldn't imagine how our readers felt.

I took off one day to attend Agathe's burial in the morning and to visit Esther in the afternoon.

I took the bus to Highgate Cemetery and followed Sir Malcolm's directions to the grave site. When I arrived, the boys were there with both Abby and Sir John, along with a vicar and four men from the mortuary. Everyone wore their darkest colors and looked as subdued as the leaden skies that promised rain.

The vicar gave an abbreviated Church of England service in English while the breeze blew his liturgical robes against his trousers and around his ankles. The men from the mortuary, who had lowered Agathe's coffin into her grave, kept glancing at the sky. From the way he kept looking around, I wasn't entirely certain Heinrich understood what was happening, but from the grief carving his young face, I knew Gerhard did.

Afterward, the vicar said a few words to each of us. I stood between the boys, a hand on each of their shoulders, and translated the reverend's words that their mother was in heaven singing with the angels. Heinrich looked from the vicar to me, but Gerhard stared at the dirt at his feet.

As we walked away, I thanked Abby and Sir John for bringing the boys all this way.

"How could we not?" Abby asked. "We've promised them a Lyons' House lunch for after. Would you care to join us?"

"I'd love to."

I hoped lunch might keep my mind off the sunny, windy day my mother had been buried.

At least the rain held off until we reached the restaurant. It was damp, stuffy, and crowded, as any restaurant is on a rainy lunchtime, but the food suited Heinrich. Gerhard appeared to have lost his appetite.

Neither boy spoke more than a half-dozen words, which inhibited the adults from speaking either. Abby tried to start a conversation with me, but my thoughts were back two decades to the loss of my mother and I was no help.

When we parted, Heinrich and I hugged for a long time, and I promised I would visit in a few days. Gerhard didn't want to be touched.

The oppressive atmosphere followed me indoors when I arrived at Esther's, where her baby was being fussy, and the tension between Esther and her grandmother was so thick you could spread it on bread. The charming book I'd brought from Berlin could do nothing to lighten the mood, and I cut my visit short with a plea to Esther to rest. Meanwhile, baby Johnny screamed.

I was glad to return to the newspaper the next day.

Adam and I had made plans to visit Abby and Sir John on Friday evening and stay until Sunday afternoon. I hoped I'd be able to search Agathe's things while Gerhard was busy elsewhere so he'd never know what I did.

My suitcase was packed and by the front door when Adam came in. Even his kiss felt distracted. "What's wrong?" I asked when I broke away.

"I have to stay in town and work this weekend. All leave has been canceled. I'm sorry."

"Is it war?" That was my fear every time he had to change our plans.

"Not yet. Mussolini is making demands on France and now that Madrid has fallen, the Spanish Civil War is all but over."

As much as I wanted to stay home in the hope he had time to come by the flat, I had a job to do as well. "Do you mind if I go down to Summersby House alone? I'll go in the morning if you can spend the evening here."

"I'd like that." His smile was only a quick flash across his lips. "I hope you do go down to Sir John's tomorrow morning. No sense in us both having a boring weekend."

I called Summersby House and reached Abby. "How are the boys doing?" I asked.

"Our two are here now with term ended and they're having a great time exploring the area and teaching them cricket. The boys are learning English from them much faster than from John and me."

"That's good to hear. Adam can't get leave for the weekend, so I'll come down by myself in the morning."

Abby promised to meet my train and we rang off.

Adam and I went out for dinner and then spent a quiet evening at the flat. After he left in the morning, I got ready and made my way to the station to catch the next train.

Abby was alone when she picked me up at the station. She answered my question with, "The boys are off I don't know where, hiking, exploring, or playing with the lads on the village green."

"They obviously haven't missed me." I was glad. They were much better off in the countryside. "Has there been any trouble with them being German?"

"Not so far. And with Matthew and Mark, or John, showing them around, they've been accepted as refugees who are also children. They've become known as the boys who are staying with us. No one sees them as a danger. And whatever you said to Sir Malcolm did the trick. We have official permission from the Home Office to foster the boys."

Abby glanced over at me and added, "Speaking of

which, we're sorry Adam couldn't join us."

"All leave has been canceled. There's something brewing," I told her.

"Ask your father about it. He's down here this weekend, too."

"Glad to know the Foreign Office isn't worried," I said, my annoyance rumbling through my tone.

"They are," Abby said as she downshifted through a curve, "but this is more of a military situation."

"Terrific," I grumbled.

"If you think it's bad now, wait until the war starts." In a serious tone she added, "You could have years ahead of you to worry about Adam. Can you handle it?"

"I have to." I stared out the window at the scenery flying past. Abby's words struck very close to home and stirred up all my worries. Had my mother worried about my father in this way during the Great War? I'd never know.

We were silent the rest of the way to Summersby House. The maid took my suitcase up to unpack in the guest room I always used while I followed Abby into the drawing room. Nobody was there, and the house seemed silent.

"Where are Sir John and my father?"

"They went over to home farm. More for a walk than anything. Do you want to go out to the garden?"

"You go ahead. I want to go upstairs for a few minutes."

I walked up the stairs as Abby went out the French doors in the dining room. Glancing around to make sure no one else was about, I went into the nursery.

The boys were already making the space their own, with old primers, stories of sports heroes, and small figures of farm animals. I went over to Gerhard's bed and looked underneath. A battered suitcase was still there, shoved to the back along with Agathe's bag.

I sank onto my knees and pulled the case out to set it on the bed. When I eased it open, I found the clothes in the same jumble Charles had left them in on the ferry. Now that I had more time and privacy, I began a systematic search.

And I found something.

No wonder Agathe had been nervous. I was surprised she hadn't done a better job of hiding the documents from the Nazis. She was lucky they'd missed checking her suitcase or she never would have escaped Berlin. The papers, sewn into the lining, weren't hard to find since I had an idea of what I was looking for. Charles had to have been careless to have missed them.

There were four sheets of paper in all, written in a nonsensical German with strange symbols and small drawings. Making certain there were no other papers hidden in the case, I closed the suitcase and slid it back to where it had been. Her bag contained nothing hidden. Feeling guilty for snooping, I hurried to my room.

The maid had already finished with the few clothes I'd brought with me, so I pulled my case out of the wardrobe and put the papers inside. Then I put my suitcase back and closed up the wardrobe before I headed downstairs and out into the garden.

Abby immediately put me to work. By the time we cleaned up, lunch was served. All four boys returned with enormous appetites and a dozen stories they wanted to tell at once. As Abby sent them upstairs to clean up, my father and Sir John arrived.

"Mrs. Mullins gave me a pot of honey. Said she owed it to you for some winter lettuce," Sir John said. "I left it in the kitchen."

"And your boots?" Abby asked.

"In the mudroom," Sir John answered with an innocent air. I thought there must be a story there that I didn't want to hear.

"Those boots fit very well, Abby. Thank you," my father said before he turned to me. "Hello, Olivia."

"Hello, Father." It appeared it would be a chilly weekend, which would be fine with me. I was already in a bad mood since Adam couldn't be here.

He looked around. "Where's Adam?"

"All leave's been canceled."

"Pity. I was looking forward to seeing him," my father replied. "Are we back in time for lunch?"

"It's good to see you, too."

Fortunately or not, my father never appeared to notice my sarcasm. "Of course."

Abby could tell a fight was brewing from miles away, no doubt having had practice from dealing with her sons. "Shall we go into the dining room? The boys should be down in a minute."

"Will we need to speak German? Those two lads don't appear to speak English," my father said.

"They don't speak much of it, but they understand fairly well. Particularly when the subject is sports or farming," Sir John said. "Our boys speak to them in English for the most part, and they're picking it up."

As I sat down at the large dining table, I said, "That is good news."

My father unfolded his serviette. "You know about these two Germans, Olivia?"

"I asked Abby and Sir John to take them in. They came on the last Kindertransport with me."

"What were you doing on a Kindertransport?"

"Sir Malcolm sent me."

I might as well have thrown a grenade into the room. "What were you doing, traveling for Sir Malcolm? And to Germany, of all places. That's dangerous. Good grief, Olivia." If my father grew any redder, he'd have apoplexy.

We could hear the boys clattering down the staircase. "Why don't we discuss this later?" Abby said with a pointed look at my father.

For once he took the hint.

While the maid served the soup, Gerhard and Heinrich told me in German, with a few English words thrown in, about their adventures of the last few days with Matthew and Mark. Apparently, they'd fished, fed chickens, practiced cricket and football, and hiked everywhere. Matthew had gifted Gerhard with his old bike and Gerhard had been showing Matthew how to "improve" it.

Matthew and Mark added their observations in

English, which the younger two seemed to follow. They'd both ask the older boys if they didn't understand a word or an expression. I noticed they didn't ask the adults. I suppose since Gerhard and Heinrich had become accustomed to speaking to us in German, they didn't feel comfortable speaking English to us. Or maybe they'd been corrected by adults too harshly in the past.

Lunch went by quickly with much juvenile good cheer, and then the boys asked to be excused. They planned an outing following the local creek as it meandered toward the Channel.

Sir John chuckled. "No farther than Ratherminster. We want you home in time for tea."

The boys agreed and with a nod from Abby and Sir John, they rushed out of the room.

"I am glad to see Gerhard and Heinrich doing so well," I told them. "And they do seem to understand a great deal of English. Matthew and Mark have worked a miracle."

"The boys all took to each other immediately. Since our boys have outgrown the nursery, they don't mind Gerhard and Henry, as he's getting to be known in the neighborhood, being there," Abby said.

"A quick word in Matthew's ear about their parents dying at the hands of the Nazis has made its way around the district—very quietly, you understand," Sir John added.

"There hasn't been any trouble with your neighbors?" I asked.

"None. They've heard how brutal the Nazis can be. I

suppose they feel sorry for the boys," Sir John said as he began the process of lighting his pipe.

"Olivia, I want to know exactly what your role was in all this," my father said.

"You know I can't tell you. Official secrets and all that." How often had he said those words to me when I was younger and wanted to know where he was going and why? It felt good to give him some of his own medicine.

And then I felt guilty. He'd had no more choice in what was an official secret than I did.

My father turned an unlovely shade of pink and replied, "I am your father and responsible for you. What is going on? And who are those boys?"

Chapter Nineteen

"Shall we go into the study for our coffee?" Abby said as I opened my mouth to give my father a dressing-down. He was not responsible for me. I was an adult, a widow, earning my own living, and working for a secret intelligence section of His Majesty's government.

My father glared at me, nodded to Abby, and rose when she and I did.

Once we were seated in the study with our coffee, my father said, "What are you doing, aiding Sir Malcolm?"

"I wouldn't have come to his attention if you hadn't been involved with him," I countered. I didn't remind him of how quick Sir Malcolm had been to incarcerate him in a secret prison when he'd discovered the body of a British spy in his drawing room. We were all aware of that disaster the previous autumn.

"That's different."

"No, it's not." We glared at each other.

Abby, probably worried for the safety of the delicate coffee cups we held, said, "Sir Ronald, what your daughter did was noble. She worked with Quakers on one of the Kindertransports to rescue over two hundred children, plus the two boys who are staying with us who would have been killed by the Gestapo if she hadn't found a way to spirit them out of the country. I think you should be proud of her."

"Abigail, there is no one I respect more than you, but I think this is a private matter between my daughter and me." My father was sounding stuffier by the moment, and I needed to stop him now.

"Anything you say to me you can say in front of Abby and Sir John. They are family, too." Well, by marriage. Abby was my late husband's cousin.

"You don't understand the dangers involved in working for Sir Malcolm. None of you do." He had taken on his mulish expression.

"Of course I do. I wouldn't trust him as far as I could pick you up and throw you." Which, at that moment, I would have liked to do. Preferably out an attic window.

"It's more than that. The Nazis have complete control over a large swath of Europe and are ready to attack at any time. Sir Malcolm is sending young people into Germany and the occupied territories to carry out his missions with no expectation that any will survive and return to England. When they do, he counts it as a bonus."

"Sir Malcolm has me trying to find out who killed a Quaker woman here in London. The fear is the killer is a Quaker."

My father slowly shook his head. "Why would Sir Malcolm be interested in a murder in London? Think about that."

"Her family are good friends of his." Probably not true, but I couldn't say that Sir Malcolm was really interested in the Quaker who was using the Kindertransport to pass government secrets to the

Nazis.

"Nonsense. The woman was one of his spies."

"I'm sure she wasn't." My father had to be wrong. Alice Waterson was the daughter of a peer, a pacifist, and from all I'd heard, not someone to take orders from anyone, especially Sir Malcolm. Would she?

Doubts began to form. If Alice were one of Sir Malcolm's spies, it would explain Sir Malcolm's interest in her and the Kindertransport he manipulated the Quakers to send me on. I could have investigated her murder without leaving London, where she'd died, but being on the Kindertransport let me try to catch a particular chaperone passing secrets.

"The only reason Sir Malcolm would interfere with a London murder, which should be investigated by Scotland Yard, was if one of his people had been on the trail of a Nazi agent."

"She was a pacifist."

"Pacifists can be spies." When I didn't respond, my father said, "Ask him. Ask Sir Malcolm if she worked for him. Much like you. And," he added, "I don't want to see you suffer the same fate."

Pushing my doubts aside, I was sure my father had to be wrong. Still, on Monday, I would ask Sir Malcolm.

Sir John chose this moment to ask my father if he'd care for a round of golf at the local club. I suspected Abby had given her husband some sort of signal, but if she had, I missed it. Once the men were out of the way, Abby put me to work in her flower garden.

"I have the boys help in the kitchen garden, since

they can see the connection between their work and their lunch. I'm afraid I wouldn't be as lucky if they were working with flowers."

I had to grin. "You mean they have no interest in winning a prize at the county flower show."

"Something like that."

We worked in companionable silence until nearly teatime, when we went in to get cleaned up. I hoped when my father returned, he'd be less combative.

The boys returned, tired and hungry, and quickly cleaned up to join us for tea. I wondered at Abby's vast array of sandwiches until I saw all four boys devouring them as if they hadn't seen food in a week.

"Slow down," Abby said as Matthew reached for his fourth. "How far did you walk?"

"Only to Ratherminster. We ran into some friends on the green and talked as we kicked a ball around. Then we were late and had to run back along the lanes," Matthew said.

"We had to keep waiting for Henry since he has short legs," Mark added. "I was afraid we'd miss tea and I was starving."

"And it was ever so far," Heinrich said. It was the first English I'd heard him say, and he was already developing an English accent.

It was also the first time I'd heard him called Henry. He didn't seem to mind. I guessed he was adapting to his new country quickly.

Gerhard, older and more serious, didn't seem to be adjusting as well, although he appeared to get along well with Sir John, Abby, and their sons. He was obedient, but he remained silent, slowly eating his sandwich as the other three talked in English.

Abby had told me Gerhard could speak some English when it was necessary, but he chose to stay silent if he could, particularly around adults. "What has that child been subjected to?" she had asked earlier while yanking out a stubborn weed.

What had he been subjected to? Wasn't being taken from his home, losing both his parents, and being forced to live with strangers and speak a foreign language enough? Apparently not, since he was the one who took charge of his mother's suitcase. The case where I'd found the coded letter.

I needed to tell him what I'd taken. After tea.

Then my father and Sir John joined us for tea, and as my father and I sparred over every word the other said, the boys slipped out at Abby's nod. Talking to Gerhard would have to wait.

"Now that the boys have left, I can speak frankly," my father said. "I don't know what Sir Malcolm has planned, but he is certainly using you."

"I know that," I told him, letting my annoyance seep out in my tone.

"She can't tell him 'No,'" Sir John said around his pipe stem as he attempted to light his pipe. "You know that as well as anyone."

My father nodded at the truth of his words. "You've got to be careful. The Nazis have spies in place here. Some of them have been here for many years. Sir

Malcolm's responsibility is to find them and remove them before they can do any damage."

"As soon as war is declared, they'll be even more dangerous," Sir John said. "And Sir Malcolm and his minions will be free to take any measures they want."

Everything they said was true. What I couldn't believe was that a Quaker, a pacifist, would spy for Germany. Or that plain, bossy Alice Waterson was killed because she was working for Sir Malcolm to catch a Nazi spy.

That was my father's theory, but was it true? I needed to see Sir Malcolm as soon as possible. If my father was right, I had to rethink everything I had thought about the Quakers. Such as one of the lovely, caring people I had traveled to Berlin with could be a cold-blooded killer.

And a spy.

"All right, I'll be careful. But I'm having trouble believing a pacifist would be a spy. Spying is like taking up arms against the enemy. It means being a combatant and taking actions that could lead to someone's death."

"Do you really see it that way?" my father asked.

"Yes."

"Perhaps the Quaker spy doesn't see it in quite the same terms."

Sir John broke in with, "Or perhaps the spy is only posing as a Quaker. Perhaps he doesn't agree with the tenets of their faith. With their pacifism."

"All of the members I've met have known each other for ages." Except two. Except Alice's fiancé and Wil

Taylor. But that didn't mean one of the other Quakers on the train with me hadn't had a change of heart not shared by his fellow Quakers.

"Quaker or not, someone is skilled at breaking necks," Sir John said. "Be careful, Livvy."

By mutual agreement, we changed the subject and took a walk to the Summersby House farm, referred to as the "home farm" by Sir John and Abby. Sir John had a litter of piglets he wanted to show off.

It was a mild evening, and we returned in the lingering light in time for dinner. "For once the boys are waiting for us," Abby said as she walked in the kitchen hall door.

Three boys were lined up in the doorway that led to the main part of the house. "Where's Gerhard?" I asked.

The boys glanced at each other from the corners of their eyes, guilty expressions on their faces. "Well..." Matthew began before he trailed to a stop.

"Um," Mark said, and then appeared to change his mind about saying anything.

"He's really angry," Heinrich said in his almost British accent. "He's not coming in until somebody says they're sorry."

"About what?" I guessed I already knew.

"Someone's been in Mutti's case. He found everything mixed up from the last time he looked in there. He doesn't want anyone touching her stuff." Heinrich, Henry to his friends, looked very stern and more than a little unhappy.

"He's been very protective of your mother's things,"

I said.

He nodded solemnly. "It's all we have of her. And Mutti made him promise..." He trailed off, looking guiltier than he had before.

"What did your mother make him promise?"

He shook his head mulishly.

None of the boys would answer, despite Sir John telling Matthew he was the oldest and needed to set a good example for the younger boys. Matthew looked miserable, but he stuck by whatever deal the four youngsters had made.

Abby sent the older two boys upstairs to clean up for dinner. They claimed they already had. Sir John told Heinrich it wasn't helping Gerhard if he didn't tell us what was going on, but his lips remained firmly sealed.

"Where is he?" I asked. "I can't make this right if I can't speak to Gerhard," I said, sounding as reasonable as I could.

"It was you? You went through Mutti's things?" Heinrich demanded.

"That's for Gerhard to work out, isn't it?" The young boy wouldn't meet my gaze. "If you aren't going to tell me anything, why should I tell you anything?"

Hunching his shoulders, Heinrich murmured, "He knows about something Mutti hid. Something that's gone now. He's angry, because he didn't keep it safe, and he promised."

"Do you know what it is?"

He shook his head. "He and Mutti wouldn't tell me. They said I was too little. That I couldn't keep a secret.

And I can." He stomped one foot. "I'm not too little."

"Olivia," my father said in the tone he used to upbraid careless servants, incompetent tradesmen, and me, "do you know about this?"

I decided not to answer him. "Heinrich, where is he?"

He shook his head.

"Then I'll just have to go look for him. Don't wait dinner for us." I started out the back door.

"You might try around the garage," Matthew said from the stairs.

"Fink," Mark said, gaining him a glare from his brother and both parents.

I walked outside to the entrance to the garage. Opening one of the wide doors, I called out, "Gerhard, I understand you discovered I took something from your mother's case. Something meant for the man your father and I both work for."

Silence greeted my words. I couldn't see anything in the unlit garage. I couldn't hear any movement around me.

"Gerhard, show yourself so we can talk about this. And get some dinner," I added as an afterthought. "Abby's cook does a very good job on roasts, and I'm hungry." I hoped Gerhard was, too.

The silence lengthened. I shut the garage door and walked over to the barn. Opening a door, I repeated my speech to no avail.

Nothing moved. Nothing breathed. Where was he? Had he decided to run away?

Chapter Twenty

"You should have asked me," a small voice said behind me in German. "That's my Mutti's case. You shouldn't have snooped."

I spun around, seeing Gerhard in silhouette against the house. Releasing a long breath, I realized he would never depart and leave Heinrich behind, and for that I was grateful.

I replied in the same language. "Since you know all about it, I should have. If you hadn't, I would have upset you terribly. Your parents made a choice to help the British defeat the Nazis. It was a courageous decision, and they tried to protect you from its consequences. That made me think they hadn't told you about passing secrets to Britain."

"Everyone treats me like a child. I'm not stupid." He sounded frustrated and near tears.

"You are a child, but you're anything but stupid."

"Then why didn't you ask me if I knew about the message?" came out almost as a shout.

"I misjudged how much your parents wanted you to know. I won't do that again." I looked at him, standing still, looking so small and fragile in the darkness, and asked, "Do you know what the code is based on?"

He shook his head. "Mutti said not to worry about the words. The British who should have the papers will be able to read it." Then in a skeptical tone, he added,

"What are you going to do with them?"

"Take them to the man I work for. He was supposed to receive the documents, and he asked me to bring them to him for your parents. If the papers hadn't already been stolen." I shut the barn door behind me.

Gerhard nodded, still looking sulky.

As long as I had the opportunity, I decided to ask. "When are you going to start speaking English?"

"I do to the lads already. I'm just not ready to be English. Not around the adults."

I thought about his words for a moment. "Does it feel disloyal to your parents to speak English and to live with Sir John and Lady Abby?"

"No. Sir John and Lady Abby have been wonderful to Heinrich and me, teaching us English, feeding us, and letting me tinker with the bicycles while Heinrich feeds the animals. But it feels wrong that my parents are dead."

"It is wrong that brave people like your parents died. I wish I knew why your Mutti was murdered. We can't do anything about your father's killers until the war is over, but someone English killed your mother and they should be punished for the crime."

"You mean someone on the train with us?"

"Yes. We were locked in those train carriages." I saw Gerhard shuffle his feet on the path. "Hungry?"

"Yes."

I moved toward him. "Let's go into dinner."

* * *

The next morning, we went to church for the main

Easter service, all of us piling into Sir John's car. I had Heinrich on my lap and Gerhard was perched half on Matthew's knees and half in the footwell. Seeing my father squeezed into the front seat with Abby and Sir John would have been humorous if I weren't being squished by four squirming young men.

Mercifully, it wasn't far. We arrived in the village with our clothes wrinkled, and the boys exploding out the back doors with shrieks of laughter as we parked on the lane.

All four boys were well behaved in church. I didn't pay much attention to them because I was studying the possibilities of holding a small wedding in the beautiful old medieval stone church. It would be hard to schedule because Hitler wasn't about to tell me when he'd start a war just so I could book a wedding.

And I knew the army wouldn't hand out passes to suit my plans. Between the nagging style of the sermon and my unhappy thoughts, I left Easter service in a dark mood.

Afterward, as Sir John and Abby greeted neighbors, I heard more than one comment about how well the German boys were fitting into the area. I heard plenty of talk about the approaching war; I heard nothing said against the boys.

After an excellent Sunday dinner, I said good-bye to the boys and then Sir John and Abby drove my father and me to the train station, asking why neither of us had off on Easter Monday. My father didn't have any better excuse than I had.

And I didn't want to admit I was still looking for a killer.

While we waited on the platform, I noticed the ring of keys on the belt of the platform manager's uniform, and it made me think.

We had been locked into the train while we'd traveled across Germany. Agathe had been alive when we left and dead of a broken neck by the time we had reached the border. I hadn't seen anyone unlock a door and come in while we were moving along the tracks at speed.

However…

I wasn't sure if it were possible to enter our carriage without this person killing themselves in the attempt, but somehow the murderer had climbed in and out of our carriage and doing so must have involved a key. There was no other way in.

I couldn't believe the killer was Dorothy, Betsy, or Wil, despite his prison record. Betsy and Wil were never out of my sight from the last time I saw Agathe alive until I found her dead. They had helped me break up the fight between the teenaged boys.

That had to have been when Agathe was attacked, and I couldn't see Dorothy breaking anyone's neck. She was neither big enough nor strong enough, nor did she have the stomach to kill someone using her hands. There was no one else in the train carriage to commit the crime.

Someone got in and out again. Therefore, they had obtained a key from somewhere.

My father nudged me into following him into a first-class carriage heading to London, and I had to drop my thoughts for a few minutes. Once we were on our way, I leaned back and shut my eyes.

I pictured myself standing in the aisle during the fight, so anyone from the front of the train would have had to push past me to kill Agathe. The murderer had to have come from the back, where the other car of Kindertransport children was. With Charles, Tom, Gwen, and Helen.

I could rule out Helen because I couldn't fathom where she would have learned to snap someone's neck. Of course, Mary Wallace would have gladly choked Alice for her flirtation with Tom, but she was back in London. If Gwen could spot a broken neck on a corpse, what else had she learned as a nurse? Still, I doubted quick methods to kill were a part of the curriculum.

Tom and Charles were my best choices, and Tom had been with Alice surveying those families in London taking in relatives who were arriving on the Kindertransport. I had only his word for it that Alice had walked off to speak to someone. What I couldn't imagine was their motive.

Could either of them be a spy?

* * *

The next morning, I awoke to a drizzly London street scene outside my window. The weather matched my mood. There was no sign Adam had been in the flat while I was at Summersby House, and I had no idea when he'd return. I put on a blue wool dress, had a cup of tea and some toast, and donned my wet-weather outerwear.

Crossing Central London by tube, I came out at St. James's Park and walked the rest of the way to Sir Malcolm's office, my heels and hose getting splashed along the way. Once again, a soldier escorted me upstairs.

Fortunately, I didn't have to wait. The soldier knocked on the dark wood door and we were immediately told "Come."

When we opened the door, we found Sir Malcolm seated at his desk studying the papers in a folder, ignoring us. For an instant, I wondered if he ever left his seat.

The soldier hesitated, but I did not. "Sir Malcolm, we need to talk."

"Thank you, soldier." The soldier backed out and shut the door. "I wondered when you'd have something to report."

"Was Alice Waterson working for you?"

"'Working' is a strong word for what any of you do," he said with a sneer.

"'Assisting' you, then, in finding a Nazi sympathizer among the Quakers involved in the Kindertransport." I hoped that was specific enough to get a direct answer from him.

"With every Quaker Kindertransport, the Nazis picked up valuable intelligence. Information known only in a few government departments. I've known Lord Waterson since the Great War. I felt certain I could trust his daughter." He looked at me from under bushy eyebrows. "Alice undertook the same task you are doing now, and it got her killed."

Thanks for warning me of the danger. "It makes sense that whoever killed Alice also killed Agathe, probably for this message." I handed over the coded letter.

Sir Malcolm glanced over the four pages. "Do you know the code?"

"No, and their sons don't either. Would Douglas MacFerron know?"

"There's no reason why he should, and he's in Berlin. Never mind, we'll soon have this deciphered and see what Konrad Dietrich gave his life to tell us." He set the paper aside. "Any luck finding our killer?"

"I think it's either Tom or Charles. They were in the other railroad carriage, but if they had managed to get hold of a key, it would have been possible to slip out to the next carriage to murder Agathe. Being supposedly locked in, if no one knew about the key, they would have been above suspicion."

"How would they have known Agathe was on the train?"

I shook my head. "Perhaps they knew what she looked like. Or someone followed her and told the killer."

He gave me a hard stare. "Good luck, Mrs. Denis. Keep up the search." He waved the notes I'd given him. "We're grateful for this last piece of intelligence from a very brave man."

I nodded to him and walked over to open the door. The soldier was at the end of the corridor, waiting to escort me downstairs. When I glanced back at Sir Malcolm, he was frowning at the coded note.

I returned to the *Daily Premier,* hoping I was not so late that Miss Westcott, my boss on the women's section, would notice. However, when I hung up my coat and hat and went to my desk, she walked over to say, "I'm so glad you could make it this morning."

Miss Westcott knew when I was absent due to an assignment from Sir Henry Benton, the publisher, and she knew my last absence was not at his direction. I pasted on a smile and said, "I'm glad to return."

"Good. Take Miss Seville and go to Hampstead Heath. There's going to be a promenade of dogs and their owners since it's Easter Monday." She smiled. "And watch where you step."

It wouldn't take much time and very little writing. *What Miss Westcott thinks of my abilities.* It would mean a good soaking. I had to be her least favorite reporter in the office. I packed my notebook and pencil in my bag and went down to the photo section to find Jane Seville.

We took a cab to the edge of Hampstead due to Jane's heavy assortment of camera equipment. Then I helped her carry the black leather boxes to the edge of the parade route, keeping an exuberant retriever from carrying anything off or putting its muddy paws on us. Giving up on us and our interesting collection of cases, the retriever trotted over to sniff the hindquarters of a pug.

"I had dinner with someone like that recently," Jane said before shooting me a smile.

Unlike Jane and me in our heels and city clothes, the human participants of the promenade sensibly wore wellies, tweeds, and oilskins. They all seemed to know each other. Only half had their dogs on a lead. I worried for my blue dress.

After speaking to a few of the participants that Jane had taken photographs of, I put my notebook back in my bag. The rain, misting lightly before in a cheery sort of spring shower, now began to soak the ground and anyone not under an umbrella. Only the dogs appeared impervious.

Jane and I carried her equipment to the road and looked about for a taxi. As I glanced up the hill to my right, I saw a man hurrying along, his umbrella covering part of his face. But what I saw made me certain he was Douglas MacFerron.

What would he be doing in Hampstead? Sir Malcolm had just said he was still in Berlin at the embassy.

"I'll be back in a minute," I told Jane as I hurried up the road. The climb in heels left me breathless, and I was still too far away to call out to him.

He turned a corner and I rushed up the street. I was gasping as I reached the corner. Looking around, I couldn't see him anywhere. There were two alleys and a cross street ahead close enough that he might have gone down any of them.

Pressing my hands on my knees, I breathed in deeply a few times before I headed back to where Jane was standing. Before I reached her, a taxi pulled up and she loaded her equipment bags inside. I strode to her side in time to climb in after her.

"Where did you find the cab?" I asked.

"I went into the store, and they had a number I could ring. Apparently on weekends, visitors are always looking for taxis after a stroll around the heath." Jane stared at me. "What made you run off like that?"

"I thought I saw someone I knew. Someone who shouldn't be here."

"Another assignment for Sir Henry?" Jane was aware I had done special assignments for our publisher in aid of helping his late wife's family, and others, escape the Nazis.

"No. He's now taken to loaning me out." I gave her a rueful smile.

Jane shook her head. "Be careful."

Good advice. I should be able to find out if Douglas MacFerron was in England or if the man I'd seen only bore a very strong likeness. My late husband had worked in the German section of the Foreign Office. I still had a few friends there.

"I'm going to have to disappear for a few minutes to make a phone call or two," I said as we got back to the *Daily Premier.*

"After you help me carry in all this equipment," Jane said in a no-nonsense tone. Once I did, she relented and led me to a small office with a phone. "Keep it short," she murmured before she shut the door.

In just a minute, I was connected to Lester Babcock,

a friend to both my late husband Reggie and me. "Lester, I need your help. Nothing illegal. I just need to know if Douglas MacFerron is at work in our embassy in Berlin at the moment."

"Odd you should mention Berlin."

"Why?" This didn't sound good.

"It's Easter Monday. Half our embassy staff is on a long weekend. Half the city is on a long weekend. I'd be on a long weekend if I could arrange it."

"So he could be anywhere."

"He could have come to London if he'd arranged for an extra day or two."

"Had he?"

"I have no way of knowing," Lester told me.

I wondered if MacFerron had come over to visit Agathe. Her photos made them look like more than friends.

Chapter Twenty-One

"Doesn't anyone have any idea where he went?" I hated the thought that MacFerron came to London to see Agathe and discovered without any warning that she was dead. I was sure from those photos she had that it would be a shock.

Lester said, "I doubt it, and there are very few people at the embassy to ask. Why do you want to know?"

"I thought I saw MacFerron in Hampstead just a little while ago. His umbrella masked part of his face, but I could have sworn it was him."

"Anything is possible," Lester said, "but I'm sure it's no mystery. It's a good weekend for spring holidays and traveling. And a lot of our embassy personnel are looking for housing in England for when the war starts." He lowered his voice. "I can't talk now. If anyone mentions talking to him, I'll call you at home tonight."

"Thank you. Tell Mary and the baby hello for me."

"He's hardly a baby. You must come over and see us."

"Soon. I promise." I made a mental note to call Mary later in the week and invite myself over for tea and gossip.

I hung up, wondering if the man I saw was truly MacFerron. Was he still in Berlin, and the man I saw just a random stranger? What might MacFerron have learned about the Nazi informant working with the Quakers on the Kindertransport? Why did the oberst tell me to watch MacFerron? And who had turned in the forger Schumacher to the Gestapo?

I looked at the clock. Before I did anything else, I needed to go upstairs and turn in my copy on the pooch promenade to Miss Westcott.

It was a struggle. Writing copy had never come easily to me when I didn't see any point to the story. An excuse for a mass dog walk when all of Europe was braced for war? Not worth anyone's time.

After it was completed to my satisfaction, I turned the copy in and watched Miss Westcott write on it with a red pencil until it bled. "How long have you been working here, Mrs. Denis?"

"Over a year," I responded quietly.

"And still you can't write a decent lead." She sighed and made a few more marks on my copy.

"Yes, ma'am." What else could I say?

"It's not as exciting as international news, but perhaps you could make an attempt to write up the engagements column. That shouldn't be beyond your ability. Just put a little more effort into the column than what you just turned in." Her voice dripped with annoyance.

"Yes, Miss Westcott." I picked up the engagement announcements on my way back to my desk.

By quitting time, I had finished my tasks and was slipping on my coat and hat as fast as the other girls. Instead of going home, though, I headed to Bloomsbury to see if I could find Tom Canterbury in the Refugee Children's Movement office.

I was in luck. He was in his crowded office, his eyeglasses perched on his long, thin nose as he peered at the papers in front of him. First, however, I needed to pass Mary Wallace, and she was no more welcoming than she was the first time I met her.

"Mrs. Denis." Her tone was as sharp as broken glass.

"Miss Wallace. Planning your next Kindertransport?"

"Of course. Which is why we don't have time for dilettantes."

"Relax. I'm not planning on going on the next trip. But I do need to speak to Tom."

"Don't dally. We have important work to do." She sounded angry.

When I walked around the corner of the desks, I could see his office door was open. I had no idea if he had heard us, or if he was even aware of our presence. I knocked on the door frame.

He looked up, sliding off his wire-framed glasses. "Mrs. Denis. Come back to travel on the next Kindertransport?" he asked as he rose.

I could see he wore a new, high-quality black suit.

"Sadly, no. I came by for two reasons," I told him. "The first is to congratulate you and the others on a successful journey that showed your careful planning."

He beamed and blushed at the same time. "We try. And you helped us avoid some difficulties. Tell me, how are the woman's sons?"

"Settling in with some friends of mine. I think they'll be all right in the end."

"Well, thank you, Mrs. Denis." He didn't seem to have anything else to say.

"The second thing is, I need a favor. I was in one of the train carriages, but I have no idea what went on in the other. I hoped you could tell me, in as much detail as possible, what occurred in your carriage."

"For your newspaper article?"

"Of course." I had already forgotten about that, but I instantly saw how useful the article could be.

"Well." He closed his eyes and remained silent for a moment. "I read to the children. Trying to distract them as we pulled out of the station. We were already locked in. Sealed in. The windows were all shut, and we had strict orders not to open any windows. I remember being worried that it would be stuffy on the train, but the weather was cool enough that it wasn't a problem. Is that what you mean?"

I nodded. "Where did you sit?"

"Toward the back of the car, facing backward. Facing away from your carriage."

"The whole time?"

"Yes."

"Where were the other three?"

"Gwen sat a couple of rows ahead of me entertaining some of the older girls. Helen was near the other end with the younger children. Charles was being Charles, moving around, entertaining the children with magic tricks. Later on, Gwen took some of the older girls to help with the youngest ones."

"Can you think of any other details?"

"Well, there was one, but it's not quite proper…"

"Go on."

"Charles came up to me at some point, we were still in Germany, and said the toilet smelled very badly. He said he thought it was a Nazi ploy to kill us all with the stench. But by that time, the children were getting dehydrated and the toilet was getting little use, so I didn't worry." Tom turned a deep red and rushed his words.

"Nothing else?" There had to have been something to distract them, if anyone wanted to slip into the next carriage.

"Nothing. It was a very quiet trip. A couple of the children were musicians and played for us. Violin and recorder. Gwen and Helen were both very good with the children, calling on the older girls to give them a hand with the youngsters. By afternoon, everyone was so tired we could have fallen asleep where we sat."

After hours of strain and stuffy air, we'd experienced the same thing in our carriage. "Did you doze off?"

He shrugged. "I may have for a few moments. Once or twice. But once we hit the border, there was no sleeping for anyone."

"The welcome by the Dutch was kindness itself," I agreed. "I don't think some of the smaller children could have survived until the ship without some nourishment."

"Cookies and hot chocolate aren't nourishment," Tom corrected me. "Still, it was a kind thought and much appreciated."

"The apples and juice were desperately needed. The cookies and hot chocolate just filled out the supplies, quite nicely from my point of view," I told him. I had been glad for anything to eat or drink at that point. The children were thankful for everything, too.

"Why are you asking me these questions? It was the same in your train carriage. Or do you think one of us killed that poor woman?" He stared into my eyes without blinking.

"It would only have been possible if one of you had a key."

"None of us did. Do you realize what you're saying, Mrs. Denis? That one of us, pacifists to our bones and determined to save as many children as possible from Nazi cruelty, would kill another human being?"

"That is something I don't understand," I said in a placating tone. "How do you stay a pacifist in the face of all you've seen in Germany?"

"Do you think violence countered by more violence is the answer?"

"I'm not arguing with you," I told him. "I'm trying to understand something foreign to my upbringing."

He settled back in his chair, apparently mollified. "I've attended Friends' meetings all my life. My parents taught me as a child to be a pacifist at home and later at school. They would be very disappointed if I didn't follow our rules. It's become second nature to me, as well as a religious belief."

"And you've known the whole team on this Kindertransport, except me and Agathe, all your life? They were all brought up the same way you were?"

"Not Wil. He became a Friend when he married Betsy. And he finds our pacifism difficult. Although not so difficult after his earlier experiences. You've heard about his time in jail?"

I nodded. "And Charles? He seems so...changeable."

"Changeable? No. Charles was raised the same way I was, but he went away to university and then traveled. It has made him perhaps more cynical, but he believes in our faith. Completely and absolutely."

"Your faith would have to be absolute, wouldn't it? You couldn't be a part-time pacifist."

Tom laughed, causing Mary to walk over to look into his office at us. "No, we couldn't," he said as she came into the office.

"If you've finished gossiping," Mary said, "we have work to do before your appointment. Serious work."

"So do I," I told her. "It's just a different sort." I slipped into my coat. "Oh, by the way, where did Charles go to university?"

"Cambridge. He finally finished up about ten years ago."

"Which college?"

"Trinity," Tom said.

"He told me Jesus," Mary said, glancing at him with a frown.

"Well, one of those," Tom said with a shrug.

"Where does he work?" I asked.

"Gray's Inn," Tom said.

"Oh, I think he's left there," Mary said in a haughty voice.

"He doesn't have to work," Tom explained, "and I think it makes it hard for him to focus."

"Then I'll try to find him at home."

"Good luck. You'd do better to try the newest nightclub," Mary said. Her face showed how distasteful she found gaiety in any form as she huffed out the words.

There were too many nightclubs in central London to know where Charles would be dancing. I went home, hoping to find Adam in residence.

I was in luck.

"Livvy, how was your weekend? Mine was colossally boring," Adam asked as he came out of the drawing room and met me in the hall of my flat.

It was several minutes before we finished greeting each other and I could again gain breath to answer. "I had a lovely time at Abby and Sir John's, but I missed you."

"I missed you, too. Right now, I need to do something to shake off this funk I'm in. I would love to act like a civilian and go dancing at the hottest spot in town."

I began to picture myself making both Adam and Sir Malcolm happy. Then I began to become suspicious. "Is there something going on that makes you think if you don't act like a civilian now, you won't get a chance to?"

He leaned away from our embrace. "You know I can't answer that."

"You just did." I felt my temper rise, but then I thought, why waste time when there's a war coming and I could use this to my advantage while I kept an eye out for Charles? I pasted on a smile. "Where's the hottest nightspot in London?"

It turned out Adam knew. I slipped on a silvery-gray frock with a plunging neckline in back and a cut that hugged my curves, silver heels, a silver beaded bag, and my black cape. I twisted my hair up and pinned it while looking in the mirror.

I looked good. Adam, in his evening jacket, looked like a matinee idol. I wished I would get half the admiring stares he would receive tonight.

"Where are we going?"

"Just wait."

We caught a taxi and rode into the area around Piccadilly Circus. The Easter Monday crowds were out looking for a night of entertainment in the face of horrible international news and the hint of spring in the air. We stopped on a side street off Shaftesbury Avenue in front of a French restaurant.

"Dinner first," he told me. Adam was a firm believer in getting his dinner. I wondered if the army starved him when we weren't together.

We had soup, and I followed mine with fish in a delicate sauce while Adam had a slice of roast. We talked easily of events that didn't touch our jobs and simply enjoyed each other's company. I was just thinking that marriage might not be that bad when Adam said, "Dancing is downstairs."

"I thought I heard a dance band playing." He rose and I followed.

"They've done a great job soundproofing the nightclub."

They did such a good job that we had to collect our wraps and go outside to enter by a narrow staircase down to the basement. Adam followed me down, standing on the stairs behind me while I waited on a group of four ahead of us. When the door was opened for them, a distinctive jazz tune poured out, leaving me tapping my toes.

Then Adam gave his name, he was found under reservations, and after we surrendered our coats once again, we were ushered to a tiny, white damask covered table about halfway toward the dance floor. Only the dance floor and the bandstand were brightly lit. The rest of the place was dim, foggy with smoke, and nearly empty in comparison to the crowded dance floor.

We sat down, ordered drinks, and I looked at the dance floor. There, doing a sped-up waltz, was Charles.

Chapter Twenty-Two

"I feel like dancing," I said, hopping up from my seat.

Adam, displaying good manners, rose and escorted me to the dance floor as if there was nothing else he'd rather do.

We'd only been there a minute when Charles's swoop around the area brought him and his partner next to me. His partner was Helen Miller.

"Charles. Helen. So wonderful to see you," I said in a loud jovial voice before introducing Adam. "Adam, these were two of my colleagues on the Kindertransport last week."

"Hello. Nice to meet you," Adam said as he glanced at me for a clue as to what was safe to say and what wasn't.

"So, you've discovered this place, too. The band's incredible. They'll keep this up until two," Charles told me, practically shouting in my ear so I could hear him.

"We both have to be at work in the morning. No late nights for us," I told him.

"What a pity. Helen and I can party the night away," he told me and then foxtrotted away from us across the dance floor.

"Care to tell me what's going on?" Adam murmured in my ear.

"Two women have had their necks snapped and a Quaker on the train with me is suspected. At the moment, I think it was Charles, but I'm not certain. And I have no proof."

"Snapping someone's neck is a militaristic skill for a pacifist," Adam told me. "Where would he have learned it?"

"I don't know. If they sit down, I want to join them. And you're a Foreign Office underling if they ask."

"Always ready to obey." He gave me a dip as the dance finished and we went back to our table as they brought over our drinks.

As it turned out, Charles and Helen joined us when they finished the next dance and Charles waved down a waiter. "A pink gin and a scotch and soda," he said, pulling over a chair for Helen as Adam rose from his chair like the good-mannered fellow that he was.

A waiter brought a fourth chair and we sat squeezed in for a pleasant chat that left our knees in danger of constant collision. At least, I hoped that's what Charles expected.

"How do you two manage to stay out dancing until two?" I asked.

"A bloody great trust fund," Charles said.

"An allowance from my parents," Helen said, "which saves me from actually having to work."

"Are you going on the next Quaker-run Kindertransport?" I asked Helen. "That certainly is work."

"Yes. Fortunately, it won't be for another week, so there's time for dancing before then. Will you be going again?"

"I'm not planning on it," I told her. "I have an article to write for the newspaper."

"The two little boys that belonged to the woman in your carriage who died. What happened to them?" Helen asked.

"They're staying with friends of mine."

"Golly. You mean they came over here, lost their mother, and have no family here?" Helen said. "Poor little tykes."

"My friends live on a farm south of town. The boys are doing well, considering what they've been through."

"I'm surprised they haven't tried to run away back to Germany. It's the only home they know."

"But there's nothing there for them now," I told her. I looked around and said, "Can you imagine Tom Canterbury in a place like this?"

She laughed. "I'm afraid this is too loud and frivolous for Tom. Or Mary Wallace. She considers any frivolity a sin."

"Tom doesn't, though. What's his story? No one can be that fond of work."

"He's been trying to provide for his mother and sisters in the way they want to be provided for. His sisters are old enough to go out to work and certainly capable of it. But his mother won't hear of it and Tom has been beaten down so long, he doesn't think he has the right to a little fun." Helen shook her head.

"But lately," she added, "I've seen hints that Tom has come into some extra money. Money that might make a difference in his life. I certainly hope so. He and

Mary Wallace both deserve a little luck."

Interesting. This was the first I'd heard of it. "Have you known him long?" I asked as Adam lit Charles's cigarette while they chatted.

"Tom or Charles?" Then Helen shrugged wide shoulders in her brilliantly draped green gown that must have cost the earth. "Same answer, really. My family lived near them when I was a child and we went to the same meetinghouse."

"Then you moved away?"

"Yes. My father changed companies when I was thirteen, so we packed up and moved. I had to learn a new language and everything."

"Where did you go?"

"Vienna."

"Beautiful city."

"Do you know it?" she asked, watching me closely.

"My late husband was with the Foreign Office. We traveled there regularly with his work. The country has changed since I was there, I imagine. Austria was independent when I was there."

"Perhaps more independent, but much poorer before it joined the Reich."

"You've kept in touch with friends from your days living there?" I asked.

"Of course," she answered. "It was nice coming home to England, but I enjoyed my time in Vienna, too."

"When did you come back here?"

"Oh, a while ago."

Her answer sounded evasive. I needed to check

with someone who knew her well. Still, I couldn't picture her learning to snap someone's neck.

Charles turned away from his discussion with Adam of dance bands they had heard to add, "And we were very glad when she returned. Helen is a lot of fun."

"Thank you," she said with a smile.

"Any closer to finding out who killed that woman in your carriage?" Charles asked.

"I'm afraid not. You didn't see anything from your carriage, did you?"

"Too busy entertaining the urchins. Plus, unless you were really looking, you wouldn't see anything through the tiny windows in the doors. Did you see anything, Helen? You spent a fair amount of time in the loo. It was at the end by your carriage," Charles added.

"And wasn't it ghastly. I picked a terrible day to get food poisoning," Helen said.

I made commiserating noises.

"I suppose the Nazis don't give you the newest train carriages for the Kindertransport," Adam said.

"It's not like we can afford to pay them much," Helen said.

"Old third-class carriages, no heat, poor lighting. But at least they get us there every time," Charles said cheerfully.

"And you're volunteering to ride one again in a week?" I said with a laugh. I hoped to nudge one of them to say something useful.

"Don't remind me," Charles said, chuckling in return.

"We don't have a choice. If we didn't do it, no one else would," Helen said. "Everyone is afraid we'll get caught behind German lines when the war breaks out."

"At least you speak German," Charles said. "That has to make it easier."

"Easier before the Nazis took over," Helen replied with a shiver. "Easier before we were waiting for bombs to fall."

"It's made up my mind for me," Charles said. "I'm volunteering for the Auxiliary Fire Brigade when the war comes. But please, don't let it come until I'm an old man."

"I don't think we've got that much time," Adam said very quietly.

"But until then, I'm going to dance." Charles rose and said, "Come on, Helen, let's tango." To a sultry-sounding jazz tune, Charles and Helen headed for the dance floor.

"Want one last circle on the floor?" Adam asked.

"I'd rather head home." I suspect my smile was sad. I could stay out to all hours at one time. No longer. Was I getting old and boring?

"Thank you," Adam said. "I'd prefer quieter pursuits."

Then he winked at me.

* * *

The next morning, dressed in my blue suit, a white blouse that came with a high collar and extra fabric for a neat bow, and a blue hat with a brim that swooped down over one eye, I headed into the office. I had scarcely entered the lobby along with a horde of people rushing in out of the rain when Mr. Colinswood, moving across the pedestrian traffic, called out my name. He dodged his way over to me, apologizing as he went.

"We're going to run your story on the Kindertransport this Sunday, and I want you to read it for accuracy before we go to print."

I nodded, jumping as cold rainwater ran off someone's umbrella onto my foot. "Do you want me to go upstairs with you now?"

"Of course."

I made my way to the elevator queue with him, waiting in silence until we were deposited on the news desk floor. Mr. Colinswood headed for his office, issuing a few orders without breaking stride.

I followed him, taking a chair in his office and watching him across the wide, paper-strewn surface of his desk. A young man in his shirtsleeves, wearing a sleeveless V-neck sweater-vest in a zig-zag pattern and a clashing tie, strode in behind me.

Mr. Colinswood looked up from where he was searching his desktop for my article and said, "Yes, Mathers?"

"I've got the copy on the German girls' camps. I wouldn't want to meet those young women in a dark alley. Take you right apart, they could." Then he saw me. "Excuse me, miss."

"Go ahead. I can wait," I told him.

He blushed, his face clashing with both his tie and his sweater, and said, "We may not have to worry about their army if their frauleins invade us."

I remembered the murderous assaults by Fleur Bettenard and Alicia Crawford Palmer the autumn before. Both were lethal Nazi spies, determined, slippery, and skilled in every sort of combat. So far, only one had been apprehended. "Are they taught to be killers in those camps?"

"They're taught to fight and shoot. I'm sure they learn to kill in other ways, too," Mathers told me. "Poisons and stabbings and—"

"Wonderful," Mr. Colinswood said. "We may not want to run that story right now. Not with that slant. Don't want to frighten our readers with fears of an invasion of Amazons. We'd give everyone nightmares." He reached across the desk with some flimsy sheets. "Here you go, Mrs. Denis. See what you think of what we did with your notes."

As I reached for the copy he was handing me, I knew I didn't think what I gave him had been notes. More a coherent basis for a story. Until I learned to write better, I knew I'd never get a byline in the *Daily Premier.* Especially not on a feature piece in the Sunday edition.

As if he could read my mind, Colinswood said, "You gave us everything we needed for a feature. Human interest, facts and figures, conflict with the Nazis, and ways our readers can help. All the details we needed. Thank you."

"If families offer to be hosts or donate money toward the care of these children, the Refugee

Children's Movement will thank you," I told him. Compared to that, my feelings about a byline weren't important.

* * *

The next morning, Adam called me at work to tell me he'd be at his army facility working through the night and would see me the following evening. I chose that afternoon and evening to visit Mary Babcock and then Esther Benton Powell and their new sons.

I decided it would either cure me of wanting to wed or leave me aching for a child of my own.

Mary had been my first and closest friend among the Foreign Office wives when I was a newlywed. It was good seeing her now with her baby son, George, who entertained us with his standing and crawling. I made all the appropriate comments, hoping Mary wouldn't ask about my recent call to Lester at work.

But she did before she poured a second cup of tea.

"I thought I saw someone who should have been at our embassy in Berlin, and thought I'd better check on him. As it turned out, he was on vacation," I explained. I had to tell her something.

"Has Lester heard any more about him?" Mary asked.

"Not that he's told me."

"Did this person have the type of position where sudden traveling could be an important skill?" Mary was as familiar with the more unusual Foreign Office positions as I was.

"Yes."

"I'm so glad Lester never went in for that work. Fortunately, he's more of a homebody than I am," Mary said. "Do you want me to have him call you if he hears any more about the missing man?"

"Please. Berlin is no place for a British diplomat to disappear. Not these days. Do you have any plans to leave London when war breaks out?" I'd heard a number of young families would head for the countryside if London received the bombing many expected.

"George and I have a standing invitation to stay with my parents in Edinburgh if they start dropping bombs. However, until Lester says to get out now, George and I aren't going anywhere."

When I joined Esther and James for dinner at their home, Esther said much the same thing. "Once war begins, James will be called up into some supply ministry. It's inevitable with his knowledge of manufacturing and transport," she said.

James gave her a tight-lipped smile, which told me he'd already received orders that included not saying anything. I was familiar with those sorts of orders, having been read into the Official Secrets Act.

"And you, Esther? I know your father doesn't want you and Johnny in danger in London."

"My father has bought a large home near Oxford where Johnny and I are to go if and when the bombs start dropping. My grandmother refuses to move out to the countryside, so she's joining Aunt Judith and her family. They and their friends have moved to Ruislip, and they'll welcome her in."

"Sir Henry bought a house in the countryside?" I raised my eyebrows. I knew Sir Henry. His idea of a large house was Buckingham Palace.

James gestured around us. Their house was a very large, comfortable, two-story-and-attic dwelling. "This, to my father-in-law, is a bungalow."

I laughed. "So, what is this large house?"

"A Victorian brewery owner's home, with a large garden, suitable for growing vegetables—"

"And chickens, and hiding an occasional pig," James added with a grin.

His wife glowered at him, appearing to grow angrier at James with each comment. "—several bedrooms, an antiquated coal furnace, and a kitchen that guarantees our cook will leave us."

"That sounds like problems your father can solve," I said, hoping to lighten the atmosphere in the room.

"Not with a war arriving any day," James told me, ruining my effort. "Sir Henry will have to hurry if he wants to improve any of the many deficiencies of that house."

"Will you close this house down?"

"Oh, no," Esther told me, "we'll move some of the furniture to the country house and then we'll rent it out furnished to someone who has to move to London for the war effort."

"I'm surprised James doesn't stay and take in boarders," I said to her.

"We've talked about that," he told me

noncommittally.

I looked from one to the other. Esther looked angry. James looked guilty. Neither would look me in the eye. "All right," I said. "What's wrong?"

Chapter Twenty-Three

"We agreed," Esther said as she glowered at James. "Now was not the time to have another child."

"You're expecting," I said, learning more about their private life than I wanted to know. I was worried about two women murdered by a possible Quaker traitor, a possibly vanished diplomat, and thousands of unhappy refugee children missing their parents. An unexpected pregnancy didn't sound like the biggest problem of the day. It wasn't like Esther and James were living in sin.

I thought of Adam and me and blushed.

"We can't undo it now," James said.

Esther gave out a sob. "And by the time it comes, it'll be autumn and we'll be neck-deep in a war. I'll probably have to give birth in a field or something."

"Essie, you're over—" James began.

"You say that because you've done your part and now you'll be off who knows where," Esther nearly screamed, "while I'm giving birth and trying to care for Johnny."

James turned beet red.

"If we are at war, and James isn't here, your father and I will get you to a hospital or a midwife. Someone good. Someplace safe," I promised her, putting a hand over her fist. "And I'll see to Johnny, although I'm sure your father will beat me to that."

"Two infants and a war on. What am I going to do?"

she said, slightly calmer.

"What you always do, Esther. Deal with everything with common sense and patience," I told her. James nodded vigorously.

"I'll have to," she said. "All I ever wanted was a say."

"That's all any of us want," I told her. "And most of the time, we have to make do with what is in front of us." If I had a choice, I would marry Adam now and keep working.

"If I had a choice, we wouldn't be facing a war. Hitler would never have been born," James said.

"You sound like that friend of yours that stopped by last night," Esther said. As James tried to shush her, she added, "He sounded like a pacifist to me."

"He's not," James grumbled.

"A Quaker?" I asked. "I've been working with a number of them lately. They won't fight, but they serve in other ways."

"He's not a Quaker," James said. "At least I don't think he is. He's more your sort," he added. "He's Foreign Office."

"Anyone I know?"

"Maybe. Douglas MacFerron."

"Good grief. I thought I saw him the other day when he should have been in Berlin. What's he doing here?" I said.

"He didn't mention being overseas. Are you sure?" James frowned.

"I was certain he was supposed to be at the embassy in Berlin. When I thought I saw him in Hampstead, I called a friend in the Foreign Office and was told lots of people were on leave. I suppose returning to London makes perfect sense if you're overseas and you go on holiday."

"He sounded like he needed a holiday. Tense. He blamed it on overwork, but it seemed odd that he'd visit me." His frown deepened.

"Where do you know him from?"

"University. We've stayed in touch, after a fashion." James sipped his coffee, continuing to frown.

"Did he mention any reason for being here?" I wondered if he wanted to check on Agathe and the boys, but surely he would have heard what happened by now.

"Taking a breather, so he said. Taking it easy, visiting old friends. He sounded so defeatist. So alarmist. Not at all what I'd expect from a Foreign Office chap."

"What's wrong? Was it just his attitude, or did he ask you something that made you uncomfortable?"

"Livvy. What's this suspicion on your part?" James asked, raising his eyebrows and staring at me. "He did ask me what I'd be doing when the war came. Which office and what I'd be in charge of."

"Old friends. There's nothing to make you wonder, unless he pressed more than he should have." I smiled at James. "He's familiar with the Official Secrets Act."

James sucked in a breath before he nodded. "There's nothing I can point to, but he made me slightly uneasy. Questions about what I'd be doing, questions about whether the house would be empty."

"He made me quite uneasy with all his defeatist

talk," Esther said, "and most of the time he was in James's study away from me."

James shook his head. "He may have been planning for his return from Berlin. When the war starts, he and his colleagues will have to come back to London and find places to live. He may have been thinking of renting here."

"I thought he was a bachelor."

"No, there's a wife tucked away somewhere, but they avoid each other as much as possible. I doubt she'd be joining him, so yes, this is much too big a house for a bachelor. Maybe he was sounding me out for a colleague."

"That must be it." I didn't want to alarm Esther or James when all I had were vague suspicions based on nothing. "I'm glad to hear MacFerron is enjoying his leave in London and making plans for the future as we all must." I gave James a smile and turned back to Esther to ask her about family news.

She immediately asked me about my plans for the future with Adam.

Esther tired quickly after I satisfied her curiosity, and I was able to get a taxi and go back to my flat. My first chore when arriving home was to call Lester Babcock and tell him that MacFerron was on leave and had visited a university friend in London the night before. Embarrassed, I thanked him for asking and promised to try to not bother him again with foolishness.

* * *

The next day, I left for lunch early without saying a word to Miss Westcott. I hoped she'd assume I was working on something for Sir Henry.

Instead, I headed for St. Timothy's Hospital, hoping to catch Gwen as she left for lunch. I reached the staff entrance just as a group of nurses exited the building, all in light gray with white aprons and various caps denoting education and experience. I almost missed Gwen, dressed so differently than when she was on our trip to Berlin.

When I waved her down, she greeted me with, "Have you found out what happened to the woman in your train carriage? And how are her sons?"

"No, I haven't learned anything. I think it might help writing up my notes for my article if I knew what you saw from your carriage."

"Nothing of any use. Look, I need to get some lunch-"

"There's a Lyon's a block away. My treat. You can tell me what you saw while we eat."

She agreed with a smile and started off briskly to the restaurant. "Are the boys doing well?"

"Yes. They're staying with some friends of mine."

"Do your friends have children?"

"Two boys, both a few years older than Gerhard." I smiled at the memory of the four boys getting along. "I saw them last weekend, and they're settling in well."

"Good. I felt certain the younger boy would be all right, but the older was quiet. Too quiet. I hope they're getting plenty of fresh air and exercise."

I smiled again at that. "They are. They're living at the big house on a farm not far from London. There's lots of room to explore. Heinrich has become so acclimated he's speaking English all the time and the neighborhood boys call him 'Henry.'"

"Younger children adjust to things more easily."

"It sounds like you speak from experience," I said.

"In case you hadn't noticed, our Meeting is a wealthy one. It used to be much richer, but many families have lost their wealth since the Great War. We lost ours early, so I never thought much about having to go to work, and I enjoy nursing. My much older sister has never forgiven our parents for leaving her in need of finding employment when she was at the age where she wanted to party with her friends."

"I suspect the same thing happened to Tom Canterbury's family."

"Yes, his, and Helen's."

"Helen's family seems to have landed on their feet," I said.

"Yes." Gwen's eyes narrowed as she looked into the distance. "It appears that way."

"I heard Tom has had good fortune recently. He's received money from somewhere."

"Really? I'm glad for him. He deserves all the good luck he can get."

"Any idea where his good fortune is coming from?"

"None at all."

It didn't sound like Gwen had heard about his good news. Was Tom the traitor after all?

We were seated, squeezed tightly in among the small tables, and ordered vegetable soup and bread.

"This is nice of you, but I don't think I'll be able to help much," she told me.

"Just tell me where you sat in the carriage and what you saw."

"I sat at the end by Tom for the first part of the journey, entertaining the older girls with descriptions of life in Britain. Then, when the younger children grew restless and Helen couldn't manage them anymore, I had the older girls help me with comforting them. I think it helped them, too."

Our food came, and we both ate with relish.

When I had curbed my hunger, I asked, "At that point, you were at the other end of the carriage?"

"More toward the middle, but facing the opposite way. Helen excused herself and ran down to the end where the toilet was. She was in there a long time, and when she came back, she complained of food poisoning. And she said the toilet smelled terrible." She looked at her food and said, "Sorry."

I shrugged. "Could you see the toilet door?"

"No." She scrunched up her face. "There is a door between the seats and the toilet, before the one to the toilet itself."

"And beyond that?"

"The door to the platform that led to your carriage. But that was locked by the Nazis."

I nodded. "Did you know Helen as a child?"

"Yes. I come from the same borough as the rest of

the people involved in the Kindertransport. It was nice to see her come back from Munich a few years ago."

"Munich? I thought she was from Vienna."

"They originally went to Vienna," Gwen told me. "Then they moved to Munich. That's where the family must have made their money."

"When did Helen move back to Britain?"

"A few years ago. Three or four." She sipped her last spoonful of soup and gobbled down her last bites of her roll. "Thank you, but I have to get back. Good luck with your article, and I hope you find that woman's killer."

Gwen hurried away, leaving me to finish my lunch. And think.

I finally decided I would have to talk to my father. He was never my first choice as a source of information, but I needed some special information, and my father would know who to talk to.

Quickly finishing my lunch, I headed back to the *Daily Premier,* arriving back in time not to be noticed by Miss Westcott. Perhaps it was a sign that she had already given up on getting any work out of me.

After work, I found a telephone box and called the familiar Whitehall number. My father answered on the second ring.

"How are you, Olivia?" he asked when he discovered I was his caller. "Isn't Redmond around? Did you want me to take you to dinner?"

"Adam is around, and I don't expect you to take us to dinner. I was calling because I need to find out who would have a special piece of knowledge about the

Hitler Youth."

"Are you..." his voice started to rise in volume before he lowered it. "Are you doing this for Sir Malcolm?"

"Yes. This is a special piece of knowledge that wouldn't offend even you, Father."

"What is it?" He sounded skeptical. Defensive. Annoyed.

"Whether the girls in Hitler Youth, or whatever group who were given combat training, were taught to break necks."

"You mean the spies like your friend Fleur Bettenard. You could ask her."

"She's not my friend," I replied in annoyance. Then curiosity took over. "They haven't caught her yet?"

"No. Of course, if she were smart, she would have left the country. I imagine her usefulness as a spy was lost when her identity was discovered."

When I discovered her identity. My father would never give me credit for learning that. Giving up that particular argument, I said, "Do you know anyone who would be able to answer my questions?"

There was silence on the other end of the line. After about a half-minute, he said, "Yes. Come over here and I'll introduce you. He may not want to speak to you, though."

Why was he always so negative? "There's only one way to find out."

I reached Whitehall, specifically the Foreign Office, in record time and then waited for my father to come downstairs and escort me into the building.

To my surprise, he led me not to his office, but downstairs, belowground, to a part of the building I'd never been in before. We stopped in front of a door marked "Library."

"He's usually here this time of day," my father said before he opened the door without knocking and stepped inside.

From where I stood in the doorway, the room appeared to be tightly spaced rows of bookshelves packed from floor to ceiling with binders full of papers. Bright lights hung down from the ceiling. And at a table with numerous open binders spread under a lamp sat a thin, gray-haired man. In a weak voice scratchy with disuse, he asked without looking up, "What do you want?"

"Do females trained by the Hitler Youth to be spies learn how to break necks?" I asked before my father had a chance to open his mouth.

"Strictly speaking, no one in the Hitler Youth, male or female, is trained to be a spy."

"The Nazis have trained youngsters to come to England to spy and to carry out assassinations," I told him.

"Not just England. They send students all over Europe, fluent in multiple languages, to report back to the Fatherland with intelligence that could prove useful."

Now perhaps I could get him to answer. "Were any of these students female, and did their training include breaking necks with their bare hands?"

He turned and looked at me through thick glasses. "Why do you want to know?"

"An assignment from another section of the British government."

He glanced from me to my father.

My father said, "Olivia, this is Dr. Underwood. Underwood, this is my daughter, Mrs. Denis." His tone said he didn't want to be there talking to either of us.

"Your daughter, eh? Then perhaps I'll answer her." After a pause, he glanced at my father and added, "Or perhaps not."

Chapter Twenty-Four

"I don't have much time before the killer strikes again. Could you please answer my question?" I asked the thin little man, hoping I could shock him into helping me.

"The killer strikes at regular intervals, so you know you don't have much time?" he asked me in a dry tone.

"Not specifically, but he or she will kill again." That felt like an honest answer.

"Ah, a matter of life and death, is it? Then let's consult the files, shall we?" He stood, perhaps five feet tall in his shoes, and walked past us to a low shelf in the middle of a row of bookcases. There he thumbed through a row of binders until he found one that he extracted.

Carrying it back to his desk and stepping past us on the way, he sat down and started leafing through the various reports. Finally, with an "Ah-ha!" he looked up at us in triumph.

"Females make a large percentage of the young Germans trained as spies, or agents as they call them. And as for breaking the necks of enemy combatants and civilians," he began to run his finger down the page, and then went on to the next page, his finger stopping a quarter of the way down, "it is mentioned that snapping the neck is silent, quick, and efficient if an agent needs a fast escape or to prevent the enemy from providing their comrades with information they've learned."

He looked up at me, a gleam in his murky eyes behind the thick lenses as he smiled. "I think that covers anything you might want to ask."

"It does. Thank you, Dr. Underwood."

"Good. Then get out and let me get back to work."

Startled, I began to back up.

My father said, "Thank you, Underwood," turned around, and left. I speedily followed him out the door.

I waited until we were out of the building before I said, "Who is he? And what is that place?"

"The repository of old Foreign Office reports. Kept under the watchful eye of Dr. Underwood, formerly of the Bodleian."

"A very useful place."

"Yes. Which means you must never mention it," my father instructed me.

I nodded.

"Are you and Adam coming to dinner with me tonight?"

Since he'd done me a favor, I could hardly refuse even though I knew he'd be pressing us for our wedding plans. "That would be lovely."

"The Beaumont Hotel dining room, eight o'clock." With that, my father strode away. I was certain he'd already forgotten me.

When I returned to my flat, Adam wasn't there, but he'd not left me a message saying he wouldn't be here for dinner either. And there was no way to warn him of what would be the topic during the meal.

I had gone to my room to dress for dinner when I heard his key in the front door lock. I hurried to the front hall to have him say, "Don't get near me. I'm mucky from an investigation and I need to get cleaned up before I can give you a proper kiss."

"You may not want to when you hear who we're having dinner with."

He smiled. "Your father."

"You guessed."

"What time?"

"Eight. At the Beaumont."

"Then I'd better hurry. I'll be taking over the bathroom."

We air kissed and then he grabbed some clean clothes and closeted himself in the bath. A dead fish smell lingered in the hallway.

As it was, we didn't leave my flat until nearly eight. The sky was already dark and starless from the clouds closing in over the city. The doorman, Sutton, whistled for a taxi and we were soon on our way.

My father, true to form, looked elegant in black and white with his gray hair and his dour expression. "You're late," he informed me before greeting Adam with a handshake and a "How are you, Captain?"

Adam didn't have a chance to answer before the hovering restaurant staff escorted us to our table. My father had already ordered the wine for dinner. When we ordered, our soup arrived immediately.

"Did you tell Adam what you wanted to know this afternoon?" my father asked, his voice dripping with disapproval, when the waiters had moved away from our table.

"I haven't had time to tell him."

"What is it, Livvy?" Adam asked in a low, tense voice.

I told him what I'd learned.

"You should have guessed that from what you know about Fleur Bettenard."

"I wanted confirmation." I couldn't take suspicions to Sir Malcolm, not with something as crazy as a pacifist Nazi agent.

"And now that you have it?" Adam watched me, the darkening of his eyes the only sign of anger.

"I'll turn everything over to Sir Malcolm. I imagine he can get proof much easier than I can."

"You mean that's it?" My father beamed.

"That's as far as I can take it. The case requires access to official records and officials asking questions to be able to mount a case to bring to trial."

"Good. Now we can talk about the wedding."

Fortunately, the waiters appeared with the fish dish and took away the soup bowls before I had a chance to say the first thing that came to mind.

When we were left to ourselves again, I asked, "Why are you in such a hurry to marry me off?"

"Because you'd both be happier if you were married. Especially with what Adam has ahead of him."

I raised an eyebrow.

"He means," Adam explained very quietly, "that I'll know that you and any children will be provided for if anything happens to me."

Suddenly, the gleaming chandeliers, the glistening white tablecloths, the delicate china and glassware, all faded before the blood and smoke of war. Before the reality of what we were about to face. I was so frightened, of war, of losing Adam, of becoming a mother in the midst of battle, that I couldn't speak.

The blood must have drained from my face, because Adam and my father were both staring at me with concern in their eyes.

"It may seem like a game sometimes, but the danger is very real," Adam told me. "I can take some precautions to protect you."

I nodded. When I could finally speak, the words tumbled out. "Can we get married at Abby and Sir John's church?"

My father appeared ready to cheer despite being in a restaurant.

"And can we keep it quiet until the war starts? I want to keep working as long as possible."

My father's imminent cheer swiftly changed to a lecture.

Adam ignored him as he gave me a grin that melted my heart.

* * *

The next morning, the telephone rang before I'd had a cup of tea. When I answered, I heard Abby's voice come over the line sounding as if she were as distant as Scotland. "Livvy," she said between the crackling, "I'd love to have you get married here. Come down this weekend and bring Adam."

"My father?" I asked.

"Of course. Let me know what train—" and then the crackling increased until the line went dead.

As I hung up the receiver, Adam said, "Who was that, and is the kettle ready?"

"Abby, inviting us down for the weekend to make arrangements at the church for our wedding," I said, my mind on four different things, "Oh, and the kettle should be ready now."

Adam strolled into the kitchen, stretching as he went. "I'd put in for leave today, but we don't know when the rector and the church will be available, or even willing," came through the doorway.

"The church is always willing. It's a building," I called back.

"But the rector might not be. Neither of us live there. It's not our parish."

"You're in His Majesty's armed forces. You don't live anywhere at the moment. And I spend enough time with Abby and Sir John on the weekends, going to church there, that I'll probably qualify as a parishioner. Besides," I added as I joined him in the tiny kitchen, "Sir John is a church warden and donates regularly to the building upkeep."

"We'll still have to wait three weeks for the reading of the banns."

"That'll put the wedding in May. Not so bad, is it?" I asked.

He set down his mug to swing me around the

narrow space. "Unless the war has started by then."

My feet touched down lightly. My stomach landed with a thud. Adam was making the start of the war all too real and immediate. "Do you think it will be that soon?"

"I don't know. Now that Czechoslovakia is gone, they're guessing Poland will be next. If we don't protect the Poles, we'll soon follow." He looked me in the eye. "Ask your father. He knows better than I do."

"And you won't be able to get leave to get married once the war starts, will you?" May was starting to feel too far away.

"I'm sure we'll get married before the war starts, so you can again worry that you'll lose your job because you're a married woman." He grinned at me. He didn't find my worry sensible that I'd lose my job and be forced to stay home and be a wife while he was who-knows-where. It was the only bone of contention between us.

"I'm not going to tell anyone." I could hear the stubborn growl in my voice. I wondered how it sounded to Adam.

He shook his head, finished his tea, and walked out of the room without a word.

His way of telling me I'd been untactful.

By the time I finished my tea, he was ready to leave for the army office he was working in. He said farewell with a rushed, distant kiss and headed out the door.

"I'm sorry, but I want both you and the job," I called out.

He returned long enough to kiss the top of my head and left again.

I dressed in a gray and white dress with a belt and short jacket, put on my slant-brim gray felt hat, grabbed my raincoat and umbrella, and headed out to the Underground. My first stop was to St. James Park to see Sir Malcolm.

I was escorted upstairs by a uniformed soldier and then waved into a chair by Sir Malcolm. He continued to listen to the voice coming from his telephone handset, making grunts and indefinite sounds as he watched me.

Once he had hung up the receiver, I said, "I know who killed Alice Waterson and Agathe, but I can't prove it. I doubt Scotland Yard would believe a woman could efficiently kill by breaking necks."

"Not a skill you learned at boarding school?" A faint smile crossed his heavy face.

"No."

"Who is this person you suspect?"

"Helen Miller. She moved to Vienna from London with her family when she was young, but then they moved to Munich. She only returned in the last three or so years. I don't know if she took part in the spy training, but I know girls did, and they learned to break necks as a quick, silent way to kill."

"Is that it? She was in the other carriage."

"She supposedly spent a long time in the toilet. You can't see the toilet door or the door to the platform to the next carriage from the seats. If she obtained a key to unlock the train doors, she could have crossed over to our carriage and killed Agathe while our attention was on the older boys fighting."

"So, I suppose she arranged for them to fight at just the right time." Sir Malcolm looked as if he were about to start lecturing me, just like my father.

"That was pure luck for the killer. She might have made certain that Agathe was sitting alone and none of us were talking to her. She might have felt that was enough. The boys fighting at just the right time was an added gift." I considered for a moment. "Or perhaps not. Maybe she hoped we wouldn't notice Agathe was dead until we reached the border. If the Germans had discovered a dead body, murdered or not, they would have stopped us, taken Agathe off the train, possibly taken us all off the train."

"But they didn't." His tone was solemn.

"No, they didn't," I agreed. "I wondered why Agathe ignored the ruckus. When I found her dead, I had time to warn the other adults I was with, and we began to make plans."

"So, what do you want?"

"I want you to follow up and learn whether Helen is a Nazi spy. I doubt we'll ever be able to prove she killed either woman, but at least you can stop her if she is working for the enemy."

"She's not," Sir Malcolm said. "She's a Quaker. A pacifist. And a friend of Alice's. Lord Waterson vouches for her. You've got the wrong person."

Chapter Twenty-Five

"No, I haven't," I assured Sir Malcolm. "Alice wasn't stupid. She wouldn't let a stranger approach her that closely and raise their hands toward her neck. Her boyfriend, her family, and her close friends would have had the only chance of walking up to her and snapping her neck. Only someone beyond suspicion could have caught her off guard and killed her that way."

He shook his large head. "It wasn't Helen. She works for us."

"Why didn't you tell me? Why didn't she?" I found Sir Malcolm was making this investigation more complicated for me.

"It's better if my—assistants don't know each other. Better for security," he added when he saw I was about to speak.

"You recruited her or she volunteered?"

"Alice suggested Helen. We approached her, and she was willing."

"I wonder why?" I was puzzled. Someone had neatly broken the necks of two women. Not strangled, something I could do if cornered, but snapped the neck bones, a skill most people don't have. The only people in proximity of both deaths were Quakers.

"We're paying her, of course," Sir Malcolm growled. "She's a young lady who likes money. I have no illusions that she prefers Neville Chamberlain over Adolf Hitler, but she's useful."

"So, you recognize that she is an admirer of Nazi Germany, and still you hired her." I found that shortsighted. Helen was dangerous.

"That is my decision." He spoke with a note of finality.

"What are you having her investigate for you?" *And do you trust anything she tells you*, I wanted to add.

"She's watching a couple of Germans of questionable loyalty. No one you've been in contact with. She's given us bits of information we couldn't have learned any other way."

"How well do you know her? I would think her background of growing up in Nazi Germany would make her highly suspect. I'd think you would question her loyalty," I told him.

"She's useful, but we verify what she tells us. We're not stupid, Mrs. Denis."

I went back to my main concern. "Who else among the Quakers has the needed skill to break necks?"

"That's what you were supposed to find out," Sir Malcolm grumbled at me.

"The answer is no one," I nearly screamed. "There is no other answer."

"Helen wouldn't have killed Alice. They were good friends. And she didn't know Agathe, so why would she have killed her? The answer lies elsewhere, and you need to keep looking." Sir Malcolm looked back at the paper on his desk. "Dismissed."

"Don't expect me to salute." I rose and stormed out

of the door, shutting it firmly behind me.

I traveled back to the *Daily Premier* building and went up to Sir Henry's office. He was behind his massive desk, early editions of all the London morning papers spread out along the surface with his paper in the center. He looked up with a puzzled expression as he watched me march in.

"I gave Sir Malcolm what I considered to be the logical answer and asked him to put someone into digging out the background on a particular person to find the evidence. He told me I was wrong and to keep looking," I said as I dropped into the chair in front of his desk.

Sir Henry stared at me for a moment before looking down at the morning edition of the *Daily Premier*. "And you want to know if I'm willing to continue employing you while you try to find a murderer for Sir Malcolm."

I nodded. "Yes, sir."

"What answer do you want?" He was watching me closely now.

"I'd like to visit Lady Waterson today. After that, I don't see how there's anything I can do." I looked at him, my face becoming warm as I added, "I want to spend the weekend at Summersby Lodge with Captain Redmond."

His face brightened. "Ah, the army is letting Captain Redmond off the leash for the moment. I'll tell Colinswood. It could be a sign the army thinks it will soon be in business."

"He thinks so, too," I admitted.

"Well, how about if you wrap up this investigation

today, take the weekend off with your young man, and be back here ready to work on Monday morning."

I felt like dancing out of his office. My face must have glowed. "Yes, sir. That sounds like an excellent suggestion."

And if Adam returned to the flat early, we'd be able to get an early start on our journey to Abby and Sir John's. And to the church to schedule our wedding. I was beginning to feel a shiver of excitement every time I thought about being Mrs. Redmond.

I would only have to keep my secret for a few weeks or a few months. Herr Hitler would see to that. After that, I, and other married women, could continue to work.

I called Lady Waterson and asked her if I could come over and talk to her about Alice. She immediately agreed.

I traveled over to Holland Park and walked up the steps to ring the bell. The maid took my umbrella and coat while I kept my gloves on until I was led to the large drawing room, where Lady Waterson sat on the same overstuffed chair.

"Do you have news for me, Mrs. Denis?" she asked, waving me into a chair opposite her.

"I wish I did. I do have more questions, though. You know all of Alice's friends from the Kindertransport. Do you know all of their backgrounds?"

"Yes. Why are you asking me this?" She made a slight, graceful gesture and the maid came in to set the tea tray on a low table.

"Another woman was killed on the Kindertransport train in the same manner as your daughter. A woman who was under suspicion by the Gestapo and carrying a message to the head of British intelligence."

Lady Waterson sat forward. "Did the message get through despite her death?"

I continued my lie, just in case. "I don't know."

"I don't see any connection—" She looked puzzled rather than angry as she sat back. I was glad, as I didn't want to cause her more pain.

"She was traveling in one of the sealed cars with the children. Only a Quaker adult chaperone could have killed her. And these were the same people who were out checking on housing with Alice the night she died."

"You don't believe it could have been one of the older boys traveling with you?" She rose and began pouring tea. "Sugar or milk?"

Once we were both seated with our teacups, I said, "I'm sure it wasn't. Only an embassy official and I knew she would be there. She had to be recognized by someone already scheduled to be on the train with us."

"And you suspect one of Alice's friends. Oh, dear. I can see why you might." She studied the contents of her teacup for a moment. "There's someone I've suspected. Without proof, you understand."

Could she also suspect Helen? "Who is it?"

"Charles. He was constantly short of cash, and all of a sudden, he wasn't. And beneath that flighty exterior lurks a very sharp, rather devious mind. A mind very like Johann."

"Where would Charles or Johann have received military training? Breaking someone's neck isn't a skill one learns in school."

She paled. "Please, Mrs. Denis, we're talking about my daughter."

"I'm sorry." I leaned forward. "But you understand why this training is important for finding her killer."

"Yes. In truth, there are gaps in what I know of the background of several of her friends. Wil Taylor came to our beliefs only when he married Betsy. He might have done anything before. In fact, I've heard he spent time in prison. Charles traveled a great deal. All over Europe. To America once."

She gave me a weak smile. "Helen moved with her family to Austria as a girl and only returned three or four years ago. Gwen did her nursing training in Edinburgh. We didn't see her for years. I only know the whole history of people like Tom and Dorothy who have had to stay home with their families."

"Was Alice suspicious of any of her Kindertransport friends?"

"Nothing along the lines of what you're suggesting. I'd hoped she would have mentioned it if she had any reservations about any of the men. But then, she didn't have any concerns about Johann."

"The Germans have been training a corps of young people to spy, infiltrate, and sabotage. Young people of both genders," I told her.

"You believe it could be any of her friends. Even girlfriends." Lady Waterson shook her head. "What a terrible suspicion."

"I suspect the one who grew up in Germany. It would have been easier for the Nazis to convince a young girl if she were going to their schools and living in their country."

She immediately saw what I was thinking. "But Helen grew up in Austria, not Germany."

"I've been told her family moved from Vienna to Munich not long after they left England."

Lady Waterson slowly shook her head as if she couldn't believe what I was saying. "I understand, rationally, why you suspect Helen. But you don't know her. She's been a great help since Alice died. They were good friends and we saw a lot of her before Alice's death."

"Tell me, how did Johann get along with Helen?"

"They were wary of each other. Contemptuous. As if they couldn't stand each other's company."

I rose. "Thank you," I said as I set my delicate teacup on the tray.

Lady Waterson rose also. "I understand from Dorothy that you rescued the two young sons of the woman who died. How are they doing?"

It seemed safe to talk to Lady Waterson. She couldn't be the killer. "Well. They're living in the countryside with relatives of mine on a farm on the Kent-Sussex border. The younger one is adjusting nicely. The older one is very distrustful. I think he understands better that both of his parents have died at the hands of the Nazis and their agents."

"A terrible thing for those children to experience." She sighed almost inaudibly. "Thank you for stopping by, Mrs. Denis. I disagree with your conclusions, but you've put in a lot of effort on Alice's account, and I appreciate it."

"If you discover something that might be of use, let Scotland Yard know. Please."

"I will. I want Alice's killer caught. God help me, I even want that person hanged."

I pulled on my gloves and picked up my coat and umbrella from the maid. As I reached the pavement, I had the feeling someone was following me. A quick glance around gave me no clue as to who or from where, but the prickling along my spine made me suspect someone was watching.

Puffy white clouds drifted across the sky. Buds had begun to show some color in flower beds. The sun was warming the breeze. All was lovely, and someone had me under surveillance.

By the time I reached the area of the Inns of Court, I was certain whoever was watching me had lost interest. I entered the law offices where Alice's fiancé worked and asked once more for Johann Klingler.

In a few minutes, Johann came out and gestured with a sideways nod toward the outer door. We walked downstairs and out onto the pavement. After we'd stepped away from the entrance to the large brick building, he said, "What do you want?"

"For starters, I want to know how you are."

"How do you expect me to be? Suspected of my

fiancée's murder, suspected of German sympathies, not wanted or accepted anywhere. And I definitely can't go back to Germany."

"Why did you and Helen Miller not get along?"

He lit a cigarette. "I didn't trust her. I suppose she didn't trust me, either."

"Why?"

He glanced around. We were on a side street during working hours. The pavement was practically empty of pedestrians and there were few cars on the road despite the pleasant weather that would normally send Londoners out of doors. "We're Germans."

"She's English."

"You spend your youth in a place and you become part of it."

"The two of you grew up in the same country. Why would this make you distrust each other?"

He glanced around again. There was no one nearby to hear him. "Everyone in Germany knows not to trust anyone else. There are too many informants for the Gestapo. Too many petty bureaucrats holding their positions because of loyalty to the Reich. Loyalty demonstrated by turning in one's friends and family."

"Do you know of anything that makes you think she's an informer for the Gestapo?"

"No. Nor does she know any such thing about me. But without proof that someone is innocent, it is safer to believe they are guilty."

"Had you two met in Germany?"

"She's from Munich. I'm from Berlin. I can't think

where I would have met her."

"How do you know she's from Munich?"

"She told me so."

"She told people she was from Vienna." Usually.

"She had to be honest with me. She had a Munich accent. Viennese sound very different. Sort of like your Scotsmen and Irishmen."

"What did Helen think of her friend marrying a German?"

"She was against it, naturally."

"Why naturally?"

"Like I said, Germans don't trust each other. The government has taught us that lesson well."

"Was she, like you, part of the dissident movement?"

He shook his head before dropping his cigarette and grinding it into the pavement with the heel of his shoe.

"Johann, I think you're holding something back. What is it?"

"The law deals in facts. I have no facts about Helen. Just a feeling that I cannot trust her." He gave a snort of laughter. "Many people, English people, say the same about me."

"But you're out of Germany now. You're safe. They aren't going to send you back, are they?" That fear might keep him silent.

"No, I have no fear there. The Watersons have been generous in their support."

I had to try. I needed to know what this German was thinking. "Johann, what are you not telling me? You may deal in facts, but you have suspicions about someone. Who is it? And why?"

"It was something Alice mentioned. Something she wondered about."

When he paused, I stared at him, wishing he'd just tell me.

"Alice saw Helen meet with someone on the last Kindertransport in Berlin. Someone she shouldn't have met with. And later she lied about it. Said she hadn't talked to anyone."

"A member of the Gestapo? An SS officer?"

"No." He shook his head. "He was a…"

The squeal of tires and the roar of an engine made us both look toward the nearly empty road. A dark sedan roared toward us, jumping the curb.

I scrambled sideways, hitting my shoulder on the building as the vehicle brushed past my bag. I didn't see Johann Klingler. I didn't see the driver. All I saw was chrome and black paint as hot metal squeezed past me.

Chapter Twenty-Six

With a metallic screech and a clatter, the car bounced off the curb into the street and roared away around a corner.

Gasping with shock, I realized Johann lay at my feet. I crouched down and touched his forehead. "Are you all right?"

His face was ashen as he groaned. One arm lay in an unnatural position and blood seemed to leak from his side.

People started to come out of buildings and run toward us. "Help," I shouted. "Please help!"

A bobby hurried up. "What happened, miss?"

"A car jumped the curb and tried to run us down. Then it drove off that way," I told him. "Mr. Klingler needs an ambulance. He got the worst of it."

The next ten minutes, which felt like hours, was a confusing jumble of images. Loading Johann onto a stretcher, his face as white as the sheets. The ambulance slowly driving away. The bobby with a hundred questions I couldn't answer. One of the solicitors from Johann's firm taking charge, answering questions and discovering which hospital they'd taken Johann to.

Finally, I was free to go home. I rushed there in a daze to put the kettle on. After two cups of tea and a nap while buried under several blankets, I felt well enough to think.

My first thought was to visit Johann in the hospital and find out how he was. My second, more practical, thought, was to call Sir Malcolm and tell him the killer was still free on the streets of London.

Someone wanted either Johann or me dead. Or both of us. And I objected.

I called the number I had memorized by now. After speaking to a soldier, I finally reached Sir Malcolm. He greeted me with, "I heard about Johann Klingler. He's in surgery."

"Did you hear I was with him when the automobile tried to kill us?"

"Yes. I'm glad you're all right."

"How do you know all this?" I was always suspicious of Sir Malcolm. At the moment, I was livid.

"We've been tailing Klingler."

"Couldn't his tail have stopped the driver? Shot him or something?"

Sir Malcolm laughed before he said, "He at least had the sense to check the license."

That was helpful, something Sir Malcolm often wasn't. "Who does it belong to?"

"There was mud smeared over the rear plate. The attack was probably premeditated."

"Great. Someone is trying to kill me, and you won't even check on the person I still think is responsible."

"Mrs. Denis," he sighed as if my help was a burden, "the entire war effort doesn't revolve around you."

What a wretched thing to say. "But my life does. Don't expect me to help the next time you ask."

"The way things are going, next time we'll be at war and I'll be able to conscript you."

That silenced me. Any mention of imminent warfare tended to silence me. I didn't want to think about war. About losing Adam, even for a short time.

"When you are finished being petulant—"

"I'm not being petulant. Someone just tried to kill me. They may have succeeded with Johann, who was standing right next to me." I took a deep breath. I was sounding childish.

"When you finish not sounding petulant," Sir Malcolm sounded as if he were laughing, "I want to know why you keep saying 'they.'"

"I don't know who was in the car. I kept looking at the grille as it came toward me."

"Shame. My man watching Klingler wasn't in a good position to see the inside of the car."

"So, we're no further forward." That was a depressing thought. Worse, it wasn't just me. Sir Malcolm and the intelligence office of His Majesty's government were stumped, too. And Sir Malcolm still wasn't willing to investigate Helen Miller.

"We know that someone now wants to kill you or Klingler. There was no sign of that before. What has changed?"

"I've picked my frontrunner for killer and asked you to research her background for espionage training."

"You're sounding peevish again."

I waited in silence for him to continue.

"I wanted to let you know we've had a sighting of

Fleur Bettenard," he finally said.

"What? Where?" I sat up straight. Fleur was a Nazi agent trained in the same schools I believed Helen had been. While Fleur had opportunity in the past to kill me, she hadn't. I had no idea why.

"Here in London."

"It wasn't Fleur driving the car."

"How can you be certain?" Sir Malcolm asked.

"Think of the number of people she's reportedly killed. She wouldn't have missed."

"Perhaps you were lucky." With a final warning to be careful, Sir Malcolm rang off, no doubt to ruin someone else's life.

I combed and pinned up my hair, dabbed on lipstick, and put on my hat. With a last glance in the mirror, I headed to the hospital. All I learned was Johann had survived surgery and was given good odds, but would not be awake to speak to anyone until the next day.

I still wanted to know what he was going to tell me about Helen when we were interrupted by a madman in a car. Since that would have to wait, I decided to talk to the one person who couldn't have killed Agathe but knew everything about the Kindertransport and the people on it—Mary Wallace.

When I reached the office of the Refugee Children's Movement, I was glad to see Mary was the only one there. She looked up from her desk when I knocked and walked in, but said nothing.

Even if I knew nothing, Mary wouldn't guess if I

acted like *I knew.* "Mary," I said as I sat down across her desk from her, "we have a problem."

"I don't have a problem. And if you have one, it's nothing to do with any of us." She continued to work on the papers on her desk.

"Ah, but it does. Tom Canterbury will have to live with the stigma of being suspected of murder, but never charged. There will be whispers. People will look away. They'll avoid him. Any hope he may have of a new position, of a promotion, of saving up for a wedding, will vanish like fog in the sunlight." I hoped I wasn't overplaying my hand.

"No one suspects Tom of murder. Unless you put it in their minds," she nearly shrieked at me.

"Tom was with Alice on that East End street just before she was murdered. And he was one of seven people who could have killed the woman on the Kindertransport train. No mere woman could have broken her neck, and then we're down to three suspects. Charles and Wil don't need money. And then we're down to one. One person who could use the large bundle of pound notes that would be paid for a murder ordered by the Nazis."

It wasn't fair, but I needed her to let slip what she knew about this group of young people who traveled back and forth to Germany together. And I knew how gossip started out of nothing and couldn't ever be stopped.

"What do you mean no mere woman could break a neck? I'm sure any of the women on that train could have snapped someone's neck." She sounded huffy, not angry. Not yet ready to let me in on her secrets.

"That's very loyal of you to say that to protect Tom, but why do you think a woman could do it? It's not like killing a scrawny-necked chicken for dinner."

"I think it's something a nurse could do. They get used to handling people much larger than themselves. Both Gwen and Betsy trained as nurses, and Gwen still is one."

I shook my head. "We both know it isn't Betsy or Gwen. Neither of them has the killer instinct."

"Unlike Alice," she grumbled.

"But Alice didn't break her own neck."

Mary folded her arms over her chest and looked down.

I decided to push. "Neither of us want Tom to suffer if he isn't guilty."

"He's not!"

"Then who is?"

"Helen." Mary leaned toward me. "I see her watching when she thinks no one is looking. And she dislocated a boy's arm on the last Kindertransport but one for not keeping in line."

"Interesting, but it doesn't prove anything," I said, trying to goad her.

"And I heard nice English Helen speaking German to some man down the street from here as he brushed against her arm. And I saw him slip something into her coat pocket. A thick envelope."

Was it an assistant of Sir Malcolm's paying her off?

Then why would she have spoken German? "Have you told anyone about this?"

"No. Alice was there, too. She heard and saw it as plainly as I did. It was shortly before the last Kindertransport. A day or two before Alice was murdered. Maybe she told someone."

"Perhaps she did. But why would Helen break the necks of two people?"

Mary looked at me with a sly smile on her face. "Why would someone who loves money and hates to work do anything?"

I was surprised. "I thought the Nazis did everything out of loyalty and unswerving devotion to their cause."

"Not Helen. She wants to go out at night and have a good time with Charles, wearing fancy gowns and makeup and dancing 'til dawn."

"Does Charles stand to inherit a great deal of money?"

"Not as much as it was, and none at all if he doesn't settle down and stick to a job."

That matched what I'd heard. "So, if Helen marries him, she would find herself—"

"Oh, no," Mary said, "Charles isn't about to marry anyone. He's as much against marriage as he is against working. It isn't fair." She brought the side of her fist down on the desk. "Some men work hard and can't marry for all their obligations, even if he gets this new Home Office appointment, while others have everything and can't be bothered with what the rest of us want."

Shocked at what she'd let slip, she refused to say

any more.

But she'd given me a new angle to explore. Not one that involved Tom Canterbury or the Home Office.

I traveled back to the area of St. James Park for another visit with Sir Malcolm.

"Do you like my office? Would you like to move in?" Sir Malcolm asked when I was escorted in.

"Who's the Nazi money man in London?"

He leaned back in his chair and looked up at me standing across from him. "What?"

"Helen Miller likes money. The kind you don't work in an office for. She's killing on order. Whatever she does, someone is paying her top dollar to have her do it. Who is funding Nazi agents in this country? And who is acting as paymaster?"

"You've met two of their female agents, Fleur Bettenard and Alicia Crawford. They weren't in it for the money. Of course, Alicia had married money, but the fact remains they were defending a government and way of life they believe in."

"Helen is different," I told him. "Someone is paying her. If you find out who, you'll solve these murders, prevent more, and cause more trouble for the German spies."

"You believe she was paid."

"She was seen getting a payment and speaking German to the man who paid her," I told him, not mentioning Mary Wallace's name.

"You believe you can prove her guilt by following the money." Sir Malcolm stared at me from beneath bushy brows.

"Yes." After what I heard from Mary, I was certain of it.

"It just so happens we know who is handing out large envelopes of cash. We're hoping he'll lead us to where it is coming from and who is issuing orders for the Führer in Britain."

"He should also lead you to Alice Waterson's killer." And Agathe's, I silently added.

"That I'm willing to help you with. I'll let you know when we have something. Now, Mrs. Denis, if you don't mind, I need to get back to work." His dry tone let me know I'd overstayed my welcome.

"Good day, sir." This time, I shut the door quietly behind me on my way out.

I kept my expression somber until I walked outside, when a broad smile crossed my face. I had no doubt that Sir Malcolm would find the evidence to prevent Helen from causing more mayhem. I was finished with my investigation for Sir Malcolm. And I was, for the moment, free to go to Abby's and plan my wedding.

I was packed and ready to travel when Adam arrived at the flat that evening with his rucksack. After a very fond greeting, with no mention of my close call that day, we headed to the train station as we made plans for our wedding.

The station was crowded with people heading to the coast for the weekend. The weather, which was warm and fair, promised to continue for at least a few more days.

We found seats next to each other and while Adam napped, I read a mystery that took place in a village like Sir John and Abby's, except for the high rate of murder.

I had called Abby that morning and told her what train we'd take. She said she'd pick us up.

But when we arrived, she wasn't there. The stationmaster told us he would contact Summersby House as Lady Abby had directed. While we waited, he went into his office. I watched through the window as he picked up the receiver and began to talk.

He spent time listening, his face going from disinterested to concerned and then dumbstruck. He glanced out the window, saw me watching intently, and turned his back on me.

My heartbeat sped up, banging in my chest. What had happened?

Chapter Twenty-Seven

I walked to the open doorway of the stationmaster's office and waited for him to hang up the telephone receiver on the black box on the wall. As he did, he turned to face me. "Lady Abby will be down in a few minutes. She hopes you don't mind if you go past the school on your way to the manor."

"What's happened?" Already my heart was pounding.

"It seems little Henry, the younger of the two German boys living with them, has disappeared."

He might as well have punched me in the stomach as his words struck. I felt my insides collapse within my body as the air left my lungs. Then I felt strong arms holding me up and guiding me to a bench just outside the doorway as Adam said, "It's all right, Livvy. We'll find him. Probably off playing with his friends and not realizing we'd all be worried about him."

When I could finally speak again, I said, "His brother must be worried sick."

"Aren't the boys in the same village school?"

"Yes, but there's a gap of three or four years separating them. That's a big difference at that age. They'd walk home with friends their own age and think nothing of where the other is."

"It's a safe place, out here in the countryside. Nothing will happen to him." Adam smiled. "At least not until he gets home and has to face Sir John's wrath for worrying Abby."

I had to smile in return. He had the Summersbys figured out. "Because Sir John would never dream of worrying. Even though, right this moment, he is contacting everyone he can think of to check everywhere."

I watched the station clock slowly tick off the minutes as we waited for Abby to pull up in the little car park. As soon as we saw her car, Adam and I picked up our luggage and hurried out to her.

Gerhard was in the front seat next to Abby. Adam tossed our luggage in the boot while I climbed in the back seat. When Abby told Gerhard to get in back, Adam said, "No, you ride up front. You have a better idea what you're looking for."

"Did you see Heinrich after the bell rang at school this afternoon?" I asked in English.

"Yes. In the schoolyard. He was with his friends, Paul and Vince. We've already checked," he continued. "He isn't with either of them." I was pleased when he replied in the same language.

"Paul said when they were about a block away from the school, a woman called Henry over. In German," Abby said. "Henry walked off with her." She glanced in the rearview mirror and her eyes met mine. She looked as frightened as I felt.

And she didn't know I suspected a woman of killing two people, including the boys' mother.

We drove to the village school. After a few minutes

spent circling the site on foot, calling the boy's name, we drove off.

"Paul said she called him 'Heinrich,'" Gerhard offered. "She knows us. Who is she?"

"What did she look like?" I asked.

"Dark hair, green dress and hat, and those two-tone shoes," he immediately told me.

"Spectator pumps," I murmured.

"Very English, very expensive, like she lives in London, Paul said," Gerhard continued.

To a country-raised six-year-old, I decided anything fancy must seem expensive and from London.

"Did she have a car?" Adam asked, and I felt my heart thump.

"No. Paul's car-mad. He looked for that right away. What's a London lady doing walking around our village?" Gerhard demanded.

"If she's walking around the village, since she's a stranger, someone is bound to spot her," Adam said.

"We've asked everyone. No one has seen a thing," Abby said. Then she glanced over at Gerhard and put certainty into her tone. "But now everyone is on the lookout, and he hasn't been missing long. He might not have gone with her, whoever she was."

Gerhard gave Abby a look I was certain I gave my father on a daily basis at that age that said, "I'm not stupid. Be honest with me."

"If you'll wait until I change clothes, Gerhard, you can show me the various shortcuts through the woods between home and school that you don't want Lady

Abby to know about," Adam said.

Gerhard shot a worried glance at Abby. She said, staring out the windscreen, "Adam, you and Gerhard feel free to search anywhere you'd like. Just be back at the house by dark. You'll need to eat sometime. And check that someone hasn't found Heinrich already."

"Are Matt and Mark here?" I asked Abby.

"No. They went back to school Tuesday. Term started Wednesday." She glanced at Gerhard. "We could use their help now."

Gerhard, looking fixedly out the windscreen, nodded.

When we arrived at the house, Adam was out and carrying his rucksack upstairs to change before the maid had a chance to remove our cases from the boot of the car. Abby gave me a look that spoke to me of her constant reminder to wait and let the maid take my suitcase up to the room I always used.

I'd grown up without servants in the house except for the housekeeper, and she'd let me know when I was a young child that she was not there to pick up after me. It seemed strange to have a maid doing for me, but Abby had a large home and a number of servants. And she insisted I follow the standards of Summersby House.

We'd barely made it inside before Adam came pounding downstairs dressed in an old jacket and with trousers bloused into his thick socks and hiking boots. "Ready to go, Gerhard?" he called before giving me a quick kiss.

Gerhard ran in from the kitchen, stuffing a piece of

bread into his mouth, the jam smearing on his chin.

Abby said, "Wait," before she pulled out her handkerchief and swiped at his face. Gerhard was bouncing on his toes. "Go on," she said, and the boy raced out the door, Adam on his heels.

"If anyone asks, John let him go out like that," Abby said with a smile. Then her expression clouded over again.

"What can I do to help?" I asked.

"John's out with the neighbors searching the countryside, Adam will follow Gerhard through the woods to the school. I think I want to visit some of the villagers and check on the other side of the village. Coming?"

"Of course." Abby led the way as I headed back to the car and climbed in the front seat.

We saw a couple of Abby's neighbors riding horses along the edge of a field. As we drove past, Abby waved a greeting. As she slowed for a turn, one of them shouted, "Any luck?"

"No." She shook her head and drove on.

Abby parked by the school and began to call at the houses of some people she knew in one direction, while I began checking with the shops in the other direction. Most of the time I didn't get out more than a sentence or two before someone would say, "Poor little tyke."

I heard how Henry, with Paul and Vince, were called the "merry band." Vince's mother worked in the tea shop, and all the shop owners kept an eye out for him. Now that Vince had started school, he was frequently seen with Paul and, since his arrival, his new friend, Henry.

A number of strangers, who were in the village on a tour of the church, had wandered in and out of shops and by the school. The shopkeepers had seen them, but no one had seen Henry or Paul that day. Vince had been underfoot everywhere.

The old woman who ran the news agent had noticed Vince hanging around her shop's back door. Since she sold sweets and had a soft spot for Vince, "poor fatherless child," she had no trouble convincing him to talk.

"He told me he saw Henry get into a car with the nicely dressed lady, speaking that funny language of his, but he must have become frightened quickly. Vince saw him throw open the car door and try to jump out. He made it halfway before the woman grabbed him by a foot and tried to pull him back in. He was dangling and she only had one hand on the wheel. Next thing you know, she's gone off the road and punctured a tire."

I nearly came across the counter at her. "Where's Henry? Did he get free?"

"No idea. But by the time she got out of the car and kicked the tire, Henry had disappeared. Vince says he has no idea where he went."

"Did anyone call the police station?"

"I told the constable when he came by. He said he'd keep a lookout for the lad and would call Sir John."

That would mean everyone was out looking for him. "Where can I find Vince?"

"He lives over the dressmaker's shop with his mother."

"And I'll take a shilling's worth of Vince's favorite candy," I said, digging into my bag.

"You've got a wise head on your shoulders," the old woman said.

I hoped I did as I walked up the inside staircase and knocked on Vince's door. His mother answered, peeping out at me.

"I'm a friend of Lady Abby. My name's Livvy Denis," I started, since the woman appeared frightened. "I'm helping Lady Abby find Henry. Vince told Mrs. Abbott at the sweetshop that he had seen Henry trying to escape from a car. I was hoping he could tell me about it. And I brought him a present to make it a little easier," I added, holding up the bag of ha'penny candy.

Vince's mother, a thin woman with perpetual worry lines etched into her forehead and radiating from her mouth, finally decided to let me in. Vince was sitting on the worn sofa watching us.

"May I offer you both a piece of candy?" I asked, holding out the bag to Vince's mother.

Her hand dangled above the bag as if there were something inside to bite her. She grabbed a piece and popped it into her mouth before she smiled. "Thank you."

I smiled back and held the bag out to Vince. He had no hesitation in taking one and tossing it in his mouth.

"What do you say?" Vince's mother asked.

"Thank you," he mumbled.

"You're very welcome. I believe I'd like one, too." I took one and sucked on the sweet cherry candy, letting the flavor roll over my tongue.

I sat on the sofa next to Vince and said, "Mrs. Abbott told me you saw Henry trying to escape from a car this afternoon."

He nodded his head. "He did escape."

"And the woman?"

"She was all dressed up, like for church. When she ran the car off the edge of the road, the tire went flat. Then she climbed out, but Henry had gone."

"Did you see where Henry went?"

He shook his head, staring at the bag of sweets.

I wasn't certain I believed him. I held the sack out and he grabbed another piece and slid it in his mouth while his mother got up and banged a pan in the kitchen.

"What did the woman do when she left the auto?"

"She stomped her foot. Coulda broken her heel."

"She had tall heels on?"

"Yeah. Skinny ones."

I nodded.

"She called Henry in his funny language and walked up and down the street. Then she kicked the tire and walked off toward the train station."

"When she was out of sight, where did Henry go?"

"Dunno. Didn't see him." Vince grabbed a third sweet out of the bag.

"Where did this happen?"

"By the beck. Before you get to the Masons' house."

One thing puzzled me. "Paul said he didn't see a car."

"As soon as Henry walked away, Paul's mum called him. He ran off. So I went to the shops and that's where I saw Henry and that woman and her car."

"That's enough, young man. Dinner's ready. Time for you to go." Vince's mother addressed the last to me. I hadn't heard her come in from the kitchen.

I rose from the sofa and handed the woman the bag of sweets. "Thank you for letting me talk to Vince. Enjoy this, both of you."

As I climbed down the staircase, I was glad I wasn't wearing high heels. But why had this woman—Helen, perhaps—worn such inappropriate footwear to the country? And why not walk to the garage to have the tire repaired? Why the train station?

I started down the pavement when I spotted Abby coming toward me, waving. I hurried toward her, eager to tell her what I'd learned.

She spoke first. "Mrs. Mason told me some stranger changed a tire on an unfamiliar car in front of her house. Do you think it might have anything to do with Henry?"

"Yes." I told her what I'd learned. "Where is the car now?"

"They drove off."

"They?" How many people were after one little boy?

"A man and a woman."

"No sign of Henry?"

"No."

"We need to look around there. Henry jumped from

a moving car. He could be lying injured somewhere."

Abby looked at the sky. "It's getting dark, and I think it may rain tonight. All the more reason to hurry the search for him immediately."

"Let's go." Time could be running out for the child. Particularly if a killer like Helen found him first.

Chapter Twenty-Eight

Fear urged me on as I hurried in the direction Abby had come from. The stream was easy to spot, since the entire bed and the sloping sides were in shadow while the flat grounds on either side still caught what was left of the dying light. The stream ran under the bridge by a house and then continued down behind the row of shops. I suspected Vince had stood there while watching Henry try to escape.

I wished I'd had the foresight like Adam to change clothes before beginning the search.

Abby stood on the bridge over the stream calling, "Henry. Are you there, Henry?"

I began gingerly to walk down the slope holding on to an old oak tree, my smooth-soled flats sliding on the grass and mud and moss. "Henry? We're here now."

I heard voices coming from the direction of the school. Then, "Abby? Any luck?" Adam called.

Gerhard shouted, "He has to be here somewhere. He has to," as he plunged down the embankment past me.

Adam gave me a hand to level ground before climbing down after Gerhard.

"He fell out of a moving car right about here. He may be hurt," I said. "He's definitely frightened."

I could hear them splashing in the water, but I could barely make out their shapes in the increasing darkness.

"Do you have a torch, Abby?" Adam called.

"In the car. I'll get it," she called back.

Beneath Abby's footsteps and Gerhard's determined splashing, I thought I heard a faint cry. It might have just been a wild animal. Living in the city, I wasn't accustomed to their sounds.

They continued to search until Abby came back with the lighted torch and Adam took it from her. Then he and Gerhard climbed under the bridge. "He's not here," he shouted up a minute later.

I heard the weak cry again.

"Adam, I heard something. Follow the riverbed past me."

He and Gerhard splashed along, neither of them attempting to keep their feet dry or trying to be quiet. I ran along the level area above the stream, listening. Nothing.

"Oh, Henry, where are you?" I stood next to another oak tree, its roots left half exposed by high water sometime in the past.

And then I heard a whimper that seemed to come from beneath my feet. "Adam, back here."

He and Gerhard hurried over, Adam shining the torch. "He's here. In the roots." He handed Gerhard the torch and said, "Hold the beam on him while I untangle your brother."

"He's here. He's here." Gerhard was jumping up and down, splashing Adam and jiggling the light.

Adam worked to free Henry, putting his arms around the softly moaning child. The sound almost broke my heart.

"Hold the light so we can see to get back up the

bank," Adam said. Abby and I helped pull Adam up to the level of the ground as he carried a filthy, shivering Henry and then I held out a hand to Gerhard. Abby led the way to her car where she pulled a blanket from the boot and then climbed into the back seat. Adam lay the boy on the blanket spread on her lap and Gerhard climbed in next to her. Adam climbed into the driver's seat and I sat in front next to him.

As Adam drove toward Summersby House, I watched Abby in the back seat. "How is he?"

"He's shivering," Abby said, "but he's breathing. I can't tell how badly you're hurt, my boy. We'll get you home and into a hot tub of water to warm you up." She began to rock him.

"How did you know to look there?" Adam asked.

"Henry's friend Vince saw him jump from a moving car. The woman grabbed one of his legs, but lost control of the car in the process. That's how he escaped," I told him.

I glanced into the back seat to see Gerhard wrapping the blanket over his brother's scraped bare legs beneath his short trousers. "You did well, Heinrich," he said in German. "You'll be fine. I'm here."

"It was a good thing you and Adam came to find him when you did," I told him. "Henry's lucky to have a big brother like you."

"I should have been there to protect him," Gerhard said.

"Henry won't appreciate you hovering over him every minute," Abby said, stopping her rocking of Henry for a moment. "In the end, Henry has to look out for Henry just like you have to look out for yourself."

"But he's little."

"So are you, my bright boy. You don't want me hovering over both of you, do you?"

Gerhard sniffed. "No."

"Now we have to trust Livvy and Adam to find this woman and lead the police to her." Abby began rocking Henry again.

"With pleasure," I said emphatically. I felt sure I knew who we were looking for. The trick was to prove it.

We were silent the rest of the way back to Summersby House. Adam offered to carry Henry indoors, and Abby thanked him. "He's getting to be a solid little man."

As soon as we pulled up by the front door, Adam cut the engine and jumped out to take Henry and the blanket from Abby's arms. We all raced in to find Sir John coming out of his study with the village constable and a couple of the neighboring farmers. Adam, Abby, and Gerhard hurried upstairs to get Henry washed up and to check on his wounds beneath the dirt while I reported what we'd learned and where we'd found him.

When I finished, I asked the bobby, "Could you find out who changed the tire on the car that ran off the road and had a flat this afternoon? The accident happened by the Masons' house. The car was driven by Henry's kidnapper. We don't know the make or model of the car."

"Perhaps the woman changed it herself. If she could kidnap the lad, surely she could change a tire," one of the farmers said.

"She was wearing a very nice dress and high heels. She doesn't sound the type to change a tire. But if the man who changed it was a local or someone from the garage, they might have noticed something about her or the car that will help us find her."

The bobby headed for the door. "I'll report in that the lad's been found, and I'll start enquiries about who changed the tire."

"I'll give you a lift, Mac," one of the farmers said as he followed the bobby out of the house. "I've got Brownie out front pulling the wagon. Toss your bike in the back. We'll leave everything where it is," he called to Sir John, "finish the tree pruning in the morning."

"Too dark for it now." The other farmworker nodded to Sir John and ambled out.

"How is he?" Sir John asked as soon as we were alone.

"Cold, dirty, black and blue, and frightened. He'll be all right eventually. But what I don't understand is why anyone would kidnap him."

"It's not like we're the Lindberghs," Sir John said, remembering the infamous kidnapping of a baby in America a few years before. That had been for money.

I hadn't told anyone at the time, but now I had to. "Henry's mother left a note in her luggage for Sir Malcolm, but I've already delivered the letter."

"Did the kidnapper know the note was gone?" Sir

John asked.

I cringed. "No. You mean this could be my fault. That I'm to blame for Henry's kidnapping."

"It can only be the fault of the kidnapper, Olivia. Don't blame yourself."

But I did. I'd kept everything quiet about the message for what I thought had been the boys' safety. Instead, I had managed to put Henry in danger instead of protecting both boys. How could I be such a fool? "But how did the kidnappers find him out here with you?" I murmured.

Sir John shook his head, his eyes wide and his brows lifted while he looked puzzled.

Slow footsteps came down the stairs. Abby led and said, "Somebody's hungry," followed by a grinning Gerhard and Adam carrying Henry, who had thrown his arms around Adam's neck.

We assembled in the dining room and took our usual chairs, and a minute later Abby came in from the kitchen, saying "Cook's kept everything hot for us. Gerhard, would you like to say grace?"

"Thank you for showing us where Heinrich was. Bless this food. Amen," was rattled off at the speed of a train.

I saw Adam trying hard not to smile. Then the maid brought in the soup and we all focused on our meal to the exclusion of everything else.

By the time we finished the main course, Henry's eyelids were drooping. "Would you like me to carry you up to bed?" Adam asked.

The boy shook his head. "Lady Abby."

"You're too heavy," Abby told him. "Let Adam carry you up and I'll come with you."

"As will Gerhard and I," Sir John said.

When the maid came out to collect the plates, I was the only one left at the table. "The adults will be down in a minute for coffee," I told her.

"Shall I bring it in here?" she asked.

Abby did not have a routine that I knew of, and tonight was nowhere near normal. "That would be fine." If it wasn't what Abby wanted, I'd take the blame.

Adam came down a moment later. "Henry wants to see you."

I went upstairs to the old nursery that the boys shared. Henry was tucked in bed, scrapes and scratches evident, and with his eyes nearly closed. When I patted his shoulder and wished him pleasant dreams, he grabbed my hand.

"She said she was taking me to my father."

I held his hand as I said, "You know she can't do that. Your parents are together in heaven. Your father was killed by the Gestapo in Sachsenhausen." Behind me, I heard Gerhard stir. "They both wanted you to come to England to be safe. They tried to come with you, but the Gestapo stopped them. I'm so, so sorry."

Gerhard came over and sat on the side of Henry's bed. "Was the woman who tried to take my brother part of the Gestapo?"

"I don't know what she is."

"Until she's caught, I don't want either of you boys

going anywhere alone," Sir John said.

"I'll protect Heinrich," Gerhard said.

"I know you will," I told him. "Right now, you both need a good night's sleep so you'll be alert tomorrow."

"Will you be here tomorrow?" Henry asked in a sleepy voice.

"Yes. Adam and I need to go to the church to see about arranging our wedding." Despite the panic we had just experienced, I felt a wave of excitement wash over me just by saying those words.

The statement was punctuated with a tiny snore from Henry.

"And now it's time for you to be in bed, big brother," Sir John said.

"Will you keep an eye out for that woman?" Gerhard asked, climbing into his bed.

"I'm sure she's back in London now, but no one can break in with the dogs patrolling the grounds," Sir John said.

"Can Rufus sleep in here tonight?"

"If the old dog can stand to sleep anywhere but in the kitchen hall, he has my permission tonight. I'll bring him up when I go to bed. All right?" Abby said.

Gerhard nodded and snuggled under the covers. We tiptoed out and went downstairs for our coffee.

After we were settled around the dining room table, Sir John lighting his pipe as we drank our coffee, Abby said, "Well, is she? Gestapo, I mean."

"I don't know. The woman I think it is may have attended spy school in Nazi Germany."

"Fleur Bettenard?"

"No, an English Quaker who grew up in Germany and I believe went to the same training school as Fleur. What I want to know is, who changed the car tire?"

"Hopefully we'll find that out tomorrow from the constable," Sir John said from his cloud of smoke. "Nothing we can do until then."

"Except call old Rufus and send him up to the boys' room," Abby said.

"Think the mutt will end up in Henry's bed?" Sir John asked.

"I don't think I'm going to pay too much attention to who sleeps where in that room tonight," Abby replied. "Both those boys have had a bit of a shock. Better to give them a little security."

While Abby brought the dog into the formal part of the house, I took the coffee tray back to the kitchen. When I came back out, the old shaggy-coated brown dog ran up to me, wagging his tail. "Going on guard duty tonight I hear," I said as I scratched him behind the ears.

"He was a puppy when Mark was little," Sir John said, referring to his younger son, "and no one dared correct Mark when Rufus was there to protect him. Loves children."

Leaving Sir John to lock up, the rest of us went upstairs with the dog and settled him in with the two sleeping boys. Rufus sprawled out on a rug under an open window and proceeded to go to sleep.

I went to sleep thinking of how quiet and peaceful it was with a slight breeze fluttering the curtains and hoped it wouldn't start raining during the night.

I awoke at some point sitting straight up in bed with a dog barking and no idea where I was.

Chapter Twenty-Nine

It only took a moment for me to remember the attempted kidnapping, Rufus, the Kindertransport, everything. I leaped out of bed, grabbed my dressing gown, and pulled it on as I ran barefoot to the boys' room.

In the faint moonlight showing the dim outline of the open window by Gerhard's bed, I saw Gerhard struggling with a shadowy figure as Rufus barked and Henry screamed.

The figure had the top half of Gerhard outside the window hanging upside down. The boy grabbed for the ladder leaning against the house while the figure holding him straddled the windowsill.

Terrified that Gerhard would fall head first the fifteen or twenty feet to the lawn, I rushed over and grabbed one of the shadow's very solid arms as well as trying to pull Gerhard back into the room by one leg.

I was sure the figure was a he, as tall as Adam and with strong muscles, but in the gloom, I couldn't make out his features. Certainly not Helen Miller.

He tried to shake me off but I hung on, trying to twist his fingers off Gerhard's arm as I attempted to pull the child toward me into the room. I thought my dressing gown would get ripped off, but there was no time to worry about that.

Gerhard screamed in fright as a strong yank by the

kidnapper nearly sent him flying toward the ground. The man shook me off and wrapped his other arm around Gerhard's throat. He tried to climb out the window with the boy in his arms. Rufus growled and snapped. I heard the boy gurgle. Furious, I took my nails and raked them down the man's face.

He answered by punching me in the side of the head. I went down, my head ringing as Adam burst in, stepping over me and grabbing the man by the neck.

They struggled while Gerhard slipped between them feet first through the open window and down to the wooden floor. He crawled over and climbed onto his bed gasping.

Rufus ran into the fray, lunging and snapping at the unknown man, who tried to kick him off without any luck.

Adam and the assailant were half in and half out of the open window, their hands around each other's necks. I saw Adam had the heel of his hand pushing the man's chin up, holding his mouth shut. Rufus twisted between their feet, growling.

Down below, the outdoor dogs barked at the excitement occurring above them.

Sir John rushed over to help by trying to pull the unknown man into the room. Abby turned on the hall light and ran to Gerhard, who was starting to retch. Henry jumped onto Gerhard's bed and hugged his brother.

I began to rise as I heard a crash in the grounds outside and the dogs' barking increased. For a moment my heart lodged in my throat. Then, thank goodness, I could still see both men in the window.

The top of the ladder, however, was no longer in view.

The stranger broke free of Adam's grip and plowed into Sir John, knocking him over.

I was the only one between the attacker and freedom. The man who tried to hurt Gerhard. With a fury I didn't know I possessed, I dove for the stranger's knees. My momentum sent him flying. I landed with my chest on his back end.

The man tried to flip over and shove me away, but Rufus chomped down on his wrist as if it were a soup bone and held on.

"Get him off me," he yelled.

Adam knelt and grabbed the man's throat as he said, "There's no place to go. Give up."

The stranger rasped out, "All right. All right," and held up his hands once Rufus let go.

"Stay down," Adam said to the man. "Somebody get me some rope."

"The curtain ties," I said, and moved to the window to remove them.

Adam glanced toward me, and at that moment, the assailant broke free. He shoved Rufus aside as he pulled a revolver from his pocket, pointing it in Adam's face.

As the man rose, we all shrank back. Once on his feet, he used the gun to wave us away. Adam moved to the side, shielding the boys and Abby while telling us to "Stay back."

We all obeyed, except Rufus, who was barking and jumping.

I shuffled backward toward the window by Gerhard's bed. I glanced out to see automobile headlights disappearing down the drive. His accomplice? His means of escape?

When I looked back at the attacker, the light from the hallway fell on his face. Finally, I had a good look at him. Douglas MacFerron. The diplomat who had helped me in Berlin.

As much as I wanted to point out that I knew him and that his escape vehicle had taken off, MacFerron had a revolver and he'd probably shoot me in anger. He might even if I kept quiet. I had scratched him badly, leaving a trickle of blood along his cheek.

At this distance his bullets couldn't miss.

Rufus began to growl. MacFerron aimed at the dog. "Come here, boy," Sir John said and held out his arms for the dog. With one final bark, Rufus trotted to his master.

"Gerhard, Heinrich, come here or I'll shoot this nice man," MacFerron said in German.

I heard the boys start to shift off the bed. I needed to stop them. Moving closer to the window, I looked out to make certain. There were no cars anywhere around the house. The ladder lay across the lawn and into some bushes. "You're going to have a long walk. Your car drove away."

"What?" He waved me away from the window. "After I changed the tire for that fool woman..."

"Not a very reliable accompl..." When I saw the fury

on his face, I knew I'd overstepped the bounds. I shrank into the shadows and edged along the far side of the room until I reached Sir John and Rufus.

MacFerron backed around the room, his gun pointing in our general direction, until he could see out the window. There was enough moonlight to be able to tell no car waited for him and the boys.

No. Not the boys, I decided. "Just go," I told him. "You can make good enough time on your own to escape without anyone capturing you."

"No." He aimed directly at me. I gulped. "I need the stolen information that these brats' mother brought with her. I can't leave without it."

He sounded desperate. And he had a gun.

"The government has it now," Gerhard said, peering out at the man from behind Adam.

"No," MacFerron shouted in frustration, aiming the gun at the boy's face as he began backing toward the door, keeping us all in view.

I took a deep breath and tried to stop shaking. "They do. I passed it on to the government a week ago. You might as well get out of here before anything else goes wrong."

"She was supposed to find out…" he began.

"Something else Helen got wrong," I replied. "Of course, we turned in Konrad Dietrich's final message as soon as we found it. Is that what you searched my flat for?"

"That was Helen." He glanced around. "I'm not leaving without a hostage." He made a lunge for

Gerhard, who shrank back.

"Take me," I said, moving forward one cautious step. "I can move faster than the boys can."

"No. Take me," Adam said, walking slowly forward with his hands out from his sides. "I can move faster than any of the rest of them."

"No," said Sir John, rising from his kneeling position. "I'm worth more to the government. I make a better bargaining chip."

"Shall I just shoot him, sir?" came a male voice behind MacFerron.

We all looked toward the hallway where one of the farmers stood. He'd been at the house earlier when we'd come home after finding Henry. Now he stood with a shotgun aimed at MacFerron.

"If he doesn't immediately put down his pistol and surrender, yes, by all means, give him both barrels," Sir John said.

MacFerron looked at the shotgun, then around at us before bending to set his weapon on the floor.

As soon as Adam had the diplomat bound with the curtain ties under the watchful eye of the farmer, I ran downstairs to the phone. My first call was to the local police station. The second was to Sir Malcolm's office.

I came back up to find Sir John removing the bullets from MacFerron's pistol, Adam keeping a firm grip on the now-seated would-be kidnapper, and two boys watching everything through wide eyes. "I've called the local police station and Sir Malcolm's office. We should have visitors shortly."

"Then I'd better put coffee on," Abby said, rising from Gerhard's bed. "Do you boys think you can go back to sleep?"

"No, ma'am," Gerhard said, displaying good manners as well as a desire to see what other turmoil was in store for that night.

"Then you'd better come down to the kitchen." Abby led them out, looking like two ducklings in pajamas and dressing gowns followed by a shaggy brown dog with a wagging tail.

When we heard them reach the bottom of the stairs, Adam said, "Anyone want to tell me what's going on? Livvy?"

Chapter Thirty

"This is Douglas MacFerron, a diplomat posted at our Berlin embassy who came over here on leave a few days ago. He was the boys' father's handler while the father was sneaking out German military secrets to give to the British." I had everyone's attention.

"Brave man," Sir John said, "stealing Nazi secrets from under their noses."

"When our government got ready to smuggle the family out of Germany, someone conveniently told the Gestapo about the man's activity. I suspect MacFerron."

The diplomat glared at me in silence. We all glared back.

I continued, "After their father was arrested, MacFerron was the one who put me in contact with the boys and their mother."

I walked over to stare into his face. "She cared for you. I could see it in the photos she brought with her. And you pointed her out to her killer."

"She knew too much about, well, about how the smuggling was done, and what information had been smuggled. She was a danger. I couldn't let her live."

"You didn't pass along all the information that brave man took from the Nazis?" Cold fury rose up inside me. "I hope you hang."

MacFerron stared at me with a smirk on his lips. "If you choose to believe that."

"Did you pass along everything Dietrich gave you?" I had to know. Gerhard and Heinrich would want the truth someday, and I suspected I'd be the only one to share it with them.

He shrugged. "I wasn't his handler. Norman was. I managed to see one of the later messages, and then told the Germans what it contained and who had stolen the information."

I wasn't sure if I believed him. "You weren't present to kill Agathe Dietrich or Alice Waterson. Who killed them? It had to be someone you met up with at the Berlin train station." I hoped to make him admit who his fellow traitor was.

MacFerron turned his face to the side.

"No matter. We'll catch up with her soon."

"Her?" the farmer said, still at the ready with his shotgun.

"Oh, yes. Helen Miller is deadlier than most of our soldiers. Comes from an education taught by the Gestapo." I turned back to MacFerron. "Was she the one who recruited you?"

In a voice so low I could barely hear him, he said, "Yes."

"But why?" Treason in the diplomatic corps seemed incomprehensible.

He gave me a look that said he thought I was mentally defective. "Money, of course."

"Money? You'd sell out your country for money?" Sir John asked, horror in his tone.

MacFerron turned to face him with a sneer. "Most of

the Foreign Office has money. Like you. Big houses. Status. Titles. Puts the rest of us at a disadvantage. I just want what you already have."

Sir John shook his head.

"Where would Helen go when she abandoned you?" I asked.

MacFerron gave me a smug look and said, "I'll save that for Sir Malcolm, I believe. I need something to bargain with."

MacFerron didn't speak again through all the time it took the local police to come out, question all of us, and drive him away.

The sergeant told Sir John that Sir Malcolm had been in touch and Whitehall would be taking charge of the prisoner in the morning.

The farmer, who'd been alerted to the intruder by his daughter, the housemaid Mary, left with all of our thanks ringing in his ears. I suspected when he left us, he stopped by the kitchen to see his daughter and the cook, who both lived in, for an early, well-deserved breakfast and gossip about the excitement upstairs.

"Are we safe now, Miss Livvy?" Henry asked.

"I think so. Even if they don't arrest Helen tonight, they'll want to question her, and she'll know it won't be safe to come back here with everyone looking for her. The Germans don't want to waste an agent on a lost cause, and since Sir Malcolm has the note your mother carried, bothering you two is a lost cause."

"But can she find someone else, someone we don't know, to help her take either of us away?" Gerhard asked.

Abby immediately said, "There's no reason to take either of you away. Once they learned the note had gone to the government, there was no reason to try to kidnap you."

"I made a mistake by not letting everyone know you no longer had the note. I'm sorry," I told them.

"I'm glad now that you took it," Gerhard said, and he gave me a smile.

I was relieved. I didn't think he'd ever forgive me for taking the note from his mother's suitcase without telling him first.

"Could the driver be anyone besides this Miss Miller?" Sir John asked.

"I doubt it. I suspect she's been working with MacFerron for a long time," I said. Despite what Sir Malcolm believed.

"I didn't like him," Henry said.

"Yes, you did," said his brother.

That started an argument consisting of silly threats until Sir John said, "Enough," and sent them both to bed. "Silently," he added as they clattered up the stairs, arguing and shoving.

"Well, I'm glad to see they're feeling more themselves," Abby said. "I hope you won't think I'm unsociable if I return to bed."

We all agreed that sounded good and headed upstairs, knowing the morning would arrive too soon.

* * *

Abby, Adam, and I, feeling droopy from our

shattered night's sleep, arrived at the church at eleven that morning for our appointment with the Reverend Garner. He waved us into his office in the rectory and then sat at his desk, studying several forms.

"Lady Abby tells me you want to be married in Saint Athanasius," he began. "Which of you belongs to this parish?"

"I do," I told him, trying to sound calm despite my fear that he might think I was stretching the term "family" a little too far. "Lady Abby is my family, and when I can come home on weekends from my employment in the city, I come to church here."

"I'm a member of the British army," Adam added before I could tell any great lies, "and as a result I don't have any roots. We hope to be married before the war intervenes."

"Oh," the rector said, "that may not be possible. There are counseling sessions and, after that, publishing the banns. We have no idea when Herr Hitler plans to engage us in war."

"*Engage* us in war?" Adam whispered so only I could hear him, his eyebrows raised.

The Reverend Garner was a stickler for the rules, but I loved the beautiful old stone-built church with its whitewashed walls and stained-glass windows. It had a beautifully rumbling organ played by Mr. Conway's deft fingers. Its dark wood pews were polished by hundreds of years of pious posteriors. Beyond the medieval graveyard was the village green. And its six ancient bells in the bell tower could ring out for our wedding.

The church was perfect even if the Reverend Garner wasn't.

"Counseling sessions?" I asked.

"You are both more mature, so I would say two would be all that is necessary for you to attend. After that, the banns must be read three times, and one of you must be here for each reading."

"Late May?" I asked.

"Oh, dear me, no," the reverend said, studying the calendar. "I can fit in the first session this afternoon after tea if that would be convenient, but with you only being here on the weekends, the earliest would be the last of May, and that is booked up. In fact, we are booked up with weddings and christenings until the eighth of July." He frowned and added, "I don't know what I'll do if we have a funeral."

"Why so booked up?" I asked.

"It's this war threat. The parents, or grandparents, remember how their lives were upended the last time the Germans rattled their swords. So now all these young people feel the need to be married before they're split up by events. And we've had a bumper crop of babies. Of course, it is spring."

"I wonder how many of the weddings and christenings are related," Adam said once we were out of the rectory. "With us facing engagement in war. Or other things."

I couldn't help giggling.

"Stop it, you two, or he won't marry you," Abby said. As she started up the car, she said, "The war won't start before then, will it?"

Adam didn't reply. If it did, I'd never forgive the Reverend Garner or myself.

* * *

The rest of the weekend was sunny and fair for springtime, and I returned to London and work on Monday morning with a light heart. Perhaps it was the Reverend Garner saying we were well suited in our first counseling session.

I'd called Sir Henry when we returned to town on Sunday night, warning him I'd be late the next morning while I wrapped up a few details.

"Does that mean you've finished your task for Sir Malcolm?" he asked.

"Yes."

"Thank goodness."

I wondered how much of the relief in his voice was because of all he'd learned at the newspaper about how close we were to war.

I arrived at Sir Malcolm's office to find him in his usual place, his back to the small green leaves budding on the tree branches outside his window. "Did you arrest Helen Miller?" I asked.

"We were too late. Apparently, she's gone back to Germany. We found a car belonging to Charles Brooks at a dock on the south coast and then located the boat that carried her and her luggage to France. The car contained a case for MacFerron in the boot." He raised his eyebrows.

"Did Charles play a role in this?" I'd finally decided

he truly was as easygoing as he seemed.

"No. When we told him about the car, his first thought was how to get to the south coast and retrieve it before his father found out."

"That sounds like Charles."

"We notified the French police immediately and told them about the murder charge against her. We have every hope they'll catch her before she reaches the German border. When they do, they will send her back, in irons, and then..." Sir Malcolm looked like a cat who'd caught the rat.

He continued. "We believe she knew MacFerron would tell us everything he knew as soon as we arrested him. Which he has. Since he didn't kill anyone, he hopes to avoid hanging by talking."

"Will he? Avoid hanging?"

Sir Malcolm shrugged one beefy shoulder. "You were right about Helen being the murderer. She truly believes in the Nazi cause, according to MacFerron."

"And you believe MacFerron?" I wasn't certain I would in Sir Malcolm's position.

"He couldn't have killed either woman."

I nodded.

"You were right. Alice did work for us, and said she suspected a fellow Quaker of passing secrets every time they went to Berlin to rescue the children. The last time we spoke, Alice hadn't figured out who was the traitor. MacFerron said Alice told Helen on the night she died that she suspected her. Helen killed her to keep her quiet." Sir Malcolm appeared to have tasted something sour.

"MacFerron had told Helen about the Air Ministry plans stolen by Dietrich and pointed Agathe out at the train station. He probably knew what she'd do. With her contacts, it would have been easy for her to get a key to the train carriages."

"What have you heard about Johann Klingler?" I asked when he finally paused for breath.

"He's awake and on the mend. Apparently, before he was struck, he was going to tell you Alice had seen Helen with a member of the British embassy staff. Someone she had no business meeting. Turns out it was MacFerron."

Sir Malcolm had his answers. I was only sorry it had taken two lives to root out these traitors.

"What will you do now?" he asked me.

"Go back to being a reporter and pray you lose any recollection of me."

I could hear him laughing as I walked out of the office. "Good luck, Mrs. Denis," he called after me.

"Good-bye, Sir Malcolm," I said to myself as I left the building, heading back to the women's pages desk of the *Daily Premier* and dreaming of dinner with Adam that night.

The war hadn't started yet. I hoped it wouldn't. Ever. But I doubted we'd be that lucky.

I hope you've enjoyed **Deadly Travel**. If you have, you may enjoy *A Christmas Mystery*, a free short story

you can claim by signing up for my newsletter at
https://dl.bookfunnel.com/95m240nos7.

The Christmas in questions is 1938, between
Deadly Deception and **Deadly Travel**, that gives you
an extra glimpse into Olivia's life on the cusp of World
War II.

If you enjoyed this or any of my stories, please leave
a review at your favorite retailer or at
www.Goodreads.com or at
www.Bookbub.com/authors/kate-parker. Most people
choose their next book from personal suggestions. Let
everyone know your opinion.

Author's Notes

Due to the huge numbers of Jews trying to escape countries under Nazi control, in the summer of 1938 in Evian, France, several dozen nations met to try to raise immigration quotas. All these nations still suffered high unemployment due to the Great Depression. The conference was a failure.

Then came Kristallnacht in November, 1938 and the need grew exponentially.

Some forward-thinking citizens approached the British government with a request to allow Jewish children and teenagers to enter temporarily. The government required a fifty pound guarantee (several hundred pounds in today's money) for each child so they didn't become a burden on the taxpayers, but allowed 10,000 children under seventeen to enter the country.

The children came from Germany, Austria, and Czechoslovakia, and entered Britain via the Kindertransports. These were organized by Jewish, Quaker, and other religious groups who raised the funds for their guarantees and also found homes for the children once they reached Britain.

The story of this particular Kindertransport, of passing messages between spies and their spy masters, and escapes from Nazi territory, is fiction...so far as I know.

Acknowledgments

I've received several notes from British readers that I sound too American to do Olivia justice. To correct that, I've brought Les Floyd onto my team to remove my Americanisms. I appreciate all his help. Any mistakes in terminology are my own.

Any book needs lots of editorial guidance. I'd like to thank Hannah Meredith, Jen Parker, Elizabeth Flynn, and Jennifer Brown for their help in making this story the best I could do. Once again, any mistakes are my own.

And I'd like to thank you, my readers, who encourage me to keep writing. Who give me a reason to continue with this solitary effort. Who lift my ego with your praise and gently chide me when I fall short of your expectations. Thank you.

About the Author

Kate Parker caught the reading bug early, and the writing bug soon followed. She's always lived in a home surrounded by books and dust bunnies. After spending more than a dozen years in New Bern, North Carolina, the real-life location for the town in The Mystery at Chadwick House, she packed up and moved to Colorado at the request of her husband. When he died, she traded in mountain scenery for the rivers, gardens, and beaches of the Atlantic coast with a return to North Carolina.

Along with the fifth in the Deadly series, Deadly Travel, she put out Murder at the Marlowe Club this past spring. She's already at work on the next Deadly series mystery, to be called Deadly Darkness. She reports she is having fun creating new stories to entertain readers and chaos to challenge her characters.

Follow Kate and her deadly examination of history at www.KateParkerbooks.com

and www.Facebook.com/Author.Kate.Parker/

and www.bookbub.com/authors/kate-parker/

Made in United States
Troutdale, OR
02/27/2024

17988768R00179